DEMON
IN THE
WHITELANDS

NIKKI Z. RICHARD

Month9Books

Trade Paperback ISBN: 978-1-948671-41-5
ePub ISBN: 978-1-948671-42-2
Mobipocket ISBN: 978-1-948671-43-9

Published by Month9Books, Raleigh, NC 27609
Cover Design by Danielle Doolittle

Month9Books

For my father.

DEMON
IN THE
WHITELANDS

1

amuel sat beside the lit fireplace, woolly blanket draped over his slim shoulders, leather-bound scriptures perched on his lap. He squinted as thin shadows danced across the pages, forcing the words to bleed together. He pushed his mother's thick-framed glasses farther up the bridge of his nose and leaned forward. He was hungry, and he craved something other than stale oatmeal and bluefish. Snowy winds beat against the cabin, causing the wooden walls to creak as if they were in pain. All these things made it impossible for him to focus. But it was more than that. No matter how many times Samuel read the verses, he felt nothing.

His father leaned forward in his chair.

"We have company."

Samuel looked through the rattling window. Two white beams cut through the snowstorm. The twin headlights grew in size and

 1

brightness, and the icy ground crunched under the weight of the approaching vehicle. Samuel stood and set the scriptures on the wooden desk next to the tattered black-and-white photograph of his mother. She was eighteen when the photograph was taken, a few years older than he was now. Her sun-kissed skin showed she was no native to the whitelands. That, and her inviting smile. She was executed soon after giving birth to him. His father refused to speak about her, admitting it was all a transgression that had been covered by Azhuel, the one true god, and His holy roots. Samuel was living evidence of a forbidden act.

The headlights from outside halted, then vanished completely, causing the darkness of the night to return. An impatient pounding hit the door before Samuel had a chance to undo the locks. When he slid back the iron bolt, the door swung forward. Frigid winds and snowflakes flew into the cabin, and the sheriff of Haid scurried inside. Samuel pressed his shoulder against the door and sealed it shut, his face burning from the cold gusts. The sheriff pulled down his heavy hood and dusted the white powder from his thick coat.

"Damn snow."

The sheriff wiped his peppered mustache. Fresh new wrinkles were forming around his cheeks and forehead, causing him to seem older than he really was. He sucked in air through his large nostrils, stripped off his leather gloves, and reclined in the open chair by the table, across from Samuel's father.

"Cleric."

"Sheriff. How can I serve?"

"Tea to start with."

Samuel's father nodded as Samuel habitually gathered the supplies. He boiled a pot of water over the fireplace and pulled tealeaves from a glass jar, ripping each one into little pieces. A few years prior, his father had stumbled upon a small patch of camellia shrubbery near the lake in the eastern woods. His father said it was a miracle of Azhuel that the tea plants managed to grow and survive in such a harsh climate. To Samuel, it was a miracle that anything or anyone lived in Haid at all.

"You know the Littens?" the sheriff asked.

Samuel's father scratched his beard. "The butcher."

"Old man's losing his body and mind. Dementia mixed with pneumonia and a handful of bad luck. Doc says he won't last the night."

Samuel mixed the crushed leaves into the pot, thinking of the butcher and his sharp tools. Once, from outside the shop's back window, he watched as the old man effortlessly gutted a pig beside the cackling furnace. Samuel had never seen a pig before, but that day he saw more of a pig than most. The butcher's skeleton-like fingers slit the animal's guts with ease, peeling back the flesh as if it were merely paper. Blood leaked down the old man's wrinkled arms as he yanked out the intestines and dropped them into a silver pan. Samuel didn't dare step inside the butcher's shop or try to speak with him about the finer points of his craft. No upstanding citizen would want to be caught socializing with a cleric's illegitimate son. That was Samuel's experience, at least. While there were citizens who believed in Azhuel, none of the faithful seemed keen on having Samuel's father as the town's stationed cleric. How could a lecherous, oath-breaking sinner like that hope to guide a spirit back to the holy roots? Samuel recalled a disgruntled logger saying something like that when his father performed the rites for his dead daughter. She was six. A fever took her.

"What about the shop?" Samuel asked while stirring the pot.

The sheriff loosened his gun holster, grunting as he slid the silver revolver on the table. He was the only person in town who never seemed scared or bothered conversing with Samuel or his father. But, as the sheriff of Haid, Eugene Black had certain responsibilities that most citizens didn't. Retrieving his father for the rites was one of them, along with keeping the peace.

"His daughter will run it, I suppose. Ain't like her husband's gonna quit his cozy little job for the mayor. Still, there's no way a family will be able to live on that salary alone. Not in this town."

Samuel nodded as he poured the steaming liquid into a cup and handed it to the sheriff. The sheriff reached into his pocket and pulled out a flask, adding a splash of liquor before taking a sip. "Perfect," he said, wiping his mustache.

Samuel set the pot back on the counter. He wasn't sure if the sheriff was talking about the tea.

"Anyway, the old man wants a cleric. Storm as it is? I'd let him croak. Do the ritual at the burial. But the law's the law. If he wants his dying fantasy, it's your job to give it to him."

"I pray all men find comfort in Azhuel's roots," his father said.

"Knew you'd say that." The sheriff snorted, then took another swig of tea. "I like you, cleric. It's like you really do believe in your god and the damn roots. Whatever that's worth to you. A real righteous man."

His words slurred. He peeked at Samuel.

"Righteous as any man can be."

His father stiffened as the sheriff finished his tea. Samuel turned his attention to the window, watching the snowflakes as they crashed into the glass. Clerics were sworn to celibacy; they were banned from any form of human touch. To perform the rites for the dead and reconnect passing souls to Azhuel's holy roots, clerics of Azhuel had to remain pure, untainted by the sins and lusts of men. Samuel's existence would forever be the stain on his father's holy vows.

"It will take me a while to get there," his father said. "The storm is growing worse, and I'll need to watch my pace."

"You don't need to tell me about this storm. Mayor's got a crew of my patrolmen posted outside of his estate tonight."

Samuel readjusted his glasses. "In that?"

The sheriff snorted. "Entitled fool. Swears he got robbed a few nights back. Missing some cash and jewelry and ... a radio? Now he wants half my men posted by his gates at all times. Had us laying out gaming traps the whole day. Traps so nasty they could rip a bear's leg in half. Which reminds me. Stay clear of the western woods for now, if you know what's good for you."

Samuel went back to the kitchen and cleaned the pot. It was common knowledge the western woods had the best pine. What were the loggers going to do?

"Anyway, no thief in his right mind would be out there now. Most of my patrolmen will probably be frozen dead by morning. And don't be stupid, cleric. It'll be my ass if you don't get there in one piece. You'll ride with me."

Samuel did his best to mask his surprise. The town of Haid had five working vehicles: three large trailer trucks for the loggers to haul their lumber and two jeeps, one for the sheriff, and one for the mayor. Ordinary citizens were forbidden from owning vehicles; that right was reserved exclusively for the politicians, their sheriffs, and a select few businesses involved in multistate trade. Samuel's father had told him how, long ago, nearly everyone owned a motor vehicle, regardless of their profession or status. But that was before the blackout, before the technology bans, before the three states were formed, back when there were many religions and their conflicting moralities forced the old governments and their citizens into countless wars. Before, when praying to any god other than Azhuel was permissible, and when it wasn't against the law to touch a cleric. That was an offense punishable by public flogging, and in some cases, execution.

Like with his mother.

Samuel petted his shaggy hair to the side, brushing his bangs from his eyes. Touching a cleric was one thing; conceiving his bastard son was another. The penalty was death by hanging. The high council, a group of seven clergymen appointed by the states to govern over the clerics according to their own religious laws, oversaw the public execution, and ultimately decided to give his father a harsh beating before reassigning him to a logging town in the whitelands. Someone would need to raise the child, and they weren't heartless demons.

"Would you mind if the boy comes along?" his father asked. "He's getting near the age, and he'll be ordained soon. He could use more observation."

"Like I care." The sheriff scooped up his revolver and eased it back inside its holster. "I'll get the engine running. Be quick."

The sheriff put on his gloves and hood before exiting the cabin. Samuel dressed himself speedily, donning his coat and knit cap before his father had laced his boots. Samuel had seen the rites performed dozens of times, but he didn't know if he'd ever get the chance to ride in a motor vehicle again. He shuffled back and forth on his feet as his father went over to the desk and collected the scriptures, tucking the brown pages inside his jacket.

"Get the knife, Samuel."

Samuel climbed up the rickety ladder to the loft space that he and his father shared. In his excitement, he'd forgotten the most important tool for the rites, save for the scriptures. There could be no rites without blood.

Samuel reached under the mattress and retrieved the hunting knife, making sure the blade was secured inside its leather sheath before stashing it in his back pocket. As soon as he stepped outside, he could tell the storm was growing worse by the minute. Powdered snow swirled violently around him, and the gusting wind was so sharp it choked the air from his lungs. His glasses fogged, and he could only see white. He held his coat's furry hood tight against his head as he followed the hazed object he assumed to be his father. He tuned his ears to the strong hum of the jeep's engine, the wailing of the wind, and his father's voice beckoning him to keep close.

After twenty steps, Samuel's teeth began to chatter uncontrollably. The raining snow was seeping through his clothes, numbing his muscles. Before he needed to yell out for assistance, he found the inside of the jeep. The metal door slammed shut, and for the briefest moment, he felt his father's warm body against his own. His father casually scooted to the opposite side. They weren't supposed to touch, but every once in a while, it happened. Samuel curled his arms together. How do you raise a child without touching him? His father did his best to try. But in those brief moments when their skin would meet, his father would calmly retract his body and pretend nothing had happened. Had he treated his mother the same way after he spilled his seed inside of her?

Samuel took off his glasses and wiped the lenses clean with the tail end of his jacket. After he put them back on, he glared into the rectangular mirror hanging near the sheriff's head.

"You don't have a sensitive stomach, do you?"

The sheriff studied Samuel's reflection as he reached for the black rod sticking out beside the driver's seat.

"No, sir."

"If you hurl, you clean it."

Two black wipers began to move back and forth across the windshield, knocking away the white powder that had piled on top of it. The engine groaned as the jeep dashed forward, and Samuel sank into his seat. The sheriff guided the rod down, forcing the speed to increase. He angled the wheel slightly and the vehicle moved to the right.

"I feel funny," Samuel whispered. His stomach bubbled. He had spoken too soon.

His father almost smirked. "Relax."

Samuel pushed himself deeper into the seat. The nausea didn't last long since the ride was short. Barely ten minutes had passed, and they'd already ridden over the train tracks and on through the neighborhoods south of the town square. The sheriff parked the jeep next to the house directly behind the butcher's shop. When he removed the key beside the steering wheel, the engine was silenced, and the black wipers froze in place.

"Let's see if the old bastard is still kicking."

Samuel and his father hopped out of the vehicle and went into the rowhome with the sheriff. Samuel was immediately impressed with its size. The living room was nearly as large as his father's cabin, but it wasn't luxurious. It was fairly dark and empty, save for a large sofa and several chairs seated alongside the fireplace and a lone mirror with cracked glass hanging on the left side of the wall.

The sheriff stripped off his coat and tossed it onto one of the chairs. His boots thumped as he kicked them against each other. He looked up, stretched his arms, and strolled down the hallway.

"Come on."

Samuel and his father followed. The narrow hallway was adorned with several lampstands mounted to the sides, the wicks from the candles lit and the flames dancing. Samuel had never seen working electricity before, but neither had most others in Haid. No one in town had access to the ancient power lines buried underground, except for the mayor. The use of electrical energy in the whitelands was expensive and only permitted on a limited basis for ruling politicians and their families.

Samuel thought about the burial rites soon to be performed. How had some of the ancient faiths practiced their burial rituals? Did they care for their gods? Were they as benevolent and kind as Azhuel? Did they, too, require sacrifices of blood?

Passing several closed doors, Samuel and the others came upon a back room with the door cracked open. The sheriff pushed the door farther back before entering the room. A large lantern dangled from the ceiling, and a woman stood near the corner of the bed. She wore a patterned dress and thick sweater tights. Her hair was pulled into a tight bun. With damp eyes and feeble steps, she approached the sheriff.

"Eugene. You're here."

"Of course." In his warmest tone, the sheriff still sounded cold.

"Harold hasn't come back yet from the estate. I'm worried."

"This storm is something else, Laura. Your man's probably just stuck inside the estate waiting for it to blow over."

"Or the mayor has him working overtime again," Laura said stiffly. "Well, if you need anything, something to drink or eat, my daughter should be near the kitchen. I didn't want her in here. My father is not himself."

The woman gave Samuel's father a tender look, which was odd

to Samuel because many people never even bothered looking in their direction. She opened her mouth as if to speak, but decided against it, and turned away.

"You're late," a voice called from across the room.

The doctor stood up from the butcher's bedside, her medical tools resting on top of the nightstand. Elizabeth Tulsan. She was a middle-aged woman with plain features, not skinny, but by no means overweight. She patted away the creases in her white apron and crossed her arms. "You said an hour. It's been nearly two. He's been fighting to hold on for this long."

"Good thing I'm here now," the sheriff mumbled. He turned to Samuel's father. "Don't just stand there."

His father stepped cautiously into the room. Samuel followed. His eyes went to the large bed in the back of the room.

The old butcher was curled up on the mattress, wrapped in a bundle of sheets and quilts. His exposed skin was mottling and doused in sweat. His breaths were forced and unnatural, like a landlocked fish sucking in useless air. Samuel rubbed his fingers together. Working in his shop, the old butcher seemed so strong. But now he was just another dying man.

Samuel grazed the knife's handle with the bottom of his palm, knowing full well what was going to happen next.

"Cleric," the doctor said as she bundled her medical tools together and dumped them inside her leather bag. "It has been some time."

His father bowed, and Samuel followed suit.

"Miss Elizabeth."

The doctor gave her condolences to the butcher's daughter, apologizing that she couldn't do more to make him comfortable. She then went to the sheriff. "Are you going to be a gentleman, or am I going to have to walk home in this storm?"

"I'm not a chauffeur," the sheriff said in annoyance, but he gave a nod, nonetheless.

The sheriff and the doctor exited the bedroom quietly, closing the door shut behind them. The butcher's daughter peered with anticipation as Samuel's father went over to the old butcher's bed. He got down on his knees. He removed the scriptures from his jacket pocket and propped them against his legs. Samuel inched up beside his father. The old butcher moaned, forcing out nonsensical sounds. It made Samuel uncomfortable. It wasn't as if he'd never seen death. He'd seen it several times before: a logger who'd taken a nasty fall and punctured his own lungs, a baby who'd caught the bumps, and the tailor who'd gone septic after suffering for years under some chronic ailment. For the most part, Samuel's father performed the rites for those who were already dead. But occasionally, the dying would make a request for a cleric. This act was permissible by law.

His father carefully removed his coat, folding it together and placing it on the dresser near the door. He adjusted the sleeves of his shirt around his muscular arms, pulling them back and exposing his skin. Black lines of ink curled from his wrist down to the end of his forearm like the limbs of an old sycamore. A few of the thicker, longer lines branched out past his elbow up to his bicep, with smaller lines protruding out at the ends. It was a visual representation of

Azhuel's holy roots, and the required mark of the clergy.

"I'm here," Samuel's father said. He stretched his leg back, passing the scriptures to Samuel.

Samuel held the book, clumsily shuffling through the pages as his father removed his gloves. He forced himself to pick a passage, knowing it wouldn't be long before he'd be ordained. His father would eventually take him to the high council, where the bishops would say a prayer of commission before he received the mark of the clergy. He'd be sixteen in a couple of months, a man nearly grown. He did not feel like a man.

"'We are dirt,'" Samuel read softly. His voice lacked conviction, even though he tried to force it. He pushed his glasses farther up the bridge of his cold nose. "'And to dirt we return. For Azhuel will draw out your flesh and pain, and in Him you will grow again, connected to the roots. In Him, there is always life.'"

Samuel exhaled and gave his father the knife. His father drew the blade out from its sheath and sliced it across his own palm, making a cut that would bleed but not scar. When Samuel was younger, he'd asked his father why a cleric had to cut himself to perform the rites. Because nothing good is free, his father had told him. If you want to reach a power greater than yourself, to connect yourself or others to Azhuel's roots, then there must be a sacrifice. The price is always blood.

Samuel's father squeezed into his palm, and red drops splattered from his hand over the butcher's face. The old man groaned as Samuel's father wrapped the wound with a thin strip of gauze the doctor must have left behind on the nightstand. The doctor did that on occasion. She never said much to Samuel or his father, but a part of him felt like they had more in common than most. Who else, besides clergymen and medical practitioners, spent so much time interacting with the dead or near-dead?

His father laid the knife down. He folded his hands together and prayed for the man's soul, praying that Azhuel would purge his sins and embrace him with His roots. The butcher's breathing worsened, his chest convulsing as if it was being crushed from the inside. Without warning, the old man's bony fingers shot up and latched onto his father's forearm.

The Litten woman ran toward the bed in a panic.

"Don't touch him!" she yelled as she wrenched away the butcher's wild hand.

Samuel's father stepped back, his prayers silenced. The old man spewed nonsensical mutterings, his head bobbing back and forth like a thrashing toddler. The Litten woman tried restraining his arms, but she wasn't strong enough. The butcher pushed her back, savagely clawing out for Samuel's father.

Samuel was petrified, unsure what to do. The Litten woman persevered nonetheless, trying to cajole the old man back into lying down. "Father. Calm yourself. Please. Enough."

The old man ignored his daughter's pleas and thrashed his torso upward in blatant defiance.

"It's all right," Samuel's father said firmly. He stepped forward and allowed the dying butcher to once again take hold of his marked arm. "Here."

The old man's grip instantly softened, and his breathing calmed. The Litten woman relaxed her hands, her lips quivering. She slowly retracted herself to the back wall.

"There is goodness in this world," his father said as he allowed the old man to cling to his arm. "I've seen what can come out of darkness and pain. Sometimes the branches must be pruned in order for the tree to sprout again. Do not be afraid. Azhuel sees all. And tonight. You will find comfort in the embrace of His roots. You will be connected to Him for eternity. You will find peace. Peace."

Samuel waited as the butcher's tongue drooped out of his open mouth, waited for what seemed hours until the old man's breathing stopped altogether. His father lowered the old man's arm back to the bed. How had the butcher's desperate fingers felt against his father's arm? He could still see the red marks where the man had squeezed.

His father seemed unbothered by the whole affair. He wiped the bloodied blade across his jeans before slipping it back into its sheath. The butcher's daughter held her cheeks, her shaking slight but apparent. She looked to Samuel's father, no longer able to hide her confusion and fear.

"What am I supposed to do?" she asked. "He wasn't in his right mind. I know he wouldn't have … what will they do to him? To his body? What will they do to us, cleric?"

Samuel held tight to the scriptures as his father walked to the door. He reached for the door handle but stopped.

"Tell no one."

A fresh fire had been lit in the center fireplace, helping to illuminate some of the shadows. Samuel sat beside his father on the Littens' large sofa, waiting for the sheriff's return. He bounced his heels against the pine floor, unable to stop seeing the decrepit butcher grabbing his father's marked arm.

"Thirsty?" his father asked.

"I'm okay."

"Something has been prepared for us."

Samuel straightened his back and looked up. A thin tray with two porcelain cups hovered above his knees, both filled to the brim with some sort of steaming brown liquid. A girl around his age stood in front of him, delicately holding the tray. She wore a gray woolly dress, similar in style to her mother's. Her chestnut hair had been braided into two separate strands that came down on opposite ends

of her collarbone, exposing and elongating her neck.

"My mother asked me to bring this," the girl said.

His father nodded solemnly. "Might I ask your name?"

She kept her eyes on the tray. "Claudette."

"Thank you, Claudette." Samuel's father took both cups and gave one to him. "I pray that Azhuel gives you and your family comfort in this time."

"Yes," the girl said.

The brown liquid smelled like tree bark and dirt. Samuel put it to his mouth and drank. It was bitter; he had expected as much, but it somehow had a soothing effect. His lips puckered. "What is this?"

"It's coffee." The girl grinned. "Have you never had it before?"

Samuel shook his head. He took another sip before shoving his glasses farther up. Coffee was a delicacy that had to be imported from the greenlands. He wondered how many coins it cost the Litten family to brew a single cup.

"It's really good," Samuel said sheepishly.

He couldn't help but notice the girl's fingers. They were thin and long like the old butcher's but free of wrinkles and bulging veins. He wondered what they would feel like on his arm. The girl must've noticed him staring. She clutched the tray tightly, bowing slightly before walking down the hallway like she'd done something terrible.

Samuel breathed deeply. Although he wasn't a cleric yet, most treated him like he was. It wasn't against the law to touch the bastard of a cleric, as far as Samuel knew, but he understood why the citizens avoided him. His arm had not been inked with holy roots, but it may as well have been. What future could the bastard child of a cleric hope for besides the mark of the clergy?

About halfway through his cup of coffee, the sheriff returned. The ride back home seemed far less eventful to Samuel. When he and his father went inside their cabin, he tossed off his boots and put his father's knife under the bed. The fire from several hours before had cooled to nothing more than glowing coals. His father lit a candle, laying the scriptures beside the picture of Samuel's mother.

Samuel gazed at the tattered photograph. His mother had left him her smooth black hair, petite height, thin figure, and bad vision. He wore her old pair of glasses. His father had saved them in case Samuel's sight worsened with age, which was a wise choice. By the time Samuel turned seven, he could hardly see a thing without them. Even with them, certain shapes and colors, like the speckled patterns of yellow and green on the pine leaves surrounding the log cabin, were hard to decipher. He told his father he needed lenses made specifically for him, but eyeglasses were expensive and hard to come by. All specialized goods needed to be brought up by train carts from the greenlands, which was always costly. And it wasn't as if his father was in a high-paying profession.

"Father?"

"What is it?"

"Why'd the butcher touch you?"

Samuel had been too scared to ask before, and the Littens' house didn't seem like the right place to bring it up.

His father glanced at the photograph of his mother. He'd said her name only once before, but Samuel had never forgotten it. Atia. It was a southern name, and to him it sounded warm and free.

"Death often supersedes the worries of the living and can break the hardest of men. What is another day on this earth in comparison to eternity?"

His father often spoke this way, incorporating the scriptures into daily dialogue.

"Do you think the butcher's daughter will report you?"

"No," his father said calmly. "She is grateful that her father passed in peace. I know that much. If she reports the incident, she and her family might be the ones who suffer the consequences. As a public citizen, she welcomed a cleric into her home. To perform the rites, yes. But this wasn't a ceremony. Our combined stories together may still leave much for speculation. My word would be of little help."

"The sheriff would defend you, right? He could speak on your behalf."

"Perhaps. But only Azhuel knows the hearts of men."

His father moseyed through the cabin, readying himself for bed.

Samuel grabbed fresh firewood and rekindled the fireplace. He extended his palms to the cackling flame. He pictured his father working in a different profession, like logging or smithing. He had the muscles for it, unlike Samuel, whose frame and body seemed more designed to reflect his mother. His thoughts often came back to her, especially recently. If his father had been something else, would his mother still be alive? Would Samuel have despised his future so much, the inevitability of religious piety and isolation? Like many orphans who'd been abandoned by their families, his father had been selected by the high council to be raised and trained in the faith by a lead cleric. Many impoverished citizens would try to voluntarily give their sons over to the cloth, if not merely to guarantee that their children would be fed on a regular basis.

"Do you ever regret it?" Samuel asked. "Being made a cleric, I mean. Do you ever wish you weren't?"

Samuel's father blew out the candle near the nightstand. "I'm honored to serve. That's the beauty of Azhuel's mercy. In the end, we all have a choice to be cleansed by the roots. To be forgiven our faults. To be made whole again. All men need this."

Samuel glanced at the photograph of his mother, imagining how the warmth of his mother's skin must've felt when she held him as a baby.

"Do you think she regretted it?"

His father, as he often did, ignored him.

"It's late. Come to bed."

The storm ended early the next morning. Samuel's father left at sunrise to examine the fishing lines by the iced-over lake. To busy himself, Samuel chopped firewood and checked the ground snares near the left end of their cabin. The snares were empty, but one of the bushes nearby had begun sprouting blackberries. He picked all the ripe berries and put them inside his pockets, eating a few along the way back.

After an hour of shoveling snow away from the doorway, he decided to take a break from his daily chores. He got the hunting knife and chose a large pine behind the cabin as the target, carving an X into the bark. He stepped back ten paces, angled his body, and threw the knife with all his might. He missed the target on the first attempt but landed near the mark every time afterward. He dug the blade out from the wood and decided to test his range from twenty paces back. This proved far more difficult, and he could hardly hit the tree at all, let alone the X. His father had once told him about a redlands soldier who had struck a scorpion nearly fifty feet away with his dagger. Samuel wished he could be that accurate throwing. But he had trouble judging depth, and that was something no amount of practice could fix. He blamed his mother's lenses.

By midday, his father had returned with several more bluefish. They cooked them right away, eating their fill. Samuel was surprised by his own hunger. After an early dinner, he showed his father the ripening blackberries, taking him to the bush. His father decided it was best to set up a ground snare near the front of it. Samuel dug a hole about a foot deep as his father hammered six stakes into the nearly frozen ground, aligning them into a perfect circle. They tied a rope around the nearest pine, set the snare on top of the stakes, and covered it with snow and dirt. Hopefully some four-legged creature would find the blackberries as enticing as they did.

Returning home, Samuel pointed to the red jeep parked beside their shed.

"Has someone else passed?"

His father scratched his beard as they walked.

"No. That's not the sheriff."

Samuel didn't understand until he got closer to the cabin. The red jeep sparkled in the sunlight, its metallic-style paint glistening. The sheriff drove his vehicle everywhere all throughout the day, and it was always covered in filth and grime, but this jeep looked as if it had been loaded off a trans-state train car hours before. Stacks of bundled papers and manila folders were scattered across the passenger seats. The documentation looked official.

It wasn't the sheriff's jeep.

Opening the front door, Samuel and his father were greeted by a nervous young man. He was dressed in a fine dark suit, wooly peacoat, and leather loafers. His blue eyes had a dazed look, like Samuel and his father and the cabin around were all part of some exotic world. He combed his slick blond hair to the side with his fingers and stood up from the chair.

"Cleric," he said a little too loudly. "I am here on official assignment from the mayor of Haid."

His father bowed. Samuel followed suit, his throat swelling.

"Do you know who I am?" the boy asked.

"I do not. I apologize for my ignorance."

"Charles Thompson. I'm the mayor's son."

It wasn't until he said his name that Samuel recognized him. The young man looked nearly the same as he had back when he and Samuel were boys. Six or seven years prior, the mayor's wife fell ill, and a high fever took her. All the shops in town closed, and even the loggers were given the day off, so everyone could attend the funeral and pay their respects. His father, as was custom, performed the holy rites. Samuel could recall the largeness of the crowd, the elaborate decorations that adorned the town square, and the lanky yellow-haired boy clenching onto Mayor Thompson's fine suit and wailing like an infant as Samuel's father sprinkled blood on his mother's corpse. The mayor had to restrain the boy and eventually had the sheriff drive him back to the estate, because his raucous outbursts were delaying the ceremony. A week after the funeral, the boy was sent away to live with one of his relatives down in the greenlands. Last thing Samuel overheard from a blabbering citizen was that the mayor's son was attending an elite boarding school getting a proper education. The greenlands had a reputation for expensive and prestigious schools, as well as lavish crops and agreeable climate.

"Of course," Samuel's father said. He bowed once more. Samuel did the same. "There is no reason to stand on my behalf, young sir. Would you like some tea?"

Charles nodded. "Yes. Please. It's so cold in here."

Samuel wanted to tell him better socks and shoes would make the cold much more bearable, but he decided against it. He poured a dash of tealeaves into a pot, and noticed his fingers were stiff and shaky. Had the butcher's daughter talked to anyone about that night? Why else would a politician be inside his father's cabin? What sort of pleasant business could Mayor Thompson have with the cleric?

Samuel's father took off his gloves and rolled up his shirtsleeves. He took a seat across from Charles, keeping his arms stiffly by his side.

"Don't know if you've heard, but my father has been the victim of a petty thief," Charles said emphatically. He cocked his head, perhaps marveling at the mark of the clergy. "He had the sheriff set up some animal traps in the woods, and he now has at least six patrolmen stationed outside the estate at all times."

His father folded his hands together, his demeanor calm. "I've been informed of as much. How might I be of service?"

Samuel stirred the boiling water with a spoon until it was ready. He poured Charles a cup, the liquid steaming. The mayor's son wiped his bangs from his forehead before sipping the tea. For a moment, the hair no longer covered the yellowing bruise swollen over his left brow. "I can't tell you more than that. But you need to come with me."

His father rose and bowed. "I'm honored to serve."

Charles gave a quick smile. He shook the teacup. "It tastes good."

"I'm glad," Samuel said.

"Do you go with him? The cleric, I mean. You're his son, right?"

Samuel rubbed his fingers across his jeans. "Yes. And sometimes."

His father cleared his throat. "He will stay behind."

"No." Charles stood up, drinking more tea before turning to Samuel. "He can come with us. It'll be fun. I can give you a tour of the estate. Unless you want to stay here and freeze to death."

Samuel tried reading his father's stoic face but couldn't. "I suppose I can."

Charles grinned as he rose. "Great! Oh. And cleric? Bring the scriptures. I'll get the engine going."

When Charles exited the cabin, Samuel sprang into action. He climbed up the ladder to their bed and pulled the knife from underneath the mattress. His father went over to the desk, collecting the leather-bound verses. He stood near the door, waiting for Samuel to get down from the loft. Then, unexpectedly, his father grabbed his arm. The skin of his palm was warm yet calloused. Samuel tensed. He recalled the butcher's bony fingers as they'd clutched onto his father's inked mark. His father got closer. He whispered in his ear. "If something happens to me. If they take me away. No matter what they threaten or do to me, you never saw the butcher touch me. Understand?"

Samuel nodded, and his father went outside.

Samuel's heart beat rapidly as he draped his jacket's hood over his head and followed, his boots crushing the snow below. His father's touch still burned on his skin. Why did he touch him? Something must have made him terribly afraid. He looked up. The afternoon sun shone brightly all around, so much so that he could nearly feel the warmth on his garments. He'd put on his gloves, but he didn't need them. The wind was still, and there wasn't a cloud in the sky; it was by far the warmest day they'd had in months.

They rode the jeep through the neighborhoods and down into the town square. The shops in the square were open and busy.

Passing between the shops on opposite ends, Samuel could see clearly through the shops' glass windows. The baker gathered sacks of wheat from his shed, yelling curses to some invisible presence. The tailor took measurements for a customer. The postman sorted through the pile of fresh mail scattered across his desk, a pair of chained spectacles draped around his neck. The blacksmith, a dark-skinned foreigner with burly arms, was hammering away at a slate of smoldering steel. The inside of his open shed glowed red from the roaring furnace. He wore a long apron and heavily tinted goggles, looking almost like a creature from another world. He was more than likely building more tools for the loggers: axes, saws, chains, and hooks. Whatever they needed. He occasionally made knives and other such items for the townspeople, which he sold at a fair price. His shop was where his father had gotten the hunting knife. He'd bartered a pile of chopped firewood and an old pocket watch for it. But despite the blacksmith's incredible talents, Haid was a logging town. The blacksmith's priority was to supply the workers with chopping, cutting, and hauling equipment. That was the business that kept him fed.

Samuel noticed the butcher's shop was closed. "Where are we headed?"

"The jailhouse," Charles said. "You've seen it before, right?"

He scratched his leg, glancing at his father. "No."

The jailhouse was a relic from before the blackout; there was no telling how many hundreds of years old it was. The old building was constructed of cracked stone and a tiled roof. There was one barred window visible on the left side. The whitelands had very few stone buildings because quality stone was expensive and a poor conductor of heat. Unless specifically employed by the wealthy elite, masonry was no longer a practical trade, especially in the whitelands.

A crew of patrolmen stood guard outside of the jailhouse, their arms cradling rifles and their expressions blank. When Samuel's father hopped out of the seat, he whispered a prayer of protection. It did nothing to ease Samuel's nerves. What if it was some sort of trap, some elaborate scheme to capture his father without making a public scene? His father had trusted the Litten woman, believing she would take their secret to the grave. But any citizen touching a cleric was an unforgivable sin. Perhaps she simply reported the offense without hesitation, fearing what might happen if the secret would be discovered.

Locks from behind the steel door jingled before it opened. The sheriff leaned against the doorway for support, his breath reeking of liquor. His thumb caressed the revolver suspended from his belt. His lips scrunched. "Why's the kid here?"

"Me?" Charles asked.

"No, idiot. Him." The sheriff pointed to Samuel. "Get him out of here."

Samuel's chest burned. His father remained unreadable, his eyes forward.

"Eugene," Charles said with forced authority. "I don't know who you think you're talking to. The mayor, your boss, is my father. If he's got a problem, he'll deal with me. You're just a stupid sheriff. You can't give me orders. If you're lucky, one day I'll be giving you orders."

The sheriff grumbled inaudibly as he eased his hand away from the revolver. "To hell with it." He stumbled back inside the jailhouse and left the door open.

Charles shrugged. "Lazy drunk. Come on."

The room was small and fairly empty, lighted only by a lone candle burning on top of a desk. A rack of firearms and various weapons had been mounted to the side of the wall: handguns, rifles, knives, swords, hooks, and a variety of miscellaneous tools with sharp blades. Samuel knew what was done to lawbreakers. Months before, a logger attempted to organize his coworkers and demand higher wages from the state. It didn't take long for the man to be arrested, tried, and found guilty by the mayor for rebellion and conspiracy to incite violence. The logger's funeral was open casket, the pieces of him reassembled in a nonsensical way. Samuel saw the body with his own eyes. His father performed the rites.

Mayor Thompson sat in a cushioned chair behind the desk, his body hunched over and his teeth gnawing on the end of a wooden smoking pipe. He was the only man in town who smoked, as far as Samuel knew, because he was the only one who could afford southern tobacco. A velvet handkerchief poked out from his breast pocket, and a gold chain hung around his fuzzy neck. His round belly bulged out over his trousers. He read through a stack of shuffled papers, his forehead tight. His blond hair was slicked back and combed.

"He's here," the sheriff said.

The mayor straightened his neck. He grinned as he sucked on the pipe's stem. He guided the pipe away from his mouth and blew out a giant ring of smoke. The smell of burning earth filled the room. "Cleric," he said. "So glad you could join me."

Samuel's father bowed. "It's my duty to serve."

"Knew he'd say that," the sheriff said before spitting.

The mayor pointed his pipe to Samuel.

"You must be the son. I didn't know you were coming, but you are most welcome. I'm certain your father will need all the assistance he can get." He waved at Charles. "You can go now."

Charles frowned, his voice unsteady.

"But I thought Samuel would come with me and—"

"Pick up some parchment before you head to the estate. Should have arrived at the post office today. If not, someone will get an earful."

Charles pouted his lips. He shrugged and, without looking at Samuel, left the jailhouse.

The mayor rose from behind the desk. The sheriff sluggishly stepped ahead, moving down the dark hallway and on toward the cell. The mayor cleared his throat before proceeding forward. Samuel and his father followed the mayor, staying several paces back. The rhythm of their footsteps echoed down the stone walls.

"This conversation will never leave this building," the mayor said as they came into the cell room. "Anything you witness here is not to be shared with another soul. I'm sure I don't need to remind you of the consequences if you fail to do so."

"I am a servant," his father said. "Azhuel has taught me humility and submission. I will remain silent as instructed."

The mayor chuckled to himself. "We shall see about your god."

Rusty steel bars divided the poorly lit room into two halves, with one side for the prisoner. Directly underneath the only window sat a little girl with thick red hair, the strands flowing down her back in large ringlets. Her milky skin was nearly as pale as the snow, and her arms and limbs almost too thin. Brown freckles decorated the tip of her nose and spread out across her cheeks. Steel chains shackled her tiny ankles to the stone wall behind her. She wore a ruffled black dress that flared at the hem, the ends stopping well above her knees. The fabric of the dress seemed thick and multilayered, which was great for insulation, but the length of it was far too short to be practical for wear during the winter months. The girl's right leg was wrapped in a thick layer of frayed gauze. She was missing half of her left arm, the stub several inches below her elbow.

Her piercing emerald eyes gazed at Samuel.

"We've captured a demon, cleric," the mayor's voice bellowed. "And I require your assistance."

$\mathcal{S}$amuel shoved his glasses up the bridge of his nose, swallowing hard. The girl remained still and silent, her eyes shifting to nothing in particular.

"This is deershit," the sheriff grumbled to himself.

"Demon," the mayor repeated as he added fresh tobacco to his pipe. He struck a match and lit the ingredients inside. "Fiend. Devil. A creature of darkness."

His father clung to the leather-bound scriptures, moving slowly as he went to the bars. "I apologize, mayor. But I'm not sure I understand."

"You're supposed to be a man of faith, cleric."

"Demons work against Azhuel," his father said hesitantly. "Their darkness can consume men's hearts with all manner of impurities. If permitted, they can burn away the roots connecting our souls to our creator. But this child—"

"Will be dead by the day's end if there's any damn justice in this world," the sheriff said, stroking his revolver. "Demon." He chortled, licking his mustache. "That's really funny."

"Don't insult me," the mayor said curtly, gnawing his pipe. "I'm an educated man. Education, Eugene. Something you would know very little about."

Samuel stepped closer to his father, wondering if the mayor had gone mad. Only the most puritanical clerics believed in the physical manifestation of demons, and such talk from a politician was more than abnormal. Politicians were well learned, well read, and ruled with the common people's welfare at heart. It was the politicians' responsibility to govern with logic and justice, and the clergy's responsibility to appeal to the more primitive natures of man. These were the primary principles of the Laevis Creed. He had heard the mayor say something like that at his wife's funeral.

Samuel squinted. The cell was dark, illuminated only by the sunlight able to seep through the barred window. But he still only saw a one-armed girl.

The mayor blew more smoke. The cloud dissipated as it came above Samuel's head. "I'm sure you've heard rumors about the thief. From my own estate, no less. How can I be a ruling mayor if I cannot protect my own property?" He paced in circles, the pipe in his mouth wriggling. "So, in an effort to apprehend the culprit, I had the sheriff set traps in the western woods. This," the mayor pointed to the girl, "is what I caught. When they found it, it was tearing at its own leg like a rabid wolf." He bent his fingers. "Bare fingers ripping through the leg. Would've gotten loose if we hadn't found it when we did."

The sheriff snorted. "Not all we found, is it? Little sadistic—"

"Eugene, please." The mayor removed the pipe. "Cleric, this demon child had the strength to murder a patrolman. We found … the parts of him. Innards in its lap, blood all over the snow. Took three men to restrain the creature. The sheriff here managed to knock it unconscious barely long enough to pull the snare back and put the shackles on."

His father nodded, scratching his beard. Samuel stood silently. His father was devoutly religious, but surely he didn't blindly believe the mayor's talk about the girl being a demon.

Samuel looked to his feet, somehow mustering the courage to speak.

"If I may, how do you know? Sir. How do you know it was her?"

The mayor grinned, seemingly unbothered. "Good question, boy. Let me further explain. A steel trap was nearly halfway through its leg, and it was scraping at the wound like it was an itch. And it never once made a sound. Not a word, a groan, a whimper as it did that or when we fought to subdue it. Nothing. Its speed is uncanny to say the least. Just look at the child's hand. Those are more like claws than fingernails. Fox-like, if you ask me. Go near it and feel the instinctual terror that grips your heart. Its blood is not red. No, not at all." He pointed at the whites in his own eyes. "But really, it's most obvious in these. Irises like diamonds, pupils slit like a reptile. Not human." He twirled his hand freely. "Now. I know what the two of you must be thinking. And no, I am no closet believer in religion. What kind of mayor would I be if I prayed to the tree god? But I do realize that, although our primitive ancestors were quite fantastical in their approach to morality and the afterlife, it is very possible that their archaic vocabulary limited their ability to explain unusual things. Perhaps the writings do hold some merit. Are the apocalyptical ramblings and nonsensical prophecies glimpses into ancient wars and spectacular technologies?" He paused. "I believe with the right methodology, we can uncover the real truth."

Samuel nodded, but he didn't understand.

The mayor straightened his shoulders, his belly jiggling.

"Cleric. As your mayor, I order to you speak with this creature. Apply your doctrine, faulty as it is, and I will analyze its interactions with you. Do whatever prayer or cutting you must." He leaned in. "If you get it to listen, to respond, then I will reward you greatly."

"Are you serious?" the sheriff interjected as he pulled out his gun from its holster, spinning its cylinder. It was as if he could no longer remain silent. "You plan on keeping this ... thing around? In my jailhouse!"

The mayor dug his heel into the ground, obviously perturbed.

"My jailhouse, Eugene. I own this town."

Samuel didn't know what the mayor was getting out of this. His father closed his eyes, muttering a quick prayer to himself before speaking. "I could never accept a reward for my duties, good mayor," he said, rubbing his nose. "I serve for the honor of Azhuel. For the roots. If you will open the bars, I will pray for this child."

"Converse, pray, do whatever you need. I've said before, the demon child hasn't spoken." He chuckled. "Maybe it'll talk for a holy man. Wouldn't that be something?"

Samuel's ribs burned as he pried the scriptures from his father. His father gave a stern look, but he ignored it. He knew his father would never correct him in front of the mayor.

The sheriff rose, his lip curling.

"You can't let them in there."

He aimed the revolver at the girl, cocking back the hammer.

The girl, oblivious of the danger in front of her, traced her index fingernail across the dirt ground. Her motion was slow yet fluid. It was as if she were in no danger at all.

"How many dead bodies are we gonna have in this town?" the sheriff asked, nearly shrieking. "Tell me that, Thompson! I knew Landon back when he was sucking on his mother's tits, and now I've got to go and tell that old woman her only living son is dead. Me, Thompson. Not you, the mayor. And for what? Some stubby-armed psychotic child … thing you want to keep around? Like a pet? And now you're trying to venture off into some religious quest?" His arms shook. "Are you mad?"

The mayor's cheeks went flush. "Know your place, sheriff. Put the gun away and open the gate. Do your job, or I'll find someone who will."

Samuel stepped back. His father's breaths were short and rushed as he rolled his sleeves back, exposing the mark of the clergy.

"It's an honor to serve Azhuel as well as those whom He has appointed over us to rule as politicians."

The mayor nodded. "Good man."

The sheriff remained frozen for a long minute before throwing the revolver across the room. Samuel jumped back as the gun struck the metal bars, the sound echoing as if a shot had been fired.

The girl never stirred.

"Get yourself a new damn sheriff." The sheriff reached in his pockets, jingling the keys before dropping them on the ground. "See if I care. Go ahead. Lock me inside that cell and see what I do to that monster."

"Eugene—"

"I'm thirsty," the sheriff interjected. "Guess I'll finally take that paid vacation you've been promising me. Trip to a greenlands lake house sounds real nice right about now. Don't you think, mayor?"

The mayor's body clenched, and it took a moment for the skin around his neck to stop blotching. "Two weeks."

"Starting now." The sheriff left the room, slamming the door behind him.

"Forgive the sheriff. He will be reprimanded for his insolence, that I can assure you. However, his concern for your safety is understandable. This demon child is dangerous. But that's why we brought it here."

The girl's finger moved fluidly as she continued her dirt drawings. Samuel did his best to show no fear as his father bent down, hesitating as he picked up the keys. Eugene Black was the hardest man Samuel had ever met. He'd never seen him so angry, or so scared. His father inserted key after key into the lock until it clicked. He slid the gate back. Samuel entered the cell with his father and immediately heard the squeal of steel. He looked back and saw that the mayor had sealed the gate shut.

The mayor wiggled his arms as he refastened the lock.

"There's about five feet of slack, so don't get too close. But these are the strongest northern chains we have."

Samuel stared at the shackles, and his father did as well. If this so-called demon girl killed a grown man, how easy would it be for her to tear them apart?

His father stopped a safe distance away. He held out his arm.

"Do you know what this is, child? It's the mark of the clergy. I'm a sworn servant of Azhuel." He tapped the inked roots with two fingers. "Of the roots. I mean you no harm."

The girl paused her doodling but kept her index finger frozen in place.

His father crossed his arms. "I would like to help you. To pray for you. Do you have a name?"

The girl said nothing.

Samuel inhaled a bitter stench, nearly gagging at what smelled like a dead carcass. The gauze around the girl's right leg had taken a blackish hue, and Samuel could now see the dried blood caked on her dress, her limbs, her hair. Some spots were crimson and others black as tar. It made him wonder how much of the blood had been hers. She glanced up at him for the briefest moment before turning away. The reflecting green of her eyes seemed unnatural to any human or animal he'd seen, like ripples of film.

"Show the girl your arm, Samuel."

Samuel came alongside his father. He set the scriptures down and placed his bare arm in alignment with his father's, but careful not to have them touching.

"I don't have a mark," he said. "Not yet. Not until I'm ordained and become a cleric." He hated the words as they left his mouth.

The girl turned to face his father's mark.

"I think she's listening," the mayor bellowed, smashing his belly between the bars. "Keep going. Ask more questions."

His father edged closer and closer, stretching out his arms in open surrender.

"I'm sorry that you're in this position, child. You must be in pain. But perhaps your silence is doing you more harm than good. If you can speak, please, tell us your name. Where did you come from?"

The girl's jaw clenched as she dragged her wounded leg up to her chest. Did she remember the way the trap had clamped into her leg?

"How old are you? You can't be more than thirteen years of age. Are you of the roots? Are you natural?" His father grabbed his inked roots. He looked down. "Or are you a servant of the flames?"

The girl returned to her dirt drawings. Samuel couldn't tell if she was scribbling words, simple shapes, or complex images. A few minutes passed before his father motioned for the knife. Samuel unsheathed the blade before giving it over and then propped the scriptures on his lap.

"Read from the prophet Jeutero," his father said. "Start of chapter four."

Samuel searched for the verse as his father aligned the blade over his palm.

"I'm going to say a prayer for you."

His father got closer to the girl.

As soon as the girl noticed the knife in his father's grasp, she rose. The chains strapped to her ankles scraped across the ground, clanking loudly. She was even smaller than she seemed sitting down, her height well under five feet. She effortlessly balanced herself on her left leg, glaring at Samuel's father as the toes on her right foot barely touched the ground. His father cut into his own flesh, allowing fresh blood to trickle down his hand. The girl clawed into her thigh with her only hand, her teeth almost peeping out from her closed mouth. She glared at the knife like she starved for it.

Samuel couldn't explain the feeling that overwhelmed him, but somehow, he knew that she was going to strike. He yanked his father backward, the force surprising him, and they both fell to the ground. His father dropped the knife. The girl flung herself forward, her movements quick and precise. She would've grabbed them both if the chains hadn't held. Samuel crawled to the knife, and once he had it in his grip, he pointed it at the girl.

His father struggled to breathe; the wind was knocked out of him by the fall.

The mayor rattled the bars.

"I told you not to get too close!"

Samuel's father got on his knees, his face red as he heaved. The girl raved with madness, her body quaking with every jerk and lunge.

Samuel could take his eyes off neither of them, fearing what may happen if the northern chains didn't hold.

Samuel trudged through the snow. He and his father had gotten lucky with the ground snares. The rope leading to the blackberry bush was clearly visible, stretching above the snow and wriggling at the sound of his footsteps. He crept forward and put down the backpack. He swallowed, sliding his jacket's hood down while he moved around the pine. A white-tailed buck battled for his freedom, thrashing his body wildly as the stakes pierced and pinned one of his front legs. Deer were fairly plentiful in the eastern woods, but they were hard to catch. The deer's antlers were short and thin, only three points.

Samuel waited.

After a while, the buck quieted its struggle. It panted wildly, its dark tongue hanging out the crack of its mouth. Samuel got to his knees, drawing closer. The deer twisted its neck in horror, its dark eyes watching him. They were wide and black. The eyes of prey.

Samuel reached inside his jacket and got the knife.

"It's okay," he said softly as he straddled the deer's torso, making sure to fully secure him underneath his legs. The buck's muscles twitched, but the creature could do nothing. How had the girl felt when she'd been caught in the bear trap, iron teeth snapping into her leg? Like the buck? Did she think she'd be free? Somehow, he couldn't picture her as a deer. She was more like a scrappy wolf cub.

Or a demon.

Most of his life, Samuel never questioned the teachings of Azhuel. He knew the doctrine firmly, the scriptural explanations of creation through the roots. For a long time, it made sense to him. Life had to come from something, he supposed. But did it mean that Azhuel was really Azhuel, or that the roots were real, or that prayer actually worked, or that there was such a thing as demons? He was beginning to have his doubts. How come every time he prayed, he heard nothing? Was there something wrong with him? He knew he'd make a horrid cleric.

The buck gave one last effort to escape, but it failed to get its hoof on the ground. Samuel patted its shaking torso.

"It's okay," he reassured.

Samuel hated this part, but he was so hungry for red meat. Fresh meat. He aligned the blade over the buck's neck, closed his eyes tight, and slit the animal's throat. The buck dropped, convulsing as warm blood came rushing out. Samuel waited a bit before opening his eyes, making sure it was over. He cleaned the blade with snow.

"Thank you."

Samuel was seven the first time he killed his own deer. He'd watched his father put down ensnared animals many times before, but when it was his turn to cut the creature's throat, he forgot all the instructions. His slice was crooked and shallow, and he missed the artery. He cried after that, and his father had to come over and do it right. Samuel was humiliated. Even as his bastard, Samuel continually felt like a disappointment to his father. He wouldn't only make a poor cleric, but a poor man. He was weak, his branch-like arms and legs too dainty to overpower much of anything, and he cried way more than a boy should. He wanted to be strong, to be resilient and do whatever was necessary to survive, but did he have it in him? It was one thing for him to watch his father put a deer down, and another when he was the one holding the knife.

I know it's hard, his father had told him. *But this is something that one day you'll have to do on your own. A man must learn to provide for himself in this world. The scriptures tell us this.*

I'm sorry.

This animal is a gift. We honor it with our eating, and we honor it by returning its body to the roots.

But it's in pain.

I know. His father had wiped his blade across the snow, cleaning off the blood. *Everything on earth is subject to pain, including us. Azhuel has given man dominion over the beasts, which makes us stewards of this world. We should strive to live in harmony with the living, no matter their size or disposition. But humans need meat. This is why you must learn to put a trapped animal down. Sometimes, a quick death is the most merciful thing to give. We thank the creature for the nourishment it will provide us, and we thank the roots. It is Azhuel's gift to us. We are but dirt. To dirt we return.*

We are all dirt. The idea brought Samuel no comfort.

Samuel said a prayer of thanks, mostly out of habit. The

blackberry bush was in full bloom. He popped more berries into his mouth before turning back to the dead buck. It would be hard work dragging the deer back to the cabin all on his own, but he couldn't leave it unguarded. Not after he'd spilled all that blood. With his luck, the wolves would pick up the scent and have picked it clean before he could return with his father.

He decided to field dress the kill. He cut into the buck's body cavity and scooped out the organs, tossing the steaming entrails away. But he made sure to save the heart and liver. The liver was his father's favorite part. He grabbed the rope from the snare and undid the knots. For once in his life, he hoped he was strong enough to do this on his own.

Samuel dumped the heart and liver into the sink. He wiped his damp glasses, his breathing heavy, arms shaking. He took off his jacket and ran his hands through his shaggy hair, feeling the sweat. His father was perched by the fireplace, lost in the scriptures and his scribbled notes.

"Father?"

His father kept his sight on the holy words, mumbling to himself as he jotted down more words. The circles underneath his father's eyes had grown darker. The mayor had given him a week to thoroughly research the scriptures, learning all he could about the dark spirits and their powers of manifestation. He would then need to report every detail he could gather on demons directly to the mayor, and together, they would devise a plan to commune with the girl.

"What is it?" his father asked.

"We caught a deer with the ground snare. I put him down."

"Get the rope," his father said levelly. "I'll be out in a moment."

"No need." Samuel motioned to the window. "It's in the shed. I couldn't mount it, my arms are dead, but I brought him here."

His father's response was delayed. "By yourself? How big?"

As much physical labor as he did on a daily basis, Samuel somehow managed to remain weak. Truth be told, he didn't think he'd really be able to pull it off on his own.

"Three points."

"That's impressive," his father said with a yawn. He rose, carefully placing the scriptures on the desk. "Did you say a prayer?"

"Yes," Samuel murmured. He guzzled down a cup of water. He wished adulthood was the only thing he would grow into. In a few months, he knew he'd be standing before the high council to take his oath of servitude. In the presence of the seven high-ranking clerics, known as bishops, Samuel would have to adequately explain and defend the doctrines of their faith. Afterward, when the blood was shed and the prayers given, he would have black ink needled into his right arm.

Samuel retrieved a fresh pan as his father diced the liver.

"Did you find anything new?"

His father sliced the meat rhythmically. "There isn't much to gather. So much is open to theological speculation. I know of Azhuel and His goodness. I know of the truth that can be found in this life and the next. I know of darkness as well, but I don't care to know more of it."

Samuel held out the pan as his father tossed in the cut pieces, the juices lathering. They'd not once spoken about the girl in the jailhouse, and since then it was nearly all he thought about. Her thick red hair, her chains, her missing arm, her bloodstained skin, her near-glowing eyes.

"Is she a demon?" Samuel asked. "I mean, do you think she's a demon?"

His father wiped his forehead, palming the edge of the counter.

"I don't know. Demons do not have material bodies. But that child? She's not like anything I've seen before. I don't know what she is."

"What do you think happened to her arm?"

"I don't know."

Samuel looked to his feet. "What will the mayor do to her?"

"The mayor is a man accustomed to getting what he wants," his father said as he packaged the buck's heart into sheets of used paper. "He sees something in that child he desires. Something dark and powerful. He will attempt to harness it with or without my assistance. For now, I must serve and obey. We are but dirt."

"What if she doesn't want to listen to the mayor?"

His father washed his hands, drying them on a fresh towel.

"I suppose the sheriff would have his way, then."

"It's not fair," Samuel said softly. "They catch her in a ground snare and hurt her and keep her chained up like a dog. It's ... not right."

"You sound like *her*," his father said dryly.

Samuel guessed his father was referencing his mother, but he wasn't sure if it was meant to be a compliment. The kitchen knife sat beside the packaged organ, blood staining the paper. He rinsed the blade before stepping back outside and onto the packed snow.

4

Unlike the butcher's quaint and unostentatious burial, Landon Swen's funeral was a lavish affair. Black streamers and red poinsettias decorated the shops' display windows. A white-clothed table had been set up near the center of the town square, serving free chocolates and licorice balls to all in attendance. Many of the parents had to restrain their children from taking too much, while others said nothing as their little ones shamelessly stuffed their mouths and pockets full of candy. How many times in their lives would they get the chance to eat packaged candy from the greenlands? Sugary treats were an expensive luxury, typically reserved for the politicians and their families. The large funeral ceremony was a rarity in and of itself. Citizens were not allowed to congregate for any reasons other than labor for the state, unless a ruling politician permitted otherwise.

The patrolman's closed coffin sat on top of the makeshift

wooden stage, and a violinist, no doubt hired from the greenlands, played a somber medley as the citizens of Haid came to pay their respects for the dead. The square was crowded, with hundreds in attendance. People were barely able to move without brushing against one another. The loggers were given the day off. That in and of itself was nothing short of a miracle. Pinewood is what kept the town alive. It was the reason Haid was one of the largest towns in the whitelands.

Landon's death was labeled an unfortunate accident, but beyond that there wasn't much explanation as to what had happened to him. The consensus was a bear attack, but most wouldn't say what they really thought. The sheriff stood beside the mayor, his cheeks flushed as he petted his peppered mustache. He kept turning to Landon's mother, an elderly woman who couldn't keep the tears from streaming down her wrinkled cheeks. He must have decided to delay his leave until after the funeral. The mayor smoked his pipe, giving strained smiles and condolences to those in mourning. Perhaps paying for such an extravagant ceremony was his way of making peace with the sheriff. Samuel didn't understand how the sheriff could get away with disrespecting the mayor as much as he had. A citizen could be punished or even executed for disobeying a direct order from a politician. Citizen compliance to ruling politicians was a necessity for maintaining peace. Or so Samuel had heard. But maybe the mayor needed the sheriff more than most thought.

"The knife," his father said.

Samuel grabbed the knife from his pocket and extended the

handle to his father. They had been waiting along the outskirts of the square until the appropriate time. When the mayor gave the signal, his father marched through the snow toward the stage with the scriptures in one hand and the hunting knife in the other. The crowd parted wide enough for ten men to pass through. Even at such a packed event, no one would dare be caught touching a cleric. Samuel stayed behind, reclining against the walls of an abandoned shack. He'd told his father he didn't want to risk botching the rites, and the large crowd would only make him more nervous. In reality, however, he hated the glares and the whispered conversations.

"*Wait. Is that the cleric's bastard? He's gotten big.*"

"*You heard what they did to the poor bitch who bore him? Religious zealots can't even keep their own vows. I wish they'd all disappear.*"

"*You think he'll be a cleric too?*"

"*It makes sense; like anyone in their right mind would hire a cleric's bastard. No telling how messed up that kid is. Can you imagine having that oath-breaking holy man as your father?*"

"*True. Save our logging jobs for those who need them.*"

Samuel looked ahead. His father hovered over Landon's coffin, cut his own palm, and sprinkled blood across the closed casket. Some gazed with open mouths and furrowed brows, while others refused to watch entirely. Undeterred by the crowd size, he read several passages from the book of Hetsulu, his tone loud but level.

"Blessed are those under the dirt," his father said. "For they shall be reunited with Azhuel. Their blood shall feed the holy roots, their skin finding life once more."

Seeing the closed coffin made Samuel think about the girl in the jailhouse.

He tilted his head, looking past the main gathering.

Laura Litten, the old butcher's daughter, stood in front of the butcher's shop. A bloodstained apron was tied around her waist, and stray strands of her brown hair were caked onto her cheeks. Sweating was a hard feat to accomplish in the whitelands since summers were mild and short-lived, but somehow, most people found a way. Laura's daughter came out from behind the shop's door, and he nearly tasted the bitterness of the coffee she'd served him. Her name was Claudette. He remembered that, and how her narrow face was a younger reflection of her mother's. Mother and daughter whispered to each other before they both strolled back into the shop. He pulled up the jacket's hood over his head. The sheriff had been right about Laura picking up the butchering trade, and his father had been right about her keeping the secret of the old butcher touching a cleric. At least for now.

Something tapped Samuel on the shoulder. He turned. Charles stood behind him in a fancy coat and loafers, blinking heavily. "Hey. Samuel, right?"

Samuel froze. He'd touched him. It was only a moment, but it happened. Why did he touch him? Didn't he remember who he was? Being the mayor's son must have given him the freedom to do anything.

"Yes."

Charles took a step closer, and his ankle dropped into the snow, nearly causing him to fall on his face. Samuel almost reached out to help steady him, but didn't. He didn't want to touch the mayor's son. Not on purpose. When Charles regained his footing, he stomped angrily into the icy ground with his shoes.

"I hate this snow."

Samuel pushed up his glasses.

"You should wear boots. It'll keep your feet warmer. And it'll help with your balance walking over the ice."

Charles shrugged. "Probably right. Not like I want to live in this frozen hell anyway." He cleared his throat. "I need a favor. A cleric, specifically."

Samuel paused. "My father is almost done."

Charles dusted his tan peacoat shakily. "Can't wait. I need a cleric now."

"I don't know any other clerics. The closet one is in Thamus, I think, and that's about thirty miles—"

"You're a cleric, right?"

Samuel shifted his weight to the side. "No."

Charles stared at Samuel. "But you are his son."

"I'm not a cleric. Not yet. I haven't been ordained."

Charles's neck reddened. "Don't be so literal. I'm the mayor's son. And that means I have the same authority. Right? Isn't it the same for you?"

"Maybe? I don't know."

"Come on. It's the same thing!"

Charles nervously pulled out a smoking pipe from his jacket.

He tossed a pinch of shredded tobacco into the black bowl, lighting it with a metal lighter. He sucked in the dark smoke, then coughed heavily. After a few puffs, he moved closer. "It's the demon. I messed up. Really bad. I think it's dying."

The girl was curled up underneath the barred window, her red hair covering her face as a small ray of sunlight beamed on her milky skin. Her little chest rose and fell, but even from afar, Samuel could tell her breathing seemed uneasy. The smell of rotten flesh and waste filled the jailhouse. Samuel covered his nose to guard it from the stench. A fresh puddle of what appeared to be black blood had formed around the girl's injured leg. The girl methodically scraped her fingers across the stained dirt, her face unreadable, her green eyes gazing into nothingness.

Charles coughed as he took a drag from his pipe.

"My father put me in charge of the demon since the sheriff's leaving town for a week after the funeral. Must be worried the drunk will do something stupid, and then get himself killed for not listening to orders. I don't know why he keeps that fool around. Anyway. That demon? That thing? It won't eat or drink. I've tried, and it won't take anything. And you can smell that, right? Like rot. It keeps getting worse." He ran a hand through his hair. "He told me it was my job to keep the demon safe for now. I really messed this up."

Samuel adjusted his glasses. "She's bleeding. From her leg."

Charles let out a nervous laugh. "About that. I went in there, you know. Trying to help." He sucked his pipe. "So, I went in there and she … it! It started crawling to me like some kind of crazed mutt. And I didn't know what do. It was instinct. I kicked it and ran for cover. Self-defense."

"Help? The demon? What do you mean?"

Charles waved his hand. "Yeah. I was going to change its bandage. Or whatever. It doesn't matter. The demon showed me its teeth. Its fucking teeth!" Charles dropped the pipe. He scooped it back up. Its contents had spilled onto the floor. "I'm dead. He's going to lose it. It was my job. I was supposed to watch it, keep it safe. He's going to kill me. Damn it."

Samuel rubbed his fingers together. "Where are the other patrolmen? Can't you ask them for help?"

"Of course not. Don't be stupid. None of them are allowed in here. Just me. They're citizens. Everyone knows they have big mouths."

Samuel's muscles twitched. He could hear a clicking noise, and when he got closer to the bars, he could see the girl grinding her teeth. He watched her, helpless to do anything. "What do you want from me?"

"I don't know. Pray for it or something. My dad thinks it's a demon, right? I thought he was going mad. But then … " Charles shook his head. "You should pray for it. Keep it calm."

"My father tried that. It didn't work."

"Maybe he did it wrong." Charles clenched his jacket sleeve.

"Or maybe you could ask the roots god to help you. Something. Do something!"

"I'm not a cleric!" Samuel burst out. He knew he shouldn't have, so he quickly regained his composure. He'd never yelled at someone before. "I'm sorry. I want to help you. But I don't know what to do."

Charles plopped himself into the wooden chair stationed by the door. He buried his face in his palms, his words stifled in his hands. "He's going to kill me this time. I know it."

"The mayor?"

Charles didn't answer.

Samuel dragged his feet as he approached the bars, pushing his forehead against the cold steel. The girl continued with her finger scraping, unmoved by the outside commotion. When Samuel was a boy, he prayed that Azhuel would bring his mother back up from the earth. He prayed that his father would love him. He prayed that he'd make friends. He prayed that people in Haid wouldn't ignore him all the time. He prayed that one day he could know what it's like to be touched and embraced and kissed. He prayed that the roots would give him a sign if they were real. Anything. He prayed and prayed and prayed. Azhuel wasn't there. If He was, He wasn't concerned about his pain. But for some reason, maybe because it was all that he knew, he prayed.

"We are but dirt," Samuel said instinctively. "To dirt we return."

Charles got up.

"You know," he said, "maybe the demon is just protecting its leg. Think about it. First time the devil went crazy on that patrolman was when it was caught in that bear trap."

Samuel recalled how the girl calmly studied his father's mark before trying to attack them. And he didn't understand why Charles kept calling the girl an "it."

"She tried to hurt my father, and he never touched her leg." Samuel fumbled with his glasses. He also had a hard time believing the girl felt pain, because if she did, her face showed no signs of it. "Maybe we can talk to her. Tell her that if she doesn't let us help her, she'll die. Someone's got to get close."

"You?" Charles asked.

Samuel's knees wobbled.

"I don't know."

Charles slapped him across the back.

"You can do this," he said before running to grab a handgun from the sheriff's rack of mounted weapons. He held it awkwardly. "Don't get killed."

"Will you shoot her?"

Charles struggled to align the barrel with the girl. "If it goes bad. I don't know. You're not a coward, are you?"

Samuel ignored the insult. He reached for his hunting knife before realizing his father still had it. "Have you shot a gun before?"

"Aim and pull the trigger. Can't be that hard, right?"

Samuel trotted into the cell and then closed the gate behind him. He approached the girl with cautious steps. He could hear everything: the sound of his boots hitting the floor, the whistle of the wind as it came in through the barred window, Charles fumbling to cock the revolver's hammer, and his own stunted breaths. He pushed up his lenses, seeing a little more clearly. The girl was shivering, her pale complexion having shifted to a subtle blue. Her body heaved with every breath, steam escaping from her agape mouth with every stunted exhalation.

"She's cold."

"It's the whitelands. We're all cold."

"Hello," Samuel said to the girl.

The girl said nothing.

"Don't know if you remember me. I was here before with my father. He's a cleric." He rolled up his sleeve, showing his naked arm. "The roots. Remember?"

The girl's fingers stopped, not bothering to look in his direction. She wasn't afraid. She was nothing like the deer.

Samuel wiped his bangs before removing his coat. His hands were shaking.

"Please don't hurt me."

He held out his arms as far away from his chest as possible, covering the girl with his coat. At first, she remained still, the coat slipping off her shoulders. But then, ever so calmly, her hand grabbed the coat and pulled it up. The chains around her ankles rattled as she curled herself deeper underneath the warmth.

"Your leg," Samuel said. "It looks infected. We're going to need to treat it somehow. You might die if we don't do something. I'm going to make it better, okay?"

The girl closed her eyes.

A minuscule calmness washed over Samuel. The girl wasn't going to hurt him. Not yet, anyway. He exited the cell and rejoined Charles.

"What are we going to do now?" Charles asked as he slammed the gate shut.

"We help her. That's what the mayor wants, right? For you to keep her safe."

"How? Get your father?"

"No." Samuel shook his head. "We get the doctor."

5

amuel waited for Charles's return. He tapped his toes against the top of his boots. The demon girl slept soundly. Her eyes darted back and forth behind closed lids, and he wondered if she was dreaming. Demons couldn't sleep, could they? It took Charles a little more than an hour to return with the doctor.

"We clear?" Charles asked as she stomped into the cell.

"I'm not stupid," the doctor said as she passed Samuel without acknowledging him. She went to the bars and studied the girl carefully from behind them, her leather bag in hand. Charles unlocked the gate and waved a beckoning hand at Samuel.

"Those shackles stay on, doc. Don't touch her unless you have to. Trust me."

The doctor let out a labored sigh. Perhaps she wondered how she could do her job without touching the patient. Samuel walked in

front of the doctor, guiding her into the cell.

The girl opened her eyes.

Samuel pointed to the doctor. "This is the doctor. She's gonna help make your leg better."

The girl didn't stir, keeping her body curled underneath his coat. The doctor set down her bag. Her normally hard face was blanketed with fascination at the girl. She whipped her head back to Charles. "What is this?"

"The leg, doc," Charles said with forced authority.

The doctor's brows furrowed. Samuel reached out, fearing at any moment the girl would lash out like she had at his father. She didn't. Samuel gingerly lifted the coat up to her waist, revealing the bloodied leg. The doctor's nostrils flared as she took in the dark substance oozing from the open leg. "What happened?"

"Can't tell you," Charles said.

"Is there anything you *can* tell me?" the doctor asked, her voice rising. "I don't know the first thing about what I'm seeing here."

"Please," Samuel cooed. "Can you help her?"

The doctor unzipped her bag and retrieved a vial of tar-like liquid. She shook it, the concoction bubbling inside the glass. "It's long gone. I'll have to take it."

"The leg?" Samuel asked.

The doctor nodded.

"What did she say?" Charles asked.

"She needs to amputate the leg."

"No, you can't." Charles flung his arms. "How can you even say that? Take the leg? You haven't even looked at the wound."

The doctor grunted, no longer able to contain her annoyance. "I've seen enough. The foot is grossly swollen and white, the skin and the toenails are all but black. If infection hasn't claimed the leg by now, then frostbite has." She pointed. "See the blotches around her thigh? It's moving fast. And that blood. This can't all be hers. How'd this happen?"

Charles crossed his arms. "I can't tell you."

"Trying to do my job, little mayor."

Charles shoved his hands in his pockets.

"Bear trap," Samuel said.

The doctor uncorked the vial. "And who thought wrapping it up in a filthy bandage would make it all better?"

"You can't take the leg. My father will … he'll want you to save the leg."

"You speak for him now? So, little mayor, answer me this. Is this child better off alive or dead? She's already lost an arm. Is a leg worth her life? With your father's money, a functioning prosthetic wouldn't be the worst thing."

Charles blinked heavily.

"No. No. No. You have to try to save it. No amputation. We're not there yet."

Samuel shifted his weight. The girl didn't seem bothered that two strangers were in the cell with her, or that there was an ongoing discussion about sawing her leg off. Had she once overheard a similar conversation about her arm?

The doctor handed Samuel the vial. "She needs to drink. I'll do what I can, but without amputation, I can't promise anything."

Samuel nodded. He edged the vial forward.

"Can you drink this?"

The girl kept still, watching him lazily. He took a deep breath before extending the vial forward to her lips, tilting it downward. More than half of the medicine fell down her lips, but some of it seeped into her agape mouth.

Within a few minutes, the girl closed her eyes and sank into unconsciousness.

"Better this way," the doctor said. She moved rhythmically, grabbing the girl's leg and unraveling the frayed gauze. Samuel's nose wrinkled at the foul stench. Pus and dark blood oozed out from the jagged strips of muscle. The meat was torn in a way that made parts of the bone visible. The doctor lifted the girl's leg, carefully turning it from left to right.

"Get my scalpel. It's the little blade with the thin handle. And the tweezers. More cloth too."

Samuel fumbled around in the doctor's bag and found the tools. The doctor took the scalpel first without touching him. Like a master craftsman, she carved into the strange girl's injured leg, the meaty flesh breaking under the weight of the blade. More dark blood and pus flowed, some of it squirting onto the doctor's gloved hands.

"How's it going?" Charles yelled.

The doctor ignored the question, dabbing the leaky incision with the cloth.

"Give me the green vial. No, the other green one." The doctor dabbed one of the cloths into the bottle, wiping the areas her blade had cut with it. The girl's limb twitched involuntarily, but otherwise remained motionless.

"How is it?" Samuel asked.

The doctor shook her head. She went to say something but decided against it. He wasn't familiar with many people in town, but he knew the doctor well enough to know she was disturbed. She busied herself with cutting away the infected tissue, the black blood and ripped meat breaking under the scalpel's blade.

"Why are you here?" she asked softly enough that only Samuel could hear.

Samuel pushed his glasses up. His lips pursed. "I don't know."

The doctor didn't press further. "Give me an empty vial," she whispered.

Samuel hesitated but obeyed. The doctor popped the lid for the vial and placed the tip of it into the wound, lapping up the black and syrup-like blood. She closed the vial and tossed it and its contents back inside her bag.

"How much longer you got?" Charles asked, the soles of his feet bouncing.

The doctor brushed her hands across her lap before taking back the scalpel.

"As long as it takes."

Another hour passed. The sunlight had begun to fade, but the doctor continued her work. After she finished slicing away the rotted meat and dabbing the cuts, she wrapped the leg in clean cloth and sealed it with a thick layer of gauze. Samuel helped her clean the tools, doing his best to ignore the smell. The girl looked peaceful as she slept, not like a crazed demon. Not that he had any clue what a demon would look like. But the more he watched her, the more he questioned the mayor's story. Did she really kill that patrolman? How could they be sure? Her body was abnormal, that was true, and she attacked his father with an instinctual viciousness that was primal. But lying there, asleep with her closed eyes and slightly agape lips, she seemed nothing more than a harmless girl.

The doctor stood up and rolled her hips, turning to Charles.

"I need fresh clothes."

Charles scratched his scalp. "I think I saw a couple of folded-up shirts for the sheriff behind his desk. Why?"

"Get one," the doctor said before motioning to Samuel. "I'm going to dress her."

"What do you mean?" Charles's voice rose. He grabbed the bars, nearly shaking them. "What are you doing? Don't touch its clothes! I think that's a bad idea."

The doctor tossed several tools into her bag. She grunted. "She's freezing in that useless dress. It's disgusting and covered in blood and pus and feces and who knows what else. She needs real clothes if she has any chance of recovering in this place. Northern clothes."

"I'm just saying," Charles stammered. "I don't think—"

"She's unconscious," the doctor snapped, unable to contain her anger. "You asked me to keep her alive, didn't you? Let me do my job."

Charles eyed the doctor before sighing and leaving the room. He came back several minutes later, an oversized plaid shirt in hand. His wide eyes watched the girl intently, as if he were expecting her to jump up from her slumber.

The doctor waved at Charles. He pitched the shirt through the bars.

"This place is freezing," the doctor said. "Is there a firepit somewhere?"

Charles hunched his shoulders. "Might be one in the shed."

"Get it. The mayor wants this girl alive, right? She needs warmth."

Samuel agreed. "She does seem cold."

"Fine." Charles did as instructed, his head dropped as if he'd been scolded.

The doctor tossed the sheriff's spare shirt to Samuel. "Hold this."

Samuel took the garment. He held his breath for a minute, watching as the doctor lifted the girl up and slipped off her dress. Ugly scars decorated her flat chest and tiny back. Some were thin and lined like stripes, while others looked like smoldered circles. She wasn't wearing undergarments. He looked farther down and saw where her slit was supposed to be. He turned away quickly, cheeks flushed. He shouldn't have looked. But he did.

Like an undressed mannequin in a store window, there was nothing there.

He knew as much as his father had felt the need to teach him about procreation and female anatomy, which was very little. But even he knew there was supposed to be something there. He glanced at the doctor. She, too, seemed disturbed by what she'd seen. Unlike Samuel, she studied the child's ambiguous crotch unabashedly.

"This can't be," she said to herself.

Samuel's heart raced. Was Charles right in calling the girl an "it"? If so, what on earth could it be? He pushed the thought away. He couldn't think of the girl like that. It didn't seem right.

From the corner of his eye, Samuel saw the doctor scoot the girl's limp body into hers, pressing the girl against her chest. Samuel wondered how it would feel to have a warm body touch him like that. The chains jangled as the doctor dressed her. The shirt nearly swallowed the girl whole, reaching far past her knees.

"What is this child?" the doctor asked, the veins in her neck rising. "Why have you brought it here?"

Even the doctor considered the child an "it" now.

"I don't know," Samuel said.

"Don't lie to me. Do you realize the gravity of this? Does your father know you're here?"

Samuel shook his head. "I'm not. I'm sorry. I don't know."

The doctor moved away from the girl and began gathering up her things. What would his father think? Was the child human? Could it really be a demon? He studied the girl's body once more, knowing now it was safe to do so since she was clothed. Her freckled cheekbones were round, her lips plump and pink, and her hair long, but her shoulders were square and boxlike. Her limbs, at least the ones that were intact, were slender and lean, but also defined by muscles. She had no breasts, but that was to be expected of a girl her age. But without genitals, was there any way of telling what she, or he, or it, was?

The sound of harsh scraping filled the jailhouse. Samuel turned to see Charles scooting himself into the room, grunting as he struggled to drag the firepit along with him. Samuel looked away from the girl and covered her back up with his coat. Even though he couldn't be sure, he really felt like she was a girl.

Samuel helped Charles move the portable fireplace into the cell, but they were clumsy in getting it set up. Charles struck a match and lit the logs inside the steel chamber. The fire devoured the dried pinewood as if it were nothing, the bright flames raging as a flood of new heat and light filled the room.

"The child's dehydrated," the doctor said as they exited the cell. "Needs water. The wound will need to be re-dressed and cleaned every day." She dug inside her bag and lobbed the green bottle and a roll of gauze to Samuel. He caught them clumsily, tucking them into his ribs.

"Wrap it snug," the doctor instructed. "That way the wound won't reopen. But not too tight or you'll smother the circulation. If you follow my instructions perfectly, there's a slim chance this child will survive. But odds are she will die. I want to be clear about that. Not with that leg staying attached. You hear me? I want no part of the blame if things go wrong."

Charles embraced the doctor, then patted her back like she was a family pet. "You are amazing, doctor. Thanks. Let's keep this just between us. No need to bother the mayor with this."

The doctor stood stiff, wide eyed. "Don't touch me."

Charles let her go, wiping his forehead. "It'll work. It has to work."

Samuel returned to the cabin several hours past sunset. His father sprang up from the desk chair the moment the door opened, his back straight and his neck stiff.

"Where were you?" His father's tone was repressed, but the pitch of his voice was higher than usual. He must have been worried. "Where's your coat?"

The roar of the jeep's engine from outside faded into the distance. Charles had driven him home, and he had promised not to talk about what had happened at the jailhouse. He rubbed his bare arms. It was the only coat he owned that fit him anymore, and he wouldn't last the rest of winter without it. Somehow, he'd need to get it back from the girl. Or whatever she was. But he knew she needed it more than he did, and that gave him confidence.

"At the estate."

His father shifted his weight. "The mayor's estate?"

"Yes. I was with Charles."

His father's jaw clenched. "I don't want you going there. Not again."

"Why? I didn't have a choice. He's the mayor's son. I have to do what he says, don't I?"

"We all have a choice," his father said as he went to the scriptures. "You should have waited for me. I didn't know where you'd gone."

Samuel found himself scowling. Most days his father didn't seem to care that he was alive, and now the concern made Samuel angry. He would never be able to please him, no matter how hard he tried.

"You were busy. It was the middle of the ceremony, so—"

"I don't trust him, Samuel. Not with you. Don't go there again."

Samuel bit into his cheek, his mind exhausted and his emotions somehow feeling completely out of his control. Why was his father angry with him? He'd done nothing wrong. If anything, he'd helped saved that girl.

"I'm not a child," he said, trying not to mumble. "I'll be a man soon. Isn't that what you keep telling me?"

His father came closer, dwarfing Samuel with his height. His father was a bit over six feet tall, but Samuel was more than six inches shorter.

"You're my child. Don't forget that. You'll do as I say."

"I'm your son," Samuel said. "Am I not your sin?"

His father's eyes widened. A long silence fell between them.

"I mean, that's what I am to you."

"Don't be foolish," his father said curtly. He grabbed the scriptures from the desk, keeping his voice level as his steps fell heavy. "Everything I've done has been for you. The roots will free you from the bonds of darkness. This demon child, the mayor, everything. Azhuel will bring to light—"

Samuel swiped the scriptures away from his father's hand and hurled them across the room, his body quaking with rage. He couldn't take another lecture on righteousness and forgiveness and the holy roots. He hated the way his father always looked to the scriptures. He showed more devotion and care to that old book than he'd ever once dared to show his own flesh and blood.

"You're a hypocrite," Samuel said with a forced calm, his hands still quaking. "You don't love me. Even if you do, you don't like me. I know you don't. I see the way you look at me." He pointed to his mother's photograph. "If I'm your son, and you love me, then why don't you tell me about my mother? Am I even your child?"

"Of course you're my child!" His father lifted his arms. "Is this not enough for you? I've raised you—"

"I don't want to be your son," Samuel yelled.

His father was stupefied.

Samuel cowered back, the taste of bitterness lingering in his mouth. His sight blurred from fresh tears. "I don't want to be a cleric. I don't. You never listen to me. I never had a choice. You had a choice. I don't. And I hate it."

His father nodded solemnly as he fetched the disheveled scripture, carefully adjusting the pages before setting them down alongside the photograph of his mother.

Samuel wasn't sure what to do next, so he went into the cabinet and peeled off a strip of stale bread. He chewed it mechanically but couldn't force himself to swallow. He poured a cup of water and drank, the liquid pushing the masticated lump down his throat. His father gave the photograph a weak tap with his index finger before climbing up the ladder to the single mattress he and Samuel shared.

Samuel adjusted his glasses, relief and guilt equally consuming him. He rubbed his arms as he got closer to the fireplace, watching as the flames devoured the dead branches until there was nothing left but smoldering ash.

6

"It's a miracle."

Samuel leaned into the metal bars, looking in disbelief.

The girl sat silently, her injured leg propped up slightly by the bottom of her heel. She was hunched over, tracing her middle finger along the dirt floor. The flannel shirt the doctor had dressed the girl in the day before fit her more like an oversized nightgown than a top. Her chains rattled as she doodled indistinguishable objects. She wasn't wearing the jacket he'd left her. It was crinkled up against the back wall of the cell. The gauze on her leg was stained a bit, but otherwise held. His nostrils noticed the lack of rot.

"She looks so much better."

Charles huffed excitedly. "I know. It's only been a day. Can you believe it? That old hag was talking like the demon was as good as dead. Now look at it!"

Samuel crossed his arms. "Do you think it's a demon?"

"I don't know. What else could it be? I mean. I didn't. Not at first. But look at it! Crazy eyes. Black, inky stuff for blood. It doesn't even have any … you know. That's insane, right?"

Charles wasn't inside the jailhouse when the doctor undressed the girl. Samuel leaned forward. "How did you know that?"

"Huh?"

"About the … you know."

"Oh." Charles scratched his yellow hair. "Yeah. I saw that when I was trying to check out its leg before I got you. The demon wasn't wearing undergarments, you know. It was kind of obvious. Freaked me out. Guess I forgot to bring it up to you in all the hustle." He shrugged. "It doesn't matter how I saw. It's inhuman!"

Samuel nodded. "But she looks like a girl. Don't you think?"

"Don't think of it like that," Charles said with a wave of his hand. "It's not a person or anything. It can't even talk or do anything but doodle on the ground and try to kill people!"

Charles jingled the keys, and Samuel stepped back as the gate became unlocked.

"Okay. You ready?"

Samuel cradled the green-tinted vial that the doctor had left with him, the roll of gauze shoved deep in his back pocket. He nodded, remembering his father's rebuke and his outright defiance. They hadn't spoken since the night before. He regretted the words the moment they left his mouth. He needed to apologize, tell his father he was angry with himself most of all for waiting this long to speak out. He knew it wouldn't change anything. But he was tired of pretending.

The girl was unperturbed as Samuel went to her. The fire inside the pit had kept the jailhouse warm. Warm for Haid. Samuel stopped. In his mind, he could picture her reaching out in an unexpected moment and ripping him apart, digging her thick fingernails into his chest and ripping out his organs like prey.

"Hi."

She continued her doodles.

Samuel forced himself to take a few steps closer, bridging the distance between them. Demon? No, she couldn't be. She must have wanted to be a "she." She had long hair and was wearing a dress. Sure. She was something different. Abnormal. But whatever she or he or it was, Samuel was drawn in.

He scooted himself closer to the side of the wall, and with a slow hand, he grabbed his coat. "Can I take this back? Only if you're not going to be cold." He swallowed. "I need to clean your wound. It might hurt. But the doctor said it's the only chance you have of staying alive."

For a long while, the girl did nothing. But then, calmly, she moved her stub into her lap and shifted her wounded leg toward him. Samuel crouched down and carefully unwound the gauze. He wasn't touching her skin. He was too scared, and he didn't want to alarm her. With the unraveling of each layer, his fears grew. She could become the monster the mayor had insisted she was. The wound was wet and excreting lots of pus, but no fresh blood. The spots where the bear trap's teeth had locked were now scabbing, the medicine from the day before still giving the gashes a slight shine. Color was returning to all the dark areas around the cuts, including her thigh. It was healing, and healing fast. Unnaturally fast.

"How does it look?" Charles called. "Is the leg good?"

"It's better. Much better. It's like the infection's almost gone."

Charles huffed. "That doctor may be a cold bitch, but she does good work."

The girl paused her drawings as Samuel dabbed fresh medicine onto the cloth. He hesitantly applied a fresh coat on the wound. She tipped her chin down and watched as he carefully massaged the liquid into the tattered flesh. Her muscles twitched, almost as if they were screaming in pain. But if she felt any pain, she didn't show it.

"That's it," Samuel said as he secured a fresh bandage and rewrapped the leg.

The girl curled her leg back and returned to her drawings. She stroked her finger from left to right, up then down, then across in a rhythmic pattern. Her movements seemed so precise, like she was painting the most elaborate portrait.

As Samuel and his father entered the mayor's estate, he did his best not to stare. The exterior of the estate was lavish enough, but inside, the furnishings were even more extravagant. Three cushioned chairs faced one another in a triangular pattern by the center of the room, every one embroidered with rolling hills and pine trees. Electric lights hung from rubber cords mounted to the ceiling, the glass bulbs illuminating even though it was noontime. He stared at the artificial light, thinking it seemed more fantastical than any stories of Azhuel's divine roots. What sort of world was it before the blackout? The Laevis Creed, established and made into law immediately following the blackout more than four hundred years ago, forbade the use of technology by any person that the ruling politicians deemed to be "exceptional." Samuel supposed the use of electricity and artificial lighting didn't fall into that category.

To the left of Samuel was a large hallway. Near the chairs to the right sat a wooden table, a plastic cube with white buttons and silver dials resting on top of it. He wasn't sure what sort of object it might be, but he assumed it to be some sort of radio communication device. His father positioned himself in direct line of the hallway, his muscles tight as his brawny hands clutched the scriptures. They hadn't spoken a word to each other since that night.

The mayor stormed out from the end of the bright hallway, adjusting his bowtie as his feet thundered across the accent rug. Charles followed after him, his shoulders hunched, and his hair parted in a way that somewhat covered the blue and black bruises on the side of his face. From the sharp eyes Charles gave him, Samuel knew to keep his mouth shut. The mayor must have learned about what had happened to the girl in the jailhouse. He tried to keep a stone face, to be as unreadable as her.

"Thelma!" the mayor hollered as he sat on the biggest chair. He motioned for Samuel and his father to sit, and they did. A young woman moseyed into the room, her hair pulled back and an apron tied around her waist. Samuel had seen her several times before in the town square, carrying a large weave basket under her thin arm, meandering from shop to shop, gathering supplies for the mayor.

"Yes, good mayor," she said in a way Samuel felt was forced. He could only imagine how many of the mayor's whims she had to indulge.

The mayor clicked his tongue. "Some tea. Honey and sugar. Two cubes."

The maid kept her eyes at her feet and bowed before leaving. The mayor put a smoking pipe between his lips, and Charles sprinkled tobacco into the pipe's bowl. The mayor waved his son's hand away as he lit the tobacco with a gold lighter.

"I don't assume you keep current with politics," the mayor said nonchalantly.

His father shook his head, and Samuel did the same.

"The greenlands are in complete disarray: widespread famine, riots in the street, factories unable to produce goods, jailhouses overflowing. Their sad excuse of a governor can't control his own people." He huffed. "Greenies. They've always had a reputation for being lazy and self-entitled. They don't value work and endurance like us whitelanders. And now they've got some fresh-faced politician, calling himself a 'politician for the common folk,' making calls for reformation across all states. It's appalling. These fools have no reverence for the Laevis Creed, no understanding of how their actions could jeopardize our longstanding peace."

The maid returned with a sliver tray and a steaming cup of tea. Charles took the cup from her and handed it to the mayor, who switched from smoking to sipping.

"My apologies. It must seem like I'm ranting. I say all of this because I, and a few other mayors of the north, will be meeting with Governor Bloom to discuss the political ramifications should the greenlands' political climate continue to unravel. We are a separate state from the greenlands, governed by our own rules and culture, but we would be naïve to think these things will not affect us." He wriggled his fingers, as if annoyed that he was giving explanations. He glanced at Samuel. "I will be away for a while, but I cannot wait any longer to hear about your findings. Please, cleric. Tell me what you've learned about my demon."

"Mayor," his father projected, holding firm to the scriptures. "I'm a cleric, but there is still so much I have to learn from the holy words." He shook the book. "In the teaching of Hetsulu, the prophet mentions how the dark ones can take a mortal soul and twist it. Corrupt it. Influence it from the inside. Bring it away from Azhuel and the peace that comes with surrendering to the roots." He paused. "It is my belief that the child is not a demon."

Samuel leaned in, hanging on his father's words. They'd never discussed his father's findings.

"But she may be under the influence of a demon. Possessed. A child inflicted and tormented by darkness."

The mayor set down his tea.

"What are you trying to say, cleric?"

His father folded his hands, rubbing his thumbs together.

"In the book of Zephereli, the dark ones are described as black winged creatures that have no form. The child has human flesh."

"Possession," the mayor repeated.

"Yes," his father answered. "With prayer, with Azhuel's guidance, we may be able to bring her out from the darkness. An exorcism, if you will."

The mayor nodded to himself, and Charles tapped his shoes on the floor.

"Help me, cleric. I am not a man of faith, as I've told you before, so I want to be clear. You believe the child is not a demon, but that it is under the influence of one?"

His father nodded.

The mayor took another a sip of tea before rolling his tongue around the end of his pipe. "And you propose deliverance for the creature?"

"If the exorcism works, the child would be free from torment. She could find peace. Is that not what she deserves?"

The mayor puffed hard into his pipe, his tongue rolling against the inside corner of his cheek. "As a noble servant of Haid and the whitelands, I could never in good faith endorse the performance of a religious ceremony other than the rites of the dead. This is clearly outlined by the Laevis Creed. You should know this, cleric."

Samuel's father held the scriptures tightly. His jaw clenched behind his thick beard. The mayor rose to his feet, and Charles shifted erratically.

"You talk of that creature as if it were a human. It has the eyes of a wolf and the ability to rip a man to pieces with one little arm." The mayor glanced at Charles. "You call it a girl, a 'she,' yet it has no genitalia. Did you know that?"

Samuel's father straightened his back. "No."

"Neither did I! Until recently. Perhaps you should ask your son." The mayor removed the pipe and waved it at Samuel. "I heard about what you did, boy. How you communicated with the demon child, risking your own life. I could use more men like you."

"Pardon me, good mayor."

The mayor chuckled. "Oh, you didn't hear about our boys and the little adventure they had the other day?"

Samuel looked ahead, doing everything he could to avoid his father's gaze.

Charles cleared his throat. "It was my fault."

The mayor scowled. "Thankfully, our lady doctor knows better than to try and keep secrets from me. If things had ended differently, well, be sure this would be another conversation entirely. He may not look like much, but your bastard is quite exceptional."

Samuel's throat went dry, and he swallowed spit.

"Samuel," the mayor said warmly. "That's your name, isn't it? My son tells me the demon has taken a liking to you."

Charles gave a quick nod.

"Yes, sir," Samuel said. "I suppose."

The mayor put his hand on Samuel's shoulder, the pipe between his thick fingers. Samuel could feel the heat. His shoulders shuddered; the mayor's hand emanated authority and power. "I think I might have an offer for you, boy. The sheriff is down a patrolman. How would you like to work for our great town in a more practical way? Patrolman would be your title, of course. You'll be placed on my payroll. Basic-level salary, but for you, there will be plenty of opportunities for increase based on performance. But unofficially, you would work as the demon's caretaker. Every day you'd visit it, feed it, tend to its needs. I can't put my faith in these other simpletons. These other patrolmen are only good for following basic orders. But you, my boy. There's something special about you. You're obedient to your mayor, are you not?"

"Yes, sir."

"Well. Will you take the job?"

Samuel could hardly believe the words he was hearing. A patrolman? He would have a state-sanctioned job with a living wage? He wouldn't have to be a cleric?

He nodded a bit too eagerly.

"Wonderful," the mayor said. He squeezed Samuel's shoulder tighter. "You will start on Monday. Listen, lad. I want you to become more acquainted with the demon. Learn its preferences and tendencies. Essentially, I want you to gain its trust. By getting it to trust you, you're getting it to trust me. Do you understand?"

Samuel didn't, but he nodded.

"If I may," his father interjected. He stood up. "The boy is more than a month shy of sixteen, and a full year away from becoming of legal age. By the law of our state, he is unable to begin a profession. He's my son. As atonement for my sins and the sins of his mother, his destiny must be with the clergy."

The mayor clicked his tongue. "I will do what I want."

"Even if what you do is in direct violation with the Laevis Creed?"

The mayor removed his hand from Samuel, frowning.

"Are you implying that I'm breaking the law, cleric?"

His father paused briefly as if calculating the consequence of his next words. He loosened his grip on the scriptures, and they nearly slipped onto the floor.

"Of course not, sir."

The mayor coughed, and his belly shook. "Excuse me." He took another drag from the pipe. "I am not leaving the decision to you, cleric. It's the lad's choice to make. If he wants to be a cleric, I can find ways to arrange—"

"No," Samuel interjected.

The mayor grinned. "So. Will you take the job?"

Samuel blinked heavily, ignoring the desperate glare from his father.

There was nothing to say but yes.

7

Samuel rolled his shoulder as he hurled the knife forward. The blade hit its target. He walked over to the pine and grabbed the wooden handle, yanking the knife out from the bark. The day was nearly over, the sunlight peeping through gaps in the pine needles hanging above his head. Trudging farther back, he adjusted his frames in an effort to see more clearly. He never had trouble applying the correct amount of force behind the knife or getting the blade to stick. Once he'd gotten down the mechanics, it wasn't that hard. When thrown correctly, the knife would go about three lengths of itself per rotation. He only had difficulty with precision in long-distance aiming. Farther than six meters, the target became hazy, and it was near impossible for Samuel to hit the bull's-eye.

He drew his arm behind him and threw the knife again. This time the blade landed a few inches below the X he'd carved into the tree bark. This would be his last day living with his father. Samuel would be moving in with the sheriff, who'd returned from his trip to the greenlands the same day the mayor offered Samuel the job of caretaker. He wasn't sure what he was supposed to feel, but he was happy. He could be normal. Be touched. Even have a family of his own if he wanted to. He imagined what it would be like to be held by a lover or to hold his own child. He wouldn't have to be a cleric. The clergy was a collection of low-standing men, some of them orphaned boys and some petty criminals receiving pardons in return for serving the cloth, that kept ancient traditions alive in an attempt to appeal to the common person's fears of death and the afterlife. Samuel wasn't a criminal or an orphan, but being a cleric's bastard meant he was guaranteed to a life of clerical service. The high council vowed that they would see to it. What better way to represent Azhuel's grace than to have the living transgression of a cleric taking up the scriptures and being marked with the roots on his forearm? His dreams of being rescued from his destiny were childish. Until now.

A politician's voice would always overrule the wishes of the clergy when it came to matters of the state. Being a patrolman didn't sound that bad compared to a life of self-mutilation for the sake of the rites, a ritual most citizens viewed as antiquated and barbaric. Still, Samuel knew that nothing was guaranteed. He knew better than to assume his patrolman position would become permanent. To keep his job, he would have to work hard to fulfill the mayor's wishes. No matter what it took.

Samuel retrieved the knife. He twirled the handle around and between his fingers in a rhythmic motion. He tried imagining himself as a patrolman working alongside the sheriff and his underlings, standing aside while his father performed the rites alone. But mostly, he thought about the girl in the jailhouse. His chest grew tight as he imagined her red hair and her green eyes and her scarred body. When nighttime came, he went inside the cabin. His father sat beside the fireplace, stabbing the coals with an iron poker. Samuel took off his coat and laid the hunting knife on the counter.

"You don't have to do this," his father said.

Samuel washed his arms in the sink, drying them with a filthy towel. It had been three days since their visit to the mayor's estate. They still hadn't spoken with each other since their fight, the silence an invisible but strong presence. It was strange for Samuel to imagine life outside the cabin: the handmade furniture and utensils, the deer and hare skins mounted to the walls, the large bucket in the bottom-left corner that they used for baths, the desk with the picture of his mother. Everything was changing so fast.

"You know I do."

His father stepped forward, the floors creaking.

"You're wrong, Son. You have a choice. We all have a choice."

"I know. And ... I want to do it."

"The mayor is a wicked man," his father said with an anger Samuel was unaccustomed to seeing. "He is solely driven by his greed. He and that tormented child have nothing but darkness to offer you. Nothing."

Samuel wasn't sure what to make of his father's protest. The man couldn't simply say that he would miss him or that he loved him. It always had to be about light and darkness. "You don't even know her."

"She is bound by something sinister, a force not to be manipulated or played with. The child needs deliverance, not vain attempts at control! I can't bear the weight of another soul being kept in torment. And I can't bear for you—" His father grabbed him, his hold pinning Samuel in place. "I am a flawed man, and I have sinned greatly. But I cannot stand back as you are led astray by false promises. You can leave. Tonight."

"What?"

His father released his hold and dashed across the room, grabbing the backpack from underneath the ladder.

"We've made these trails, you and I." He threw the bag at Samuel. "Go. Go past the lake and keep going west. Move through the forest until you hit the mountains. You'll have to go through them. I know a cleric on the other side. Ulysses. He's in Kurset. He isn't the holiest of men, but he has no love for politicians. He would take you in. Grant you sanctuary."

Samuel didn't want to argue with his father, but he was being irrational. Desperate. It was unlike him. "What would you do?"

"I will find a way to perform the exorcism, and I will buy you as much time as I can afford."

"How do you know she's possessed?" Samuel probed. "Can that explain her body? What if she's something else? You said you want to do an exorcism. Do you even know how? What if it does nothing?"

"I have faith," his father said with confidence. "I don't know what the mayor's intentions are, but I'm almost certain he wants to harness the child's darkness for his own strength. The roots would never permit this."

Samuel put the bag down, propping it on the side of his leg.

"If a storm hits, especially in the mountains, I'll be as good as dead."

"No. You could ride it out. You're stronger than you think. There are caverns all along the mountains. Azhuel would protect you."

"Azhuel's roots won't keep me warm, Father. Or alive. I don't want to leave Haid as a fugitive. I want to do this. What do you think the mayor will do if you show up at the jailhouse and I'm—"

"We all deserve death," he father retorted. "I deserve death."

Samuel clenched his fists. His father always interrupted him. He never listened.

"You'll make a martyr of me like you did to my mother?" His eyes burned. "You're wrong. No one deserves to die. Not for faith or sin or anything!"

Samuel walked to the cabinets and poured himself a cup of tea while his father continued on about humankind's dark nature and Azhuel's merciful roots, his voice so loud it nearly shook the walls. Samuel found the strength to ignore him. Their last night together went on like that until his father tired out. When Samuel was sure his father had fallen asleep, he crawled into the bed they shared. His heart raced as he thought about his new life. For some reason, however, the skin on his right arm kept tingling uncomfortably, and he couldn't get it to stop itching.

"Don't stand there like a moron," the sheriff grunted, his breath burning with alcohol. "Get in. And wipe your feet."

Samuel dusted the white powder from his boots. The sheriff's house was near the east side of the town square, about a kilometer from most of the neighborhoods and right beside the railroad tracks. Samuel fiddled with the straps of the backpack. The home was a little bigger than his father's cabin, but not by much. The kitchen counter was littered with half-eaten bread and moldy cheese, and empty glass bottles of liquor decorated a tiny white table next to the front window. The sheriff pulled out a cushioned cot from behind the closet, unrolling it in front of the fireplace. He tossed a feather pillow and some cotton sheets near the foot of the portable bed. Samuel laid the backpack on top of the cot.

"I got food in the kitchen pantry," the sheriff said as he reached down and grabbed a mostly empty bottle of booze, taking a swig. "My food. If you want something, buy it yourself. Salary's not much, but it's enough to feed yourself." The bottle bounced across the sheriff's thigh, and he flagged him through the narrow hallway to the two doors facing opposite each other. "It's simple. If you didn't pay for it, don't eat it. Pissing pot's on the right, my room's on the left. Stay out of my room. Don't touch my things. Or I will break you."

"Okay."

The sheriff slipped his thumbs into his belt loops as they went back into the living room. He held his arms together as the sheriff nodded toward the dresser. "Use the last shelf, but don't put too much in it or it gets jammed. You can borrow one of my shirts for now, but go to the tailor's today and have him make you a few. Got it?"

Samuel nodded. "Okay."

The sheriff took a deep breath. "Look, I don't want you here. But I may have pushed my luck a little hard with that … individual, and now I'm pretty sure he's got you here to keep an eye on me and make sure I don't go near that monster. I won't. We clear on that? So long as that thing is in my jailhouse, I'm not going inside. Neither will any of my men. Not even if you're in there screaming or begging or crying for help. If you get your guts ripped up, it's your own damn fault. I won't waste another good man on that monster."

"Okay."

The sheriff flung open the window and spat before taking another sip of liquor. "I didn't ask for this, you know. Any of it."

"Don't touch the guns. Or the knives. Just … don't touch things. At all."

Samuel nodded. He'd learned the pattern. The sheriff sank down into the chair outside of the jailhouse and tossed Samuel the keys.

"Hope you brought something to protect yourself. I'm not giving you a gun."

Samuel reached into his coat pocket and pulled out the hunting knife. His father had told him to keep it, that he'd use one of the older knives for the rites. Perhaps it was meant to be an early birthday present.

"Good enough." The sheriff took a swig from his flask. "Got more than a hundred active patrolmen currently serving in Haid. Half of them the mayor keeps stationed at his estate, most of the others I keep posted near the logging sites, and I've also got a few others I try and keep around the neighborhoods. You'll be the groundskeeper for the jailhouse. That's your job. Take care of the place and keep the incarcerated restrained and alive. You're the only one besides the mayor and myself permitted on the premises until further notice. Understood?"

Samuel nodded as he fiddled with the collar on his neck, his body feeling too small for the sheriff's collared plaid uniform. He tried rolling up the sleeves, but they kept falling back down.

The sheriff must've noticed. "Stop." He licked his lips as he took out a handful of copper coins from his pocket. He counted out five of them and put them in Samuel's hand. "Here. An advance. Buy yourself a shirt later. Tell the tailor it's a rush order. Looks like a nightdress on you."

The sheriff laughed at his own joke.

The coins felt heavier than Samuel thought they would. He'd never touched money before. If his father needed goods, he bartered for them. And there wasn't a long list of people willing to trade with a cleric.

"Don't you have some babysitting to do?" the sheriff asked as he reclined deeper into the chair, his eyes watching the sun peep out from behind the forest of pine.

Samuel nodded as he put the knife and the coins into his pocket.

When he came inside the jailhouse and went to the holding cell, the girl's predator eyes were fixed on him. He straightened his collar once more. He was sure he looked as ridiculous as he felt. He got the green vial and the roll of gauze from the cabinet before walking inside the cell.

"Hey," he said nervously, holding out the supplies. "I'm going to check on the wound. If that's okay."

The girl slid her arm back. She probably didn't like men in uniform much. He tugged on the shirt's fabric. "Oh. This? I got hired to be your caretaker. Officially, I'm a patrolman. But really, I'm just going to come here every day and take care of you. Do you understand?"

Her muscles relaxed slightly as she slid out her legs and spread them far apart. She turned her head as he got down and re-dressed the wound. He sprinkled the ointment across her open flesh. The bite marks were beginning to scab nicely, and the areas around the wound were gaining back their color. He was in awe.

"It's amazing. You're pretty much all healed up."

Samuel reapplied fresh gauze, then wiped his hands across his jeans, trying to rid them of the sticky ointment. The girl slowly pulled up her hand and pointed to the black dress hanging in between the metal bars.

Samuel looked back.

"Would you like to put your dress back on? I'm sure it's not very warm. But it's yours. And I'll keep the firepit going."

The girl got up slowly, balancing herself on her good leg. She brushed her thick hair to the side as she coolly stripped off the shirt she was wearing. Samuel stared at the girl's naked body for a moment before turning away to get the dress. Even with the scars and her missing arm, she was beautiful. He tossed her the ruffled dress and kept his head down. She wriggled her body into her clothes before sitting again. The shackles around her feet jingled as she doodled on the dirt floor with her index finger.

He wasn't sure what he was supposed to do next. How do you gain someone's trust? What did the mayor expect him to do with her? Perhaps he wanted to have her behave without the shackles.

Samuel pushed his glasses against his nose.

"I'm Samuel. I don't know if you remember my name. What's your name?"

She didn't answer.

"You can't talk, can you? That's okay. I'll give you a name."

The girl looked at him blankly.

"I mean, only if you want. I don't want to call you demon. Or girl. I mean, I don't know if you're a girl. You were wearing a dress when you got here, and you look like a girl. I guess you're not going to tell me what you are. Or your name. So, I guess I'm on my own here."

Samuel crouched lower, thinking awhile about what to name her. "Can I call you Atia? It was my mother's name. She was pretty like you. She's dead now."

The girl halted her drawings for a brief moment, but then continued with her dirt sketches, swirling her finger in large hoops, then accenting quick strokes. He didn't want to talk anymore, so he got more wood to rekindle the firepit. The freckles on her cheeks seemed brighter in the firelight, her skin more milky, and her hair more red. *We all deserve death.* He recalled his father's words, picturing the worry on his face. They were all prisoners, really. The girl, the sheriff, his father, him. It seemed like everyone had to answer to somebody. He wanted to tell her that, but he kept his mouth shut and decided instead to share the silence.

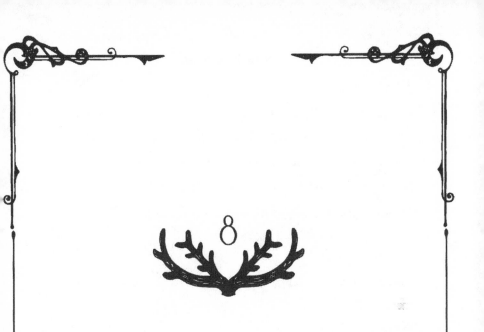

8

By the end of the week, the infection in her leg had all but cleared. Large scabs blanketed every bit of the torn flesh, the brown flakes occasionally damp with pus. The swelling had dropped significantly, and the color of the skin had returned to one shade. There was no need to call on the doctor. Samuel knew that the girl and her leg would survive. He worked hard to make her as comfortable as possible. Every day he rekindled the firepit, gathered fresh pillows and blankets for her cot, emptied her bucket, and served her water and food. She wasn't a big eater, but she liked red meat. She used the restroom like any creature, only she did so from one hole.

In addition to buying fitted shirts for himself, Samuel bought Atia more clothes as well. The tailor eyed Samuel suspiciously for buying girls' clothing alongside his patrolman uniform, but he didn't ask any questions. He purchased several winter dresses, including another

black one, but she always seemed partial to her original black dress.

She was never shy about dressing in front of him. He would try really hard not to stare, but sometimes he couldn't help it. When he would look, she would watch him watching her strip. That always made him feel guilty, and he would quickly turn away, pretending he wasn't at all curious. Her skin was so badly scarred. What had happened to her?

Every morning, when Samuel came in the cell, she never did anything to show his presence was appreciated. Then again, she didn't seem bothered by him. His fear of her diminished with each passing day. He wasn't stuttering as much when he talked to her. He wasn't afraid to get close to her. He no longer bothered bringing his knife into the cell. It was becoming abundantly clear that she was no demon. And it was becoming harder to believe the mayor and the sheriff's accusations of her being a murderer.

He was almost certain she was a mute, because the only rumble he ever heard from her throat was the soft hum of breathing. Every time he asked if she could speak, she'd ignore the question. For a while, he thought he'd never be able to understand her. By his third week at the sheriff's house, however, he got an idea. He could hardly sleep that night. When he arrived at the jailhouse that morning, she was sitting peacefully by the barred window and staring at the pine forests. It was almost as if she was looking for something. He set his stuffed backpack down by the door.

"Hi."

The girl stretched out her leg, a gesture for him to begin his examination. Her toes curled slightly as he peeled away the gauze. He twiddled the green vial of medicine playfully.

"Don't think you'll need this medicine anymore. Hey, Atia?"

She turned, her lips pursed, as if the name he'd given her was unnatural. He fiddled with the buttons on his shirt. He had uniform shirts tailored to fit him, but they still felt strange. "Want to try and walk on it? The leg, I mean. Can you try to put some weight on it?"

She slid her shackles farther back as she stood. Her dress swayed with the motion of her hips as she put more weight on her right leg. Her nose wrinkled a bit, and she leaned more on the opposite side, her muscles quivering. She gave a few reserved steps, but then glided down against the stone wall and sat.

"That's so great," he said excitedly. "Before you know it, you'll be walking around in no time."

She fingered the chains.

Samuel reluctantly shook his head.

"Oh. I'm sorry. That's not my choice." Samuel brushed his shaggy hair nervously, pushing his bangs away from his eyes. "I went shopping for more things. Would you like to see what I got you?"

Samuel grabbed the backpack, lowering it onto his lap as he knelt. He slid down the zipper and reached inside. The truth was, he'd spent his first week's pay entirely on her. He didn't mind. It wasn't like he'd lived with much before. She angled her neck slightly as he showed her the chartreuse strip of fabric. Her fingers cautiously reached out and took hold of it.

"It's a ribbon."

She rubbed the frayed ends.

Samuel swallowed. "For your hair. It's so long and pretty. I thought the green would look nice. Match your eyes."

She put the ribbon down, letting it fall from her fingers. He wasn't sure if she liked it, but decided it was best to move on. The hair ribbon wasn't the thing he was nervous about giving her. His palms sweated as he snatched out a plain leather notebook and a fresh pencil.

She peered at the gift, her nose scrunching. Was she smelling them?

"I've watched you," Samuel said as he slid over the items. "You're always doodling on the floor. You could use this to draw on. And. Maybe we could write each other notes and things like that. If you want."

She held the pencil delicately as he placed it against her thumb and index finger.

"If there's anything you want me to get for you. Something you want to tell me. You can use it. And I can always get more supplies."

Atia gingerly crossed her legs as she bolstered the notebook, turning the blank pages until she settled for one near the middle. Samuel pushed his glasses farther up his nose. She might tell him where she'd come from or how old she was. Or maybe she could write what had happened that night with the bear trap and the patrolman. He watched, speechless, as what had seemed like random scribbles in the dirt transformed into detailed images. Graphite lines filled the page, and it took several minutes before he could make out the drawing.

It was a map of the three states. On the bottom part of the

boot-shaped land, she drew the redlands, the southernmost region with a desertlike environment that harbored the military class and safeguarded the old sciences. She added detailed light shading to make the gritty impressions of the sand deserts. In the middle were the greenlands, the centermost region of the continent, which housed the majority of the states' citizens due to its vast size, comfortable temperatures, good soil, and bountiful crops. She filled the section with heavy shading and bunched circles, a representation of the diverse land with its various forests, plains, and mountains. At the top of the map, she drew the whitelands, the largest but least populated of the three states, which harbored the largest resources of lumber and coal.

The girl flipped the page around and pointed to an area on the upper left-hand corner.

"It's beautiful," Samuel said. "You're really good."

She tapped the area once again.

"Oh, uhm, I'm not sure where that is. I don't know geography all that well, but I'm guessing that's near Haid. We're in the mid-eastern region of the whitelands, about three hundred miles from the coast. From what I've been told. I've never stepped foot outside of this town and the eastern woods."

She swiped at her chopped bangs before filling in more lines, adding more details to the page.

"How did you get so good at drawing?"

Before he could say anything else, she tore the page from the notebook and laid the paper down beside her.

The copper bell above the door dinged as Samuel shuffled into the butcher's shop, his hands plunged deep into his pockets. Rows of beef were on display behind a glass counter with tiny white labels describing each cut: tongue, neck, brisket, rib, flank, chuck, tenderloin, round, shank. All imported from the south, of course. Greenland cows weren't exactly fit for northern weather. There were other selections of meat as well. Pork, chicken, venison, quail, goat, turkey, rabbit, and bison. Half of the meat was merely for show. The mayor was the only one who could afford bison meat and other premium cuts.

Breathing in the smell of blood brought Samuel back into the woods with his father, back to their simple hunting traps and his father's lessons about Azhuel gifting mankind with the mind to overcome beasts.

The butcher's granddaughter, Claudette, sprinted out from the back room to the bloodstained counter. She smiled a bit when she saw him and wiped her hands on her filthy apron.

Samuel tried smoothing the wrinkles out of his uniform shirt.

"I heard that you were a patrolman now."

"Something like that."

"Can I help you?"

He scratched his elbow.

"I've been busy. With my job and all. I don't have the time to catch my own game. And I was thinking I could try something different."

He dug back into his pockets and dumped loose coins on the table. He'd gotten his second week's pay, and this time he swore to himself he was going to save as much as possible. He'd already bought Atia more or less everything she needed for now. But still, he wanted to get her this one thing. And there was one other thing he was going to buy for himself, something other than a uniform.

"Have you tried the goat?"

"Goat?"

"Yeah." She bent down and pointed, her finger tapping the glass. "It's a different texture and taste, and not as expensive as some of the other meats."

Claudette packaged him up about two pounds, wrapping the red chops in white paper. It cost about six coins, which wasn't a bad price, considering his wages.

Before he left, Claudette asked him if he planned on attending the summer festival. It was a strange question because it had never been an option before. He told her yes, thanked her, and left. The sun was fading quickly, and he didn't know how long the blacksmith's shop stayed open.

Samuel paced back from the pine tree and flung the knife directly into the carved X. And then another, and another, each one close to the target. The daylight had nearly gone, the clouded sky spilling over with red and orange. It didn't stop him from continuing. The first half hour had been shaky, but his accuracy had increased dramatically in no time. His poor vision was hardly a factor anymore.

"Throwing precision is what these things are made for," the blacksmith had told him as he pulled back his goggles and motioned to the set of three silver throwing knives that were mounted to the wall display. Samuel touched them gently, the cold metal kissing his fingertips. The knives were simple in design, made entirely of steel, including the handle, and less than half the size of his hunting knife.

He twirled the last knife between his fingertips. It was so light, the small blade perfectly designed for flight.

He was going through the motions, but his mind was on Claudette. She'd talked to him as if he weren't an abomination. And she was pretty. A heat rose to his cheeks. For the first time in his life, he could dare to imagine a life outside of the roots. A life where he could be a normal citizen, not one bound to the faith. Perhaps one day he could marry a girl.

As he retrieved the knives to make another throw, headlights from an approaching jeep flooded over the line of pine trees. Samuel covered his eyes with his elbow as the vehicle parked and the sheriff rolled down the window.

"Don't you have a job to do?" the sheriff called out from the driver's side window. "How do you think the mayor's going to feel when he hears about you messing up good lumber?"

Samuel walked to the vehicle, his shoulders hunched.

"This isn't where they cut lumber. I thought—"

The sheriff snorted as he sipped from his flask.

"A joke, kid. Like we don't have enough pine around here to bury this whole state in. Where'd you learn to throw like that? Ain't half bad."

"My father taught me. Not much else to do ... that and read the scriptures."

"Both of those things make me want to puke." The sheriff lowered an arm out from the open window. "Looks like the mayor was wrong about the estate thief."

"Huh?"

The sheriff licked stray drops of liquor from his mustache. "Just got back from the mayor's place. He was packing up for his trip to who knows where, and looks like some more money went missing from his personal safe. Walked in on him beating the shit out of that brat of his when I got there. Kid was wailing like a newborn. He was cowering in the corner like a whipped pup, swearing he didn't take anything. Pretty pathetic."

Beat him? Samuel fiddled with the knife.

"Do you think he did it?"

"No," the sheriff said with a drawl. "Take one look at the kid and you see he's all bark. Besides. Why steal his daddy's money? Entitled little shit already gets more than he needs."

Samuel felt nauseous. "If he didn't do it, why is he in trouble, then?"

The sheriff shrugged. "I mind my own business. So should you."

"But, if the thief is still out there, then that means the girl didn't steal anything."

The sheriff snorted. "Maybe. Maybe not. Like that makes a difference now. If it's not a thief, then it's just a cold-blooded murderer. What's the mayor hope to gain from keeping that thing around? I couldn't guess. But me, you, the cleric, and the little mayor, we're all just along for the ride. Quicker you learn that, the easier it gets."

"What gets easier?"

"Everything."

"It's a bit warmer today."

Atia was lying down on her back, her glazed green eyes fixed on the ceiling. She turned to face him, but then turned back. He tried to take her dismissal of him as a good thing. She was comfortable around him. At least he thought so. The floral-patterned dress she was wearing was covered in dirt and filth from the day before. Her red hair was caked to the sides of her neck and cheeks, and visible knots were forming near the ends.

"I've got a hairbrush for you, if you want it. Would you like to bathe? I'm sure it's been a while. I think I can get the hose through the window, if you'd like."

Atia got to her feet and stood by the window.

The sun was beaming through the tiny bars, illuminating the prison cell. Samuel tossed her a towel before resealing the gate. He

went through the hall and outside the front door. He looked around for the sheriff's jeep but couldn't find it. The mayor had ordered the sheriff to stay by the prison as much as possible, but since he was out of town, the sheriff didn't bother doing more than give Samuel a ride to the prison. Some days the sheriff would come back after a few hours, but other times he wouldn't return at all, and Samuel would have to walk back to town in the dark. He was fortunate that summer was approaching. His boots crunched the snow as he went behind the prison and found the tiny utility shed. He got the hose and connected it to the outside water valve, running the water over his bare fingers. It was so cold. Perhaps this wasn't such a great idea.

He rounded the corner and found the window. Getting on his tiptoes, he guided the hose between the bars. He could hear the water splashing against the cell's dirt floor.

"It's cold," he called out. "Can you reach the nozzle?"

Samuel watched the hose for a few seconds before seeing it pulled farther in.

"Good. Just shake it hard when you're done."

He dug into his coat pocket and retrieved the map she'd sketched. The more time he spent staring at it, the more questions he had. How did she know the geography of the states so well? Had she traveled to all the places she sketched? Did she have any family that was alive? How had she survived that long wandering the woods? The whitelands' unforgiving cold was bad enough, and the wolves, bears, and wild dogs lurking throughout the woods weren't known for their peaceful temperament.

The hose shook back and forth, cuing Samuel. He reeled the hose back. He sloshed through the wet snow and headed back to the shed. After shutting off the water and putting the hose right back where he'd found it, he went back around to the front and inside the jailhouse. Atia was wrapped in the towel, drops of water falling off the ends of her thick hair. Steam rose from her bare shoulders. She was cold, he knew she was, but she didn't show it.

He scurried over to the old hope chest sitting in the far-left corner opposite the cell. It wasn't in the best condition. The wood was rotted through in several places, and various parts were covered with holes and layers of dust. He'd known better than to use it without asking the sheriff's permission, however.

"Sure," the sheriff had grumbled. "If you can open it. Thing's been locked shut before I ever got the job, and I never found a key. It's not like I go into my own jailhouse anymore."

During their time together, the sheriff often complained about how he could no longer do his job with Atia staying at the jailhouse. Since a permanent prisoner now occupied the lone cell, the sheriff couldn't make proper arrests for the minor disputes that were a regular occurrence with the loggers. "Sometimes they need to get drunk, brawl it out, and spend a night behind bars to get their senses back. Now I've got to be diplomatic and try and get them to talk things out. Not my strong suit."

Getting the chest to open at first hadn't been easy. He had to break open the rusted locks with a hatchet he found in the jailhouse's utility shed, and he'd ruined the blade by doing so. It was Atia's box now, and he filled it with all of her new clothes and things. Samuel shuffled clothes around until he pulled out a lovely cream dress, the cotton sewn in a way that really trapped in the body heat. He'd almost bought several pairs of tights to help keep her legs warm, but it would've been a useless purchase. It wasn't as if she could slip anything through the fetters that bound her ankles. He had bought her a proper pair of northern boots. They were black with several silver clasps in the front, the toes arched in a semicircle. He thought she would like them. It was impossible to comprehend how she'd made it as far as she had without a good pair of boots.

The gate squealed as Samuel unlocked the bolt and slipped back the gate. He gave Atia fresh clothes, and she dressed herself. They ate roasted goat liver together, and she consumed more than she ever had before. She drank nothing but water, occasionally snacking on bits of bread and meat. Did she like the food? Did she even need to eat? What was she thinking? He asked himself that one nearly a thousand times a day.

Although Atia couldn't or wouldn't speak to him, he felt as though he could read her moods based off her drawings. For the time being, she'd only composed landscapes. Some were beautiful backdrops, calm fields, and cloudy skies. Others, jagged mountains and dark nights. But there was one sketch in particular that amazed him. The details were impeccable. Samuel assumed it to be a painting of one of the redland cities. None of the houses in the town square were made of wood. They were all composited of nothing but mud bricks and stone. The ground was covered in sand and trees with large pine-like needles that Samuel couldn't identify. The town was right next to the ocean, and Atia had drawn the waves rolling onto the shore. One of the buildings she drew was bigger and more complexly designed than any building in Haid. The structure was comprised of six dome-topped towers aligned in perfect symmetry around a giant steeple, the towers all elaborately designed with various carvings and patterns. He'd heard once that the redlands trained their soldiers in old cathedrals various religious groups would frequent for prayer. Although the Laevis Creed forbade the clergy from congregating in any buildings that were previously used for religious purposes, the redlands military was able to reuse the old buildings as they saw fit. The redlands didn't have land suitable for crops or natural resources like the other states, but their military was well respected among the other states.

Samuel felt a connection to the picture in a way he couldn't fully explain. Perhaps because it was an entirely new world to him. From what he'd heard, as well as from what he'd seen from Atia's sketches, the greenlands seemed fairly similar to the whitelands, minus the large amounts of snow that lasted throughout most of the year. But the redlands seemed much more exotic and warm. His mother was a native of the redlands. When he looked at his own skin, he could see remnants of the bronze shade she'd left for him. He wondered what kind of life she'd lived before meeting his father. What if she was the child of some wealthy politician? She did have a photograph taken of her, and that sort of technology was expensive. She must have come from a wealthy family. Did she have any family left? What were her friends like? What did she do for fun?

Those questions always led him to questions about her relationship with his father. How did they meet? What had caused her to be so bold as to make love with a clergyman? Did she love him? His father always refused to talk about his mother and what had happened, and that left Samuel to speculate on his own. He only knew what he could deduce from the picture and occasional comments his father made. She was a redlands native; she had a warm heart, and a warmer smile. He couldn't understand what had drawn someone like her to his father.

Finishing her food, Atia lay down flat on the stony floor and stared at the wall above her. Samuel pushed up his dark-framed glasses and scooted closer.

"Atia," he said.

When the word left his lips, he wondered if it was strange that he'd given the girl his mother's name. She looked nothing like the young woman in the picture his father kept on the desk. And there was a part of him that was attracted to the girl, and that seemed out of place in conjunction with his mother. It wasn't a sexual attraction to the girl. At least, he didn't think so. To be truthful, he wouldn't really know if it was. Her fierceness, her strength, her beauty, even the mystery surrounding her enamored him. He knew there was a part of him that enjoyed spending time with her. He knew that he cared for her deeply and that he really did want to be her caretaker. He also knew that he'd never felt this way about anyone before.

Atia kept her head still, but her predator eyes moved to the left and looked at him. Samuel rubbed his hair. He needed to have more courage than this if he was going to learn more about her.

"Can I ask you something? I ask you a lot of questions, I guess. You don't speak, I know. But how come you don't write words?"

He tapped his shoes.

"You're not a demon, right?"

She remained stoic.

Samuel lowered his palm onto the ground, his heart beating. "I won't tell anyone if you don't want me to. Not even the mayor. I promise."

He meant it.

She parted her lips, the air escaping as she exhaled.

"You can understand me," Samuel said. "What I'm saying. I know you understand my language. Don't pretend you can't. Please. I want to help. I want you to know I'm your friend."

She sat up, the chains rattling harshly. She lifted her one hand and pointed to the outside window. Samuel was dumbfounded for a moment before he understood. His mouth went dry, and he instantly felt guilty.

"I'm sorry. I can't let you go. The mayor—"

Her eyes penetrated him, her jaw tightening. He pulled back, a wave of fear returning over him. Was she going to attack him? Instead, Atia closed her eyes and rolled over onto her side, pressing her stub against her chest. She laid her head on the ground, and her damp hair covered her face like a blanket.

Samuel scooted back into the bars and lowered his head. She was a prisoner. Of course she wanted to be free. But he couldn't help her that way. He couldn't fail at his job. Even if she managed to escape and the mayor didn't blame him, which was highly unlikely, Samuel would more than likely lose his job as a patrolman. The thought of going back to his father and being ordained a cleric made him sick. He couldn't decide which fate would be worse.

Returning to the jailhouse, Samuel promised himself he wouldn't push Atia with so many questions. He would have to wait and give her time. Hopefully she would trust him soon. He knew his employment was contingent on gaining her trust. How he was supposed to prove that was beyond him.

Atia was drawing another picture. Her hand moved the pencil in precise swipes as her stub anchored the sketchbook on her lap. He didn't say anything, but sat next to her and peeked over her scarred shoulder. He expected to see another landscape portrait, but this drawing was different. The entire page from top to bottom was filled with the most intricately drawn roots.

"The roots?"

She rubbed her stub across her arm.

"Like my father's mark."

She pushed her red hair back behind her shoulders and continued her drawing.

Samuel swallowed. "The ribbon would help hold your hair back. That way it doesn't keep falling on the paper when you look down. Want me to get it?"

She did nothing for a while, but then gave a slight nod.

With nervous hands, Samuel retrieved the chartreuse ribbon from the hope chest and got on his knees behind her. He gathered her thick hair in the crevice of his thumb and index finger. Her strands felt heavy and soft. He brought the ribbon up to her hair. He wasn't sure how to tie it, but he knew it was similar to a bowknot. He grabbed both ends of the ribbon and looped them around, making two knots to form a crooked bow.

Atia added more shading to the roots.

"Do you know about the creation theory? Mostly only clerics know it. Or demons, maybe. I'm not sure."

She didn't acknowledge his question. He decided to continue anyway.

"Long ago," he said, "Azhuel blew into the dark void covering the world and made the lands and the plants and the mountains. After surveying His creations, He knew that the world needed more. He added creatures: fish, birds, rodents, and bugs. But still, the earth seemed to be missing something. Azhuel took a very deep breath and exhaled as hard as He could. And out from His breath came humans. He was most pleased with the creation of humans, as they were the purest reflection of their creator. He loved them dearly and gave them dominion over all the earth."

She moved her pencil up to the branches and added more leaves.

Samuel did better on his second attempt at the bow, but the loops weren't proportional.

"But then, when the demons saw what Azhuel had created, they crept out of their realms and made their way into the earth. Demons were the enemies of Azhuel, a horde of shapeless beings who Azhuel had banished to the lower realms for their insatiable hunger for inflicting pain on other creatures. They hated Azhuel, and since they could never harm Him, they decided instead to afflict his prized creations. Demons roamed the earth freely, tormenting the souls of mankind. Human beings became clay in their dark clutches. Their once-pure spirits went dark, and soon they lost all connection to their creator. Azhuel was heartbroken."

Samuel pulled back on the left loop until it was almost identical in size to the right one.

"Azhuel decided to do whatever was necessary to save humans from the demons. He couldn't inhabit the earth in his god-form, or else the power of His presence would crush the world. So, He threw Himself into the earth's surface and spread His pieces out across all the lands and oceans. His broken body became like unending roots. He made sure to be wherever there were people, from the deserts of Kinhu to the icy mountains of Septrea. And then He brought Himself up to the surface in the form of a large tree. The life tree."

Atia gently stroked the pencil back and forth, shading the branches. Samuel adjusted the angle of her bow, centering it. He blinked slow.

"That way, Azhuel would be able to watch over His creation. His unending roots would forever be buried deep in the earth's surface. And any soul that surrendered itself to the roots in death would be brought into eternal light."

She finished her drawing and laid her pencil down beside her thigh. She tore the page from the book and handed it to Samuel. He studied the picture intently.

"The scriptures say that mankind can again communicate with Azhuel because His roots are everywhere. All we must do is shed our blood and pray. And, when we die, we return to the earth to be with Him forever."

Saying the words aloud, Samuel could hear his father's voice telling him the same story over and over again as he was a child.

"I don't know if it's true. It sounds like a wild story to me. But I know some people believe. My father does."

Atia parted her lips, her warm breath turning to steam as she scooted her body closer to the firepit.

It was early in the morning when Samuel entered the butcher's shop. He didn't need to buy more meat; he and Atia were set on food for at least a few more days. But coming to the butcher's shop was an excuse to see Claudette. She often smiled when he walked through the doors, and it made his blood rush when she would talk to him like she cared. Except this time no one came out to greet him. A loud boom erupted from the back room. He turned his head, hearing a sudden commotion past the counter, down behind the wooden swing doors. He advanced slowly, listening to what sounded like smashing tools and an animal squealing. He didn't want to interrupt, so he quietly waited.

"Stupid pig!"

Samuel leaned closer, carefully placing his palm on the left door. "Everything okay?"

"Sorry," the shaky voice called out. "I'll be out soon."

He inched the door forward but froze. He didn't want to intrude. "Do you need help?"

Silence followed, and Samuel took it as a cue to move in. He pushed through the door. In the center of the room was a long metal table covered with knives, mallets, and bloody rags. Pots and pans hung from wiry strings that were anchored into the ceiling. In the back corner, a pig frantically shuffled back and forth, bumping its plump body against the walls. The pig was bleeding from its lower neck, but it wasn't a very deep cut. Claudette was squatting in the corner on her knees, a large meat cleaver in her grasp. Strands of her brown hair had fallen out of her bun. Her white apron had blood on it, but the stains were mostly speckles. Her eyes were wet with tears.

"Are you okay?"

Claudette sniffled, wiping her nose with her forearm.

"Sorry. I'm working alone today. My mom isn't feeling well. She caught a fever, so I made her stay home. I knew we had a shipment coming up from the train carts, but I told her not to worry. I'd watched her bleed out a pig before. I tried to cut the throat, but I didn't do it right."

The brown pig squealed as it came forward and charged into the table, knocking over several utensils. Claudette buried her head into her arms.

"It's not like my father is ever around to help. He's always working at the mayor's estate. Making real money, he says. I can't do this by myself. I'm not strong enough."

Samuel came closer to her. He empathized with her because he thought he was the only one in Haid who felt that way.

"Don't say that," he said. "You're really strong. Stronger than me. Besides. It's a lot harder than it looks."

He imagined how much Claudette and her mother must miss the old butcher. He reached into his pocket and pulled out his hunting knife. "I can help you put it down. I've done this before."

Claudette poked her head out, but perhaps was too embarrassed to say anything. The wounded pig was getting closer to the wooden doors, squealing in wild frustration. Samuel stepped back to guard the exit, spreading his legs out in order to make his body wider.

"What can I do?" Claudette asked as she rose to her feet. "To help."

Samuel unsheathed the blade. He waved the knife at the pig.

"You can put down the cleaver. Probably not the best knife for this."

She left the cleaver on the table, her red eyes watching the pig with disdain.

Samuel cleared his throat. He felt nervous because he knew he wasn't as strong as most other boys his age. He was nearly a man, yet puberty had hardly left a mark on his face or body. Shouldn't he have developed more muscles by now? Not only that, many times he didn't feel he'd make a decent man at all. He was a sensitive boy, and when it came to hunting, he never enjoyed the kill. But he'd killed animals before. He probably would have to kill again. Hunger often made him do things he didn't like doing.

"We need to corner it. Trap it. That way I can latch on and get a clean cut."

Claudette pointed to the lower left end of the room. "Over there. By the drain."

With Samuel and Claudette on their feet, the pig retreated to the back part of the room. Samuel kept the knife level to the floor as he inched over. He waved Claudette to do the same on the opposite side. They got closer and closer. The pig jammed its body against the wall, huffing as its hooves smashed the ground below. Its black eyes squinted as it tried to run in between them. But Samuel expected it. He jumped onto the creature and hooked his left arm around its neck. The pig writhed, and Samuel fought to keep his grip. He had to move fast. Claudette ran up behind the pig and wrapped her skinny arms around its belly, securing it. Samuel had no idea how Laura was able to do this all on her own. He remembered the pig's superficial cut and realized it was probably much easier when the pig wasn't expecting it.

Samuel tightened his hold on the neck as hard as he could, slowly anchoring the head up and squishing the pig's face into his chest. He'd never killed a pig before, but he'd killed enough animals to know to get the artery behind the jowl. He pressed the knife below the pig's cheek and slit hard.

"Thank you," Samuel whispered.

The pig went limp within a matter of seconds, and in a minute's time, Samuel was able to push the creature down into a puddle of its own blood. Samuel took a deep breath as he moved back, blood dripping from his forearm and knife. He started mumbling a prayer of thanks, but stopped himself. He didn't need to pray anymore, and he didn't really want to. It was a bad habit.

Claudette went to the table and picked up several rags. She untied her apron and wiped her hands before giving a fresh towel to Samuel. He cleaned his knife and arms and tried to wipe off the blood that had spilled on his clothes.

"Need help cleaning? I'm guessing you're going to put it in warm water."

"My mother says it loosens the skin. But no, I can't let you do any more." She reached out a hand to Samuel. "Come with me."

Samuel pushed up his glasses with his wrists before quickly putting his knife away. He took her hand. It was warm, soft, and uncalloused. His heart raced as though electrical currents were burrowing inside of him. She led him behind the counter to the precut meats.

"Which one do you want? It's free, of course. You've earned it."

Samuel pushed up his glasses with his free hand, because Claudette was still holding his other one. He was touching someone, a girl, feeling her skin against his. He pretended to be looking at the wide selection of meats and cuts, but he really didn't care. A heat rose to his cheeks.

"I guess I'll take some chuck."

"No. That's cheap." She let his hand go. "Get something better. Something the mayor would get." She let go of his hand and pointed to the fancier cuts. "Here. How about a slice of rib? Or sirloin. That's the mayor's favorite, I think."

"Sirloin sounds good."

Claudette packaged up the meat for him, and he tried to watch her in a way she wouldn't find strange. She was as filthy as he was, but it didn't matter. She pursed her lips as she handed the package over to him, rubbing her thumb over the counter.

"Thank you," she said.

Samuel held up the meat.

"Thank you," he said back.

She tilted her shoulder down a bit, and Samuel fought hard not to stare at her budding breasts. "See you at the festival?"

Samuel had never paid attention to festivals in the past. He knew it was supposed to be a big celebration marking the end of winter. The whitelands had only two seasons: summer and winter. Summers were short in the whitelands, a few months, and after all the snow had melted away, the winter would inevitably return. The mayor would pay for fancy decorations and food and games for the citizens to partake in, and everyone would welcome the warmer weather. It was the mayor's way of thanking the citizens of Haid for their hard work. At least that's what he'd overheard one year from a logger's wife, but once she'd noticed he was listening to the conversation, she moved away. It was his own fault. He was hovering too closely. He learned how to eavesdrop from a safe distance and be as still as possible. When he didn't move, he could become invisible. He liked that. But now, all he could think about was how a girl was talking to him and had held his hand.

"Maybe," he said. "I'll have to ask the sheriff. I worked every day, so—"

"Everyone goes," Claudette said with a smirk. "Even the sheriff's patrolmen. You could meet me here if you'd like."

Samuel toddled to the jailhouse, the package of sirloin cupped between his arm and his chest. His boots sank into the melting snow and spots of ice, and he'd nearly fallen twice in his two-mile hike to the jailhouse. Fresh snow was easy to walk through, but when the snow would melt and refreeze, it became really tricky to keep balance. He decided to walk on the edge of the eastern woods, steadying himself on the trunks of the pine trees every time he felt his balance slipping. The sky was fairly cloudless, and the sun was shining brightly. If Haid was lucky, most of the snow would be gone by the end of the week.

The stone jailhouse was in view, and as he got closer, he noticed a figure standing outside the front door. He didn't see a jeep anywhere, so whoever was outside had walked there. A sudden panic struck him. Atia. Was it her? Had she somehow managed to escape? His eyesight was poor even with his mother's frames. He picked up his pace, running as fast as he could. No, the figure was too tall and massive to be her. That eased him a bit. He knew how much trouble he'd be in if she got free. But worry came trickling back because no one but the sheriff and the mayor were permitted to enter the jailhouse. It was his job to keep anyone else out. He hustled as hard as he could without slipping, and when he finally came out of the woods, he recognized the figure.

His father, dressed in his long black coat, had his back turned on the utility shed. He scratched his burly beard with his free hand, the other one clutching tightly to the scriptures. Samuel scanned the area as best as he could to make sure no one else was there.

His father kept his cold demeanor as he gave a cordial bow.

"It's good to see you, Samuel."

When his father's head came back up, Samuel saw a sadness in his eyes he'd never seen before. It petrified him.

"What are you doing here?" he asked nervously. "Father?"

His father straightened his back in a way that nearly dwarfed him.

"You look good. Well fed. The sheriff is treating you well, I see."

"As well as he can."

Samuel wanted to believe this was nothing more than a kindly visit from a lonely father missing his son, but he knew his father better than being someone who allowed his actions to be dictated by fickle emotions. Everything his father did had to align with the will of Azhuel.

"I don't think you should be here."

"I'm here to perform the exorcism." His father's large fingers rubbed the pages of the scriptures. "I must do what is right. For this child. For you."

Samuel's heart sank.

"Did the mayor give you permission to try?"

His father eyed him blankly.

"But," Samuel began to stutter. "Father. You can't. You'll be punished for going in there. I was ordered not to let anyone in. Don't you care what happens to me?"

"More than you'll ever know, Son."

Samuel scooted to the jailhouse door, nearly falling in the process. He spread his arms in between the frame, his limbs shaking as he dropped the meat. His father was much stronger than he was; Samuel would never be able to overpower him.

"Please," he begged. "Don't do this. You're acting mad. She's not a demon. She's not possessed. I know she's not. She's different, but not like that. You're wrong. I'm getting to know her, and she's really not that bad."

Samuel pressed his body harder against the door.

His father bent down to lay the scriptures on a pile of lumber.

"Forgive me."

His father clenched his right hand into a fist and slammed it into Samuel's chest. The force from the blow knocked him flat on his back, and the air left his lungs. Samuel heaved pathetically as his father rummaged through his coat pockets until he found the keys. Samuel's eyes were teary, and his glasses had been splashed with snow, making it even harder to see.

His father picked up the scriptures, moved to the door, and put the wrong key into the lock. Samuel still couldn't breathe, and his head burned something fierce, but he crawled on his knees to his father's legs. He thought about getting out his knife, but he could never use it on his own father. He coiled himself around his father's legs like a constricting snake. He couldn't let him get into that cell. He needed Atia to stay the same, he needed this job, and he couldn't witness his father's execution. His father's blind faith in the roots would kill them both. Why couldn't he see that?

His father seemed unbothered by the weight of his son, moving on to the next key and unlocking the front door. "Let go, Samuel."

The sound of a roaring engine blasted through the air, followed by what sounded like screaming metal. A large boom erupted. It was so loud it hurt Samuel's ears. He managed to catch his first breath as his father halted his pursuit.

"What is this?" the sheriff yelled as he stormed the jailhouse, his gun drawn.

Samuel loosened his grip and wiped his glasses. The revolver's barrel was aimed at his father. He rolled onto to his knees but had to hunch over to allow his breaths to fully return. He needed to move. To do something.

His father faced the sheriff.

"I am getting in that cell. I will perform this exorcism. I have to try. No good can come of keeping that child locked up and kept in darkness!"

"That's a matter of opinion, cleric."

"No creature should endure the darkness. It is Azhuel's will—"

"Damn it!"

The sheriff pulled back the revolver's hammer.

"That first shot was a courtesy."

Samuel adjusted his glasses, coughing. "Please don't." He gagged for more air. "Don't shoot. No."

"I am dirt," his father said calmly. "And to dirt I will return."

"And you will kill your son in the process," the sheriff added.

"He has nothing to do with this."

"He will, if I say the boy's the one that let you in. I swear to your tree god that's what I'll say." The sheriff waved the gun wildly. "Enough of this shit, cleric. This isn't about that little monster. It's about the boy. It's over. You've lost him. Now go."

Samuel's hands were wet and cold. He pushed them into the snow to help lift himself up to his feet. "Go," he said weakly. "You need to go. Please?"

His father closed his eyes as he stood there silently, perhaps whispering prayers in his mind. He pulled his hand away from the door, leaving the key inside the lock. Samuel had seen the man put his faith above everything: his wants, his fears, even his own son. But this once, his father relented in his conviction. He glared at Samuel, then turned away as if he were nothing. His thick boots crunched the snow as he headed back into the woods.

Samuel's eyes were still wet. He gently touched the part of his chest where his father had struck him. The sheriff growled in annoyance as he holstered his revolver.

"Can't leave you alone for a minute, can I?"

"I'm sorry."

"Save it."

Samuel could smell the liquor on the sheriff's breath. With the mayor out of town, the sheriff rarely came by the jailhouse at all. But he wasn't about to argue the sheriff's point, especially when he was drunk.

"Did he hurt you?"

Samuel shook his head. "I'm fine."

"What was he talking about? Doing an ex … "

"Exorcism."

"Shut up. Never mind. I don't want to know." The sheriff chewed his bottom lip. "I've never seen your old man so riled up before." He tossed the jailhouse keys to Samuel and waved his hand. "Don't you have a job to do, patrolman?"

Samuel looked down. He squeezed the keys. "Yes, sir."

11

amuel did his best to act normal, but he couldn't. His mind was a whirlwind of confusion and pain, and his demeanor showed it. Atia did nothing unusual as he prepared her meal. But, for once, she seemed to take a mild interest in his quiet demeanor.

She leaned her body a bit forward, almost as if she was inviting him to speak. She surveyed him with her green eyes coolly, as if she was trying to decipher his thoughts. Her stare made him feel only more embarrassed. Perhaps she *was* a demon and could read his mind. Unlikely. He ignored her gaze and didn't say anything as they shared a grilled sirloin. The meat tasted exceptional, but the tightness in his jaw made it hard for him to chew. He could still feel the weight of his father's fist on his chest. His father had never once struck him, electing instead to discipline his son with disapproving expressions and long-winded lectures on morality. He knew this wasn't typical.

Even the kindest of northern parents weren't shy about giving their children a good beating when they deserved it. He thought about Charles and couldn't imagine how he managed to deal with it.

Samuel pressed his palm against his ribs to see if the area felt bruised. It was tender. He winced. He shook his head as if to empty his mind. There was no use complaining or thinking about it. He had a job to do. He picked up the dishes, emptied Atia's bucket, and examined her leg. It had been a while since he'd paid the old wound much mind. The tissue had grown back, but the giant teeth gashes circling below her kneecap were filled with fresh flesh and pockets of pus. He patted the area with a damp rag. When he was finished, she inched her knees up to her chest and pulled her thick hair over her left shoulder and across her collarbone. She seemed content to wait for him.

Samuel pushed his thumb behind his ear, fiddling with the end of his glasses.

"Did you hear all of that?"

She said nothing.

"My father hit me. He was trying to get in here. Do an exorcism. Do you know what an exorcism is?" Samuel didn't wait for an answer. "My father's convinced you're a demon. No. That's wrong. He thinks you're possessed by one. Or something like that." He rubbed his temples because his skull was still throbbing. "He's losing it."

Atia petted her hair with her stubbed arm.

Samuel shook his head. "He could've been killed. The sheriff had his gun out. I don't know. Maybe he was bluffing. I hope he was. I don't understand him. My dad, I mean. I never have. I've lived with him since I was a baby, but I've always felt alone."

Samuel looked into Atia's eyes. If she wasn't a demon, then what was she? She was fast. He'd seen how quickly she could move when she tried. The mayor and the sheriff were convinced she was strong, but he'd never witnessed her doing anything exceptional in that regard. She did bleed black. Her slit pupils were unordinary to say the least. Her torso was covered in horrendous scars. She was missing her girl parts and half of one arm. Why? What did it all mean?

Once, when he was a boy, Samuel saw a spotted salamander with two tails near the lake's shore. And there was an old logger who had an opening in the center of his top lip that reached up to his nostrils, and from what his father told him, the man was born like that. Animals and people could be born with deformities and abnormalities. What if Atia was merely like them? Human, but different. Unique.

Samuel pushed his back again the wall.

"All of this," Samuel said with a sigh, "because nobody can figure out what you are."

Atia tilted her chin up, her teeth barely visible inside her slightly agape mouth. Her nose wrinkled, and her cheeks bunched up in a way that showed some sort of thoughtfulness. She lowered her neck and pointed to the hope chest.

Samuel got up and ran outside of the cell. His fingers fumbled as he unlatched the clasp on the wooden trunk. Was she trying to communicate with him? Why now? He dug through the clothes until he found the sketchbook and the small pack of pencils. As he got back into the cell, Atia sat with her knees lowered and her hand outstretched. He gave her the sketchbook and put the pencils down by her thigh. She propped the book against her flat chest and delicately turned pages until she came to a blank one. Near the top end of the page, she scribbled three letters that were so small he had to squint to see them.

Z E I

Samuel watched as Atia shaded heavy lines alongside the word, forming a rectangular border around it. She angled the pencil near the base of the page and drew furiously. His eyes absorbed everything as fast as they could. A steel door, similar to the one outside of the jail cell, guarded an empty room. The walls, floor, and ceiling were surrounded with some sort of bubble-like padding. Each individual pad was cut into a diamond shape, almost the same as her pupils. The room was illuminated by artificial light, a single electric bulb mounted above the door. Near the upper end of the door was some sort of rectangular box with individual numbers in order from one to nine. On the floor was something like an iron grid, the thicker bars lined with some sort of thin material that looked like netting. Around the room appeared to be tiny beams of light that ran across the floor.

Atia added a mattress to the corner of the room, the ends of the bedframe looking nearly like the prison bars. She put down the pencil and lowered the sketchpad onto her stomach, rubbing the fresh skin on her leg with the heel of her other foot.

"I don't understand," Samuel said.

He leaned closer and shoved his glasses back up. It did little good. Whenever he bent down, the frames slid down his nose. Atia scooped the pencil back up and began to draw more. She added a young girl lying on the bed, her long hair sprawled out wildly across the sheets. The girl was small, like Atia, and seemed to be near the same age. Samuel bent down farther, his nose nearly touching the page. He held his glasses in place. She had both of her arms.

She curled the pencil between her fingers and tapped the girl in the picture.

"Wait. Is that supposed to be you?"

She gave a soft nod. He studied the picture carefully, sucking in every detail he could. The room's design was something foreign to him. It nearly looked like a prison cell, only the technology seemed far more advanced than anything he'd seen before. Perhaps it was from one of the ancient buildings that had survived the blackout. Still, the Laevis Creed strictly forbade the preservation and use of exceptional technology. How could she have seen such a place?

"What is this?"

Atia circled the engraved Z E I several times over.

He concentrated on the picture, wanting badly to make something out of it.

"I don't understand. That's not a word I know. Is it an acronym? Does it stand for something? If you could write out something more, like more words or a sentence."

Atia sat up, the pencil clutched in her palm and her eyes staring coldly back into his. Her hold on the pencil made it resemble a knife. The sketchbook had fallen to the ground. Samuel held up his hands in surrender. She wasn't going to hurt him. He knew her better than that. She wasn't the demon everyone thought she was.

"Wait. I'm sorry. I want to understand."

She flicked the pencil across the cell and hobbled to the barred window, her hair bouncing out from behind her shoulder.

"Z. E. I." Samuel rubbed his arms. "ZEI. Zei? Is that your name?"

She kept staring out the window. She nodded.

Samuel swallowed. He was dumbfounded. "Your name is Zei? I knew it! You're so much smarter than they think you are. But ... why didn't you tell me that sooner? I want to call you by your name. Why did you let me call you something else?"

She didn't respond.

"You could've written it or spelled it in the dirt."

She shook her head, her jaw clenched.

She was telling him no. Maybe she wanted to write more but couldn't.

"You can't read."

Samuel felt stupid. His father had taught him the alphabetical letters and the sounds corresponding to each one. It was a cleric's responsibility to read the scriptures. Only clergy, politicians, and those wealthy enough to afford an education could read. What use did a logger or farmer have for reading? It wasn't as if they could afford newspapers or books. Samuel's ability to read and write was something he'd taken for granted without even realizing it.

He picked the pencil up and set it down beside the fallen sketchbook as she lazily reached her hand out to the bars on the window as if to touch them. They were too high for her to reach.

"I'm sorry for upsetting you," he said. "Do you want me to call you Zei from now on? I didn't mean to name you like ... "

A pet, he thought.

She waited a moment before giving a subtle nod.

Her face remained stoic, but her eyes relaxed slightly. She was upset. He could tell. It was his fault for provoking her. He kept telling her he wanted to listen, but all he did was talk at her. Perhaps this was better. Maybe now he could stop rambling and making assumptions about her and give her the space she needed to open up. Maybe he could do something for her that she wanted.

"Well, Zei. If you want, I can try to teach you how to read. Would you like that?"

When Samuel closed the door to the townhouse, the sheriff immediately plopped himself down onto one of the wooden chairs by the kitchen. A half-empty bottle of liquor was already set on top of the dinner table. He uncorked the glass bottle with his teeth and took a long swig.

Samuel went over to the window above the sink, looking at the railroad tracks. The train that had made its way up to Haid early that morning was getting ready to leave, and he could see the conductor talking to one of the loggers as men hustled to fasten the large cuts of pinewood together in the open cart. He thought about Claudette, how good it felt to touch her.

The sheriff sucked so hard on the bottle it made a thunk.

"Why so glum?" the sheriff grumbled.

Samuel watched as the conductor climbed inside of the cab and yelled more things at the loggers, pulling hard on the whistle. Its scream was so loud it shook the walls. "My birthday is next week. Friday. I'll be sixteen."

"Is that a bad thing?"

"No."

"Sixteen." The sheriff leaned back into his chair, causing the first two legs to come off the ground. "You'll be a man in the eyes of the state. Sixteen. Best years of my life. Back when I wasn't trapped in this northern shithole. The summer months here are a complete joke. My bones can't take much more. Several more years of saving up for retirement and I'll be on the first cart out of here. I'm greenlands born and raised, and proud of it. Living in an icebox doesn't make you hard or tough. It just makes you stupid. Anyway. My folks were sharecroppers for a cotton field, a hundred miles from Emur." He eyed Samuel. "Know what a sharecropper is?"

"Not really."

"It's somebody who farms a rich politician's fields and gets paid shit for it. My family had some food and a tiny plot of land to live on. But between them, me, and my sisters, it wasn't enough. I was the oldest kid and the only boy. My dad always complained that he needed more men around the house. Made no sense to me either way. More siblings meant more mouths to feed." The sheriff stretched his arms behind the chair. "But more bodies meant more hands for harvest."

"How'd you get here?"

The sheriff pushed his tongue between his teeth. "What do you think this is? Story time?" The sheriff took another drink. "I guess you can make yourself useful and get me something to eat."

Samuel went to the counter and started gathering supplies for a pot of soup. He grabbed some carrots and potatoes from one of the pantries and decided to use some of the lamb's meat he'd bought a week back. Even inside the cooler, the meat was going bad. He could smell the stink of it.

"I hated farming," the sheriff said as he toyed with his bottle.

Samuel lit the fire.

"My old man. He wasn't the easiest guy to work with. He'd go on and on about things being done a certain way and would lose his mind if one of us didn't work fast enough. It was stupid because we were all faster than he was. I was stronger than him, and he knew it, so he'd always try and show me up by getting in my face and barking orders like he was some hardnosed solider."

The train outside began its slow climb up the tracks, the whistle blowing and the iron wheels squeaking. Samuel hated the noise the train made. It made him miss the quietness of the cabin. He rinsed his hunting knife and started chopping up the ingredients.

"And then came the day," the sheriff continued. "I was about your age. It was October, and the weather was dropping so fast everybody was worried the crops would die if we didn't harvest them fast enough. My old man knew a bad return meant less pay, and he wasn't going to have it. My little sister, Elaine, she was about six at the time. She was supposed to be out in the fields working, but she'd skipped out to play in the house for a bit. I saw her go in, but I didn't care. The kid was never really all there, in her head, if you know what I mean. A sweet girl, but not much in the way of productivity. Still, I never wanted her to be anything other than what she was. She was family. You take care of your own. That means something to me."

Samuel sliced the meat into inch-sized chunks before tossing them into the pot.

The sheriff's words were slurring more. "It's nearing the afternoon. I was working near the toolshed. I watched my father go inside the house, and then I heard screaming. I should have minded my own business, I know that now. But I was soft and young and stupid, and I thought I was a man. I went inside. He was beating Elaine with his belt. I mean, we got whipped all the time, but he was … laying into her. I guess all my rage at him, all the years of his grinding and bitching came up to the surface, and I couldn't take another minute of it. I came up behind him." The sheriff made a fist and punched the air. He then picked up the bottle and took another sip. "Knocked him out cold. One hit."

Samuel brought the water to a boil and mixed in the tomato broth. There were many times when he'd wished his father had been anyone else, but he knew his father wasn't a cruel person. He was indifferent and tough, but not mean. Minus the religious zeal, perhaps he could've really liked him. Perhaps that's why the spot on his chest where his father had struck him still felt so heavy.

"Did you run away?"

The sheriff arched his back forward and let his front chair legs hit the floor.

"No. I left. I was an adult. I packed my bag and left. My mother cried. She tried talking me into staying. 'You two can work this out,' she kept saying. She didn't know how much I hated him. Kissed my mom and my siblings goodbye: Jessie, Jaeliene, Melanie, and little Elaine. And I left." He pointed to the window. "Hopped on a train and hitched it all the way up to this stupid town."

"You paid for a ride?" Samuel asked as he tossed in the vegetables and the meat, stirring everything with his spoon. "Where'd you get the money?"

The sheriff laughed.

"I broke into one of the closed carts and hid behind this cow that kept shitting every couple of hours. When the train stopped, I snuck out and found the loggers working on the woods right outside the mayor's estate. I asked for a job, and thought I'd get one because I knew I was strong enough. But the old sheriff, Benson, was patrolling the area and stopped me in my tracks. 'Who the hell are you?' he asked. 'Eugene Black,' I said. 'Came here for a job.' That old man looked like he'd lived longer than anyone should in this frozen piece of land. He studied me over up and down and said, 'I'm getting too old to be out here all the damn time. Work for me, and I'll give you a place to crash and money enough to live. But you better do your job well, or I'll throw your greenlands hide out onto the streets as quick as I hired you.'" The sheriff waved his hands up. "Rest is history."

Samuel poured them each a bowl of soup and sat down opposite the sheriff. He gave a soft blow on his first spoonful before taking a bite, wondering why the sheriff was being so civil. He wasn't sure if it was the sheriff's way of apologizing for threatening to get him killed.

The sheriff shoved the bottle over to Samuel.

"I can't be drinking next to you," the sheriff grumbled. "Not if you're going to sulk like that. It's killing my buzz."

Samuel hesitated, but his hand eventually took hold of the bottle. He took a sip and nearly choked. It tasted disgusting, like tree bark and acid, burning his throat like liquid fire as it went down his pipe.

"No thanks," he said as he scrunched his face. His lips were puckered, and he pushed the bottle back to the sheriff, who was laughing once again.

"It gets easier," the sheriff managed to get out as he swirled the bottle back and forth. He let out a few more cackles before taking a sip of his own. "Before you know it, you'd near sell your soul for a drop. Anything to shut the mind off. Stop all the noise."

They ate in silence for several minutes before the sheriff spoke up. He lowered his spoon into the bowl and wiped his mouth with his sleeve.

"I'll give you some advice, kid. If you want to make it in this life, you've got to be hard. You can't be soft. If you're soft, no one will respect you. If you're soft, you'll die. And no one is going to take care of you. You have to take care of yourself. It's that simple. Learn that now, and you might actually have a future. Understand?"

amuel sat beside Zei in the cell, their shoulders nearly touching. He relaxed against the stone wall, watching her write all the letters of the alphabet over and over and over again. He took off his glasses and rubbed his eyes. He'd been acting as her teacher for five days, and he couldn't have asked for a more engaged student. If he wrote a letter and asked her to copy it, she would write the letter repeatedly until he'd tell her to stop. He had to buy her a new sketchbook within two days of their lessons because she'd used up all the free pages.

Samuel had no clue how to teach her to read and write. He was not a teacher. All he could think to do was mimic the ways his father had taught him. When Samuel turned five, his father had decided it was time for him to learn to read the scriptures. For weeks on end, Samuel did nothing but write the letters in the snow with a stick. Paper was expensive, so his father made him use what limited resources they had available to them. First, Samuel had to memorize the letter. Then, he'd have to write out the letter and say aloud its corresponding sound. Zei couldn't speak, so he had to modify his approach a bit by saying the letter's sound for her when she drafted each letter. By the end of the day, his throat itched something terrible, and his voice would nearly be gone. He'd never spoken aloud so much before.

"You can take a break if you want."

Zei's pencil moved furiously, her eyes sucking in the pages of her script like they were fresh meat. Samuel had tied her thick hair back so it wouldn't keep falling over the pages. He rubbed his fingers together, thinking of ways to break up the monotony.

"I've got an idea. We could play a game with the letters. Would you like that?"

Zei paused her writing and lifted her pencil from the page.

"Here. Do you mind, Zei?"

Samuel brushed the shackles around her ankles to the side. He sat up on his knees, leaning over as he turned to a blank page. He liked calling her by her new name. Giving her his mother's name was a dumb idea. Thinking about his own name, he felt that "Samuel" capsulated his identity. His mother had chosen it. He didn't know why. But that was the name she'd chosen for him.

Zei tapped her pencil on the blank page.

"Right. Okay. I will make a letter sound, like 'guh,' and then you'll have to write the letter that goes with it. And that way I'll help you spell out some easy words."

In near calligraphic design, Zei wrote the letter G.

"Yeah. That's right."

Zei realigned the point of her pencil with the paper. Samuel thought for a moment, closing his eyes.

"Buh … ih … rr … duh."

When Samuel opened his eyes, he saw the word *bird* on her paper.

"That's good." He tapped each letter with his index finger. "Buh, ih, ir, duh. But if you say the sounds fast, it makes the word *bird*. You get it?"

Zei inched her nose closer to the word, almost as if she were about to sniff it. She pulled back and then sketched a snow owl perched on a pine limb. Samuel couldn't help but smile wide.

"I knew you could do it. You're so smart, Zei!"

"Who?" a voice called out.

Samuel's skin crawled, and his muscles spasmed. He whipped around to see if he could spot the intruder. Charles stood by the doorway, his arms tucked inside his gray peacoat. He was dressed in tan slacks, a fancy collared shirt and bowtie, and a suit jacket.

Samuel stood up quickly. He took the sketchbook from Zei, closed it, and put it on the ground next to her.

"I don't think you're supposed to be in here."

Charles pointed his chin up.

"Did you give that demon a name or something?"

Samuel almost said no. It was her name, and she'd written it for him. It was best to keep that between them. At least for now. "Kind of." The chains behind him jingled slightly. "Why are you here?"

Charles shrugged. "Bored. I don't know. My dad comes back

tomorrow. I wanted to check up on you. See how our friend in there is doing. Summer festival is in a couple of days. You're coming to the festival, right?"

Samuel nearly blushed at the memory of Claudette.

"I want to," he said. "But I'll have to check with the sheriff." There was so much about being a normal citizen he still didn't know. "Am I supposed to dress up nice for it? I ... don't really have nice clothes."

"Forget the sheriff. You don't need that old drunk's permission. And don't worry about clothes. I can come pick you up, and we'll get ready at my estate. You can borrow one of my suits. What the hell are you spending your salary on anyway?"

"Stuff for her," Samuel said as he scratched his arm. "And I'm trying to save as much as I can. In case. Maybe this job doesn't last."

"How very responsible of you," Charles said with exaggerated inflections. He pointed to the cell. "Wow. Amazing. You really are a demon whisperer. It hasn't tried to hurt you or anything? If I didn't know any better, I'd think the demon looked like just a normal kid."

As if prompted by Charles's questioning, Zei popped to her feet, moving in front of Samuel. The slack in her shackles was nearly gone. Her face was cold and ferocious, the fingers of her one hand stretched out and curved like claws ready to tear apart its prey. Samuel could see the fear on Charles as he nearly stumbled back into the hallway.

"Get away from me!" Charles yelled. "Keep it away!"

Samuel almost reached out for Zei, but stopped. "Wait. What's wrong?"

Zei whipped her neck back and nearly bared her teeth at him. Samuel held his hands up in surrender.

"It's okay," he whispered. "Zei. It's okay. Trust me."

She turned her attention back to Charles, her nostrils flaring.

Charles pointed a shaking finger. "Crazy demon monster!"

"Don't call her that," Samuel said sternly. He lowered his arms. Zei stood as fierce as a bear. What had made her snap? He had to get her to calm down and remind her that she was safe.

"No one's going to hurt you. I promise. Zei. Look at me. I promise you."

"That thing is mad," Charles let out in a high-pitched cry. He awkwardly scurried farther behind the hope chest. "I didn't do anything. I did nothing to you. You hear me? Just leave me alone!"

Samuel swore he saw Zei smirk, perhaps feeling satisfaction in watching Charles cower away. She walked backward until her hand touched the stone wall behind her. She slid down onto her butt and sat with her legs crossed. Her eyes were still fixated on Charles.

Samuel swallowed. He knew that Zei wasn't a demon. He just knew it. He knew her better than the sheriff or the mayor or Charles or his own father. But he also knew, in that moment, Zei would kill Charles if she could reach him.

Samuel paced along the outside of the cell as Zei doodled in her sketchbook. He wasn't sure if she was writing more letters or drawing a new picture. As he passed by his coat hanging by the door, he pondered if he should dig inside the pocket and get his knife for protection. It was a fleeting thought. She wouldn't hurt him. At least, that's what he chose to believe.

Had his father been right about the exorcism? What if Zei needed deliverance? The thought made him smirk. She had a temper, but that didn't mean she was under the influence of a demon. Why was everyone so set on that? Why did Charles keep calling her "it"? Couldn't she just be a girl with violent outbursts? No. She wasn't normal. Her lack of sexual characteristics was anything but normal. Even Samuel had to admit she wasn't really a "she." Zei's androgynous body and gruesome scars and missing arm were proof of a past that was anything but ordinary. When it came to Zei, he felt like he was the only person thinking rationally about her. She was alone. Perhaps she'd always been that way. Even with his father, he knew what it was to be and feel lonely. He somehow knew Zei felt the same.

"What was that about?" he asked. He dangled his arms between the bars. "You had me scared for a minute."

Zei ignored his question and continued doodling. Samuel opened the gate and went over to her. Strands of her hair were falling out of the sloppily tied ribbon. He'd need to fix it again. He wasn't a skilled hairdresser, but he enjoyed messing with Zei's long hair. It was silky and thick.

"Charles isn't a bad person. He's nice. He's nice to me."

Samuel looked down at Zei's paper, crouching down to get a better view. On the paper was a giant face that looked nearly identical to Charles. She'd drawn his slicked-back hair, the fading bruises around his cheek, and a nose that almost seemed a bit too big for his face. But it was more than simply a portrait. She'd added all this shading that made his eyes look sunken and dark. His mouth was open like a beast, his jaw outstretched in a way unnatural for a human. His wet tongue hung out like he was some sort of wild beast about to devour its helpless prey.

Samuel backed away from the disturbing image. He wanted to ask Zei about it, but he wasn't sure what to say. Zei had made Charles into a demon.

Samuel sat in the cushioned chair beside the wooden box with the white buttons and silver dials. His boots rapped on the hardwood floors as he waited for Charles to return. He had brought him up to the estate and then left him in the giant living room by himself as soon as they got inside.

"I've got something I've got to do first," Charles had told him. "Get Thelma to make you something to eat if you want."

Several minutes after Charles had run out of the room and up the spiral staircase, Thelma came out from the kitchen. She looked exactly the same as the last time he'd seen her. She dusted her hands on her apron and, in a kind voice, asked him if he needed anything. He told her no and thanked her. She smiled a bit and pointed to the stairs.

"You two must be good friends."

"Excuse me?"

"You're the only person he talks about besides his father. He doesn't get many visitors."

"Oh."

The maid's insight made Samuel feel more uncomfortable about his visit. He'd never really had a friend before, and being friends with the mayor's son was probably a fantasy for most of the young people in Haid. He liked Charles. He never treated him like he was only a cleric's son. Maybe the shadow of their father's professions was a common factor they shared. But after seeing Zei's sketch, he couldn't help but picturing Charles as a monster. It made him a little uncomfortable.

Thelma put a hand on the wooden box next to her.

"Would you like to listen to the radio while you wait?"

Samuel shifted in his seat and gawked at the box. It was a radio.

"If the mayor won't mind."

"The mayor is still out," she said, sounding relieved.

Thelma's news helped Samuel to relax a bit as well. He had no desire to interact with the mayor. Thelma gently turned one of the knobs, and immediately a hissing sound came out from the netting on the front of the box. She pressed one of the white buttons, and the noise was immediately replaced with the muffled sound of people talking.

"Turn this knob here if you want it louder."

"Thank you," Samuel said with a bow.

Thelma left him and went back inside the kitchen. He leaned closer to the box, nearly putting his ear on the netting. It sounded like a discussion between two men about the greenlands, yet he couldn't make out but a few words here and there. Justice. Poverty. Equal distribution of goods. His fingers carefully turned the dial to the right until the voices got louder.

One of the voices sounded as though he was in the middle of a long description about the greenland cities currently rioting.

"The last count from Emor was 632, Borem 844, and our capital of Medda well over a thousand," the lamenting voice said. "No educated man could make a valid argument that our political system is working. Our citizens, greenlands, even redlands and whitelands, are dying, because our mayors have run them down with their greed and lack of empathy. And our governor in particular? He's holed up safely in his greenlands estate doing nothing to address the needs of those who've been placed under his care."

"Are you arguing for a united nation?" the other voice questioned. "And are you implying that you, Julius, are the solution?"

Samuel pushed his glasses back up his nose. His head was bent too far down.

"I would never be so presumptuous," the passionate speaker said with feigned humility. "I am merely a vessel speaking for our citizens, because they can't. They have no voice. Our politicians have long seen to that. The Laevis Creed has seen to that."

"You're speaking against the Creed as well?"

"Yes. I am. If the Creed doesn't work for every citizen, then it isn't working. The time for regression is over. Our ancestors once thought that our future was beyond this very earth, out into the far reaches of space, and we've given all of that away. Why? Peace, sure. But who lives in peace? Clearly not these rioters who've been branded terrorists. And why are they rioting? Because they can't put food on their tables. Tell that to our governor."

"You must admit these proclamations are beyond ambitious," the host rebuffed. "They might even be viewed as treasonous."

"So be it."

"Okay, Castor. Let's play this out. With all this unrest in the greenlands, and with men like you screaming out for reformation, what are the other states and their ruling families supposed to think? I'll tell you what they're thinking, Castor. 'He's coming for us next.' And their prides be damned."

"Yes," Castor said. "Exactly. May their prides be damned."

The sound of footsteps booming from above jerked Samuel's attention away from the radio. Charles rounded the corner and sauntered down the stairs. He was holding some sort of large package wrapped in brown paper.

"Happy birthday." He shook the package. "It's for you."

The radio buzzed on as Samuel took hold of the package. It was nearly the size of his torso. "How'd you know?"

"The sheriff said something about it. It is your birthday, right? Sixteen?"

Samuel nodded, the package feeling less heavy than it looked. Charles gave him a solid pat on the back before combing his hair back with his fingers. He spoke with more excitement than Samuel could muster.

"Don't just stand there. Open it!"

Samuel tore the corners of the package, carefully folding out the ends so he didn't rip the paper. Something about ripping paper needlessly seemed wrong to him. He reached inside and felt the softness of fabric. He pulled out the items with one solid tug. It was an entire outfit: black slacks, a peacoat with multiple buttons, a gray button-up shirt with a pressed collar, and what appeared to be some sort of polka-dotted black-and-white miniature tie. He pulled the peacoat up and held it wide. It was made of thick wool and lined with multiple layers of fabric that would probably trap in body heat better than his winter coat. He'd never touched something so expensive before.

"Put it on," Charles said as he motioned for Samuel to stand up.

He put the rest of the clothes on top of the miniature glass table and slipped on the coat. It was the perfect length, but when he buttoned it up, it felt a bit loose on him.

Charles watched him intently.

"It's a little baggy, but if you leave it unbuttoned, no one will be able to tell. I'll get the tailor to fix it right up. I figured we're close to the same size. I mean, except that I'm like way taller and cooler."

Samuel rubbed his thumb across the smooth wool. For the longest time, he imagined a life like this. And here he was, in the mayor's estate, wearing fine clothes reserved for the wealthy. It was a fantasy.

"It's really nice. Thank you."

"Don't worry about it!"

"Are you sure I can wear this? Will I look out of place?"

"You'll be with me." Charles cleared his throat and leaned a bit closer, lowering his voice. "And, uhmm, thanks. For yesterday. I'm glad you were there. That demon really has it out for me."

"But why—"

"Wait."

The raised voice coming from the radio had caught Charles's attention. His brows furrowed as he listened to the new argument for equal land redistribution and the establishment of a systematic food system.

"Ridiculous! And who exactly is gonna pay for that?"

Charles shut off the radio. Samuel shifted his shoulders, feeling the peacoat rub across his thighs.

"Why are you upset?"

Charles plopped into an open chair by the table, plopping his boots down on the end of the table. "It's nothing. It's that guy. Julius Castor. He's some greenie do-gooder trying to start a class war."

Charles reached into his pocket and pulled out a smoking pipe. He packed the bowl with tobacco before lighting it. He inhaled, blowing a ring of smoke. He scooped up a newspaper and began reading. "'Named after Isaiah Laevis, the renowned diplomat who managed to broker negotiations between the warring politicians and the religious leaders of their prospective anti-establishment rebellions, the Laevis Creed outlined the terms of cohabitation between the new state governments, the religious elites, and their citizens after the blackout. The former politicians agreed to cease any and all combat, govern their reassigned lands without territorial skirmishes, destroy exceptional technology, seal away access to the unspeakable sciences, and to share some of their treasures and lands with the elites and their families. In exchange, the religious elites conceded to disband their populist movements, encourage their followers to lay down their arms, terminate their old faith ideals, and merge into one singular religion for the betterment and safety of mankind: the roots. This agreement has kept peace on our lands for several centuries.'" Charles cleared his throat. "'Julius Castor threatens to eradicate centuries of tradition and structure for his fantastical vision of an egalitarian society where no one works but everyone eats.'"

Charles tossed the newspaper by the radio. "The whitelands politicians are in a frenzy. That's why my dad left in such a hurry. He went to a private assembly in Kairus. All the mayors are meeting up to strategize ways to be prepared for riots and foreign invasion."

"That sounds complicated."

Charles let out an exacerbated sigh. "It's the whitelands, Sam. Things don't change here. Not without a fight."

Charles bit down on the pipe, freeing his hands. "Here. Hand me that bowtie. I'll show you how to do it."

The ground covering the town square was void of snow, replaced instead by patches of rough grass and stiff dirt. Streamers and banners hung from the various shops, one of which had written in large script "Whitelands Strong." White and gray balloons were tied to every post, the two colors that composed the whitelands flag. Citizens meandered down the shops and wooden booths, laughing as they conversed with their families and friends. Large lines formed around the spots where games were being played.

One of the most popular stations, located directly outside of the blacksmith's shop, appeared to be some sort of wood-chopping competition. Piles of pine trunks were lined up in a single row, an axe reclining on each trunk. Samuel listened to the burly blacksmith's directions on the rules of the game. Each round was limited to a group of six competitors. Once cued, the participants would pick up

an axe and start chopping. The first person to split his or her trunk down the middle into two separate pieces would win the round and would later get a chance to compete in a final contest to see who was the strongest axe wielder in Haid. There were several women competing in the game, and by the looks of their biceps, Samuel had no doubt they would beat him in a test of strength.

A table sat in the left corner of the blacksmith's shed that was covered with crafted knives and hatchets. It made Samuel think about the throwing knives he purchased weeks before. He'd left them by his cot. He did have his hunting knife tucked inside his new peacoat. The only order the sheriff had given him for the festival was to bring a weapon.

"If you get a bunch of people together, pluck them out of their normal routines, then give them free booze, things are bound to get stupid."

"Won't all the patrolmen be in the square?" Samuel asked.

"Mayor's still on a quest to find his thief, so he's keeping half my force at the estate. Entitled piece of shit." He spat. "Don't let it get to your head, kid. You being armed is just a precaution. Don't try and be a hero. You hear me? You leave the real work for the real men."

Charles nudged Samuel forward with an elbow.

"Sword swallowers canceled. I was looking forward to seeing a performance."

"Sword swallowers?"

"Name speaks for itself. One time, at my school, they had this whole brigade of entertainers stop by. Watched this one guy shove a burning cutlass down his throat like it was nothing. It was insane."

"Wow."

Samuel draped his new peacoat tighter across his chest, fighting the urge to adjust his bowtie. He was uncomfortable in his garb, the clothes making him feel like an imposter. Pairs of eyes studied him as he moved along through the square with Charles, eyes that saw through his fancy garb. Samuel lowered his head, watching his own feet shuffle. As much as he wanted to belong, he knew that he didn't.

A greenlands band played upbeat music on the makeshift stage. The ditties sounded exotic, like they'd been written for a warmer and kinder place. There were four musicians on the stage. Three of them played on stringed instruments, while the one in the center beat his palms against a giant drum. They were far more talented than the last band that had played, at Landon Swen's funeral. How much money had the mayor spent to cart them up?

They came upon a group of girls close to their age. Charles stiffened his neck. The girls were huddled together giggling about something. One of the girls was exceptionally pretty, her blond hair falling down her shoulders and her round cheekbones nearly as pale as Zei's. Her blue eyes locked onto Charles before she turned to her friends and smirked. Charles picked up his pace.

"Bitch."

"What's wrong?"

"Nothing." Charles scrunched his lips. "She's mad because I'm not into her. As if I'd waste my time."

Samuel looked back, seeing if he could spot the girl. "The blond one?"

Charles yanked him back around. "Yeah. Come on. Keep moving."

Samuel didn't know much about love, but he never thought of Charles as a bold romancer. Society didn't take kindly to women having relations before marriage. Most of them ended up working in whorehouses after that.

"My dad's been on my case lately," Charles said, kicking a glob of dirt as they moved along. "Saying I need to grow up and 'be a man.' Whatever that means. So, to make him happy, I invited that stupid girl over to the estate and all. We drank whiskey, talked awhile, and ended up necking a bit. I just wasn't into her. It's always like that. I mean. She's a logger's daughter, anyway, so it's not like anything could ever happen. She was so desperate, Sam. You should've seen it. Girls like that are dumb and annoying. I don't see what all the fuss is about."

Samuel shrugged, unsure how to answer his friend. He knew little of love and passion and sex, but he was pretty sure he liked girls. He liked Claudette. Before he knew it, they were walking alongside the butcher's shop. Samuel found his feet carrying him to the glass window. He peeked inside. A lanky man with long arms and slightly sunken cheeks stood next to Laura behind the meat counter chatting with several visitors. Samuel recognized him as Laura's husband.

Claudette stood in the center of the shop holding a large tray full of tiny cuts of meat. She was wearing a red frock dress with black tights and flats. Her hair was fastened back in some sort of elaborate braid that was composed of three separate parts, one of which encircled the top of her head like a crown. Samuel could've never done something as complex to Zei's hair.

Zei. How was she? Could she hear the festival noise from inside her cell? Was it driving her mad? When Samuel left her by midmorning, she was writing a list of simple words that he'd taught her from the day before: cup, snow, sun, pig, and Sam. He wanted her to recognize his name.

Charles tapped his shoulder.

"Tavern is giving out free drinks. Not that it matters to me. But they're supposed to have some new fancy brews from Boram. Getting harder to get their good beers with all those damn riots. My dad's probably hanging out over there."

"The sheriff too. I'm going to go inside this shop, if that's okay."

"Suit yourself." Charles walked backward right into the masses behind him, and people shifted to the side to avoid being hit. "You know where the tavern is, right? Meet me there?"

Samuel nodded and waved before turning to the shop's door. If beer tasted anything like the liquor the sheriff had given him, he would be fine without it. He opened the door, and the bell above it rang. He pushed his glasses farther up the bridge of his nose as he came by Claudette. She smiled, and it made his breath quicken.

"How are you?"

She jiggled the tray slightly.

"Bored. And my arms hurt. You look handsome."

Samuel bit into his lip. "Need help?"

"You can't do everything for me."

She lifted the tray up with one hand, showing off the cooked meats with the other.

"Free sample? The mayor paid for extra meat so we could serve it to everyone at the festival."

Samuel picked a meat that appeared to be some sort of sausage. He bit into it, and his taste buds instantly took a liking to the flavor, but he was nervous about chewing funny, so he used his hand to cover his mouth. He swallowed without fully masticating, and the lump of meat nearly stuck in his throat.

"It's really good."

The people that had been chatting with Laura and her husband left the shop, and Laura glided out from behind the counter. Her hair was tucked back in her usual bun, but she was wearing a nice dress instead of a bloody apron.

"I heard what you did for my daughter," Laura said with a slight bow. "Thank you."

Samuel went stiff and bowed lower.

"It was nothing."

"Kindness must run in your bloodline."

Laura's face was nearly as hard as Zei's, but unlike Zei, he could feel warmth in her words. The law was broken that night when the old butcher touched his father, but Laura never reported the incident. A wave of silent gratitude was exchanged between them, and it had nothing to do with killing a pig. His father had helped her father pass peacefully. Unlike most, she seemed grateful for what his father had done. He was thankful for that.

Claudette sashayed in place while keeping the tray balanced.

"Can I get my break now?"

"Ask your father," Laura said.

Claudette went to the counter, laying the tray down on top of it. Samuel knew her father was a skilled laborer. His experiences with antique technology were enough to earn himself a job for the mayor. He was the personal handyman for the estate, whose main job was to help keep the electricity running smoothly. The man rubbed his hairless chin as his daughter made her request, his nose wrinkling as she spoke. He nodded, reached into his pocket, and retrieved a handful of silver coins. The amount seemed larger than Samuel's weekly allowance.

"Don't spend it all on candy."

"I'm not a child, Dad."

"Harold," Laura said in a low voice. "We have to be frugal. The shop isn't taking in the profit it should and ... "

"Forget the shop, Laura. The mayor gave me another bonus for my hard work. I told you that overtime would pay off."

"You didn't tell me this."

"Sorry," he stammered out. His face reddened. "I've been busy. Working. Providing for my family. And now, I'm trying to do something nice for my daughter, if you don't mind."

Laura frowned but kept silent.

Claudette bent her head and took the money.

"Thanks, Father."

Her father forced a grin, his teeth showing a bit of yellow.

"Go on. Buy yourself something pretty."

Claudette took hold of Samuel's arm and pulled him outside.

"Sorry about that," she said as she guided them away from the shop. "He's been acting weird lately. Now he and my mom argue all the time about money."

"Please. Don't apologize." He paused. "I know what it's like to have no money and a weird dad."

Claudette smiled.

First, they went to one of the boutique booths. Claudette bought a fancy lace hairband and several hairpins. After, they visited the candy station and purchased a packet of licorice. Once they'd eaten their fill of sweets, they made their way to the center of the square and watched the greenlands band perform more songs. Claudette didn't seem to have any shyness around him and kept the conversation going by talking about the weather and funny stories about things that had happened at the shop. She also asked him a lot of questions. That was something Samuel wasn't used to. What was his favorite color? Did he like living in Haid? What did he like to do for fun? He had to lie a bit when she asked him what he did as a patrolman.

"I just guard the jailhouse. That and watch the sheriff drink."

He somehow found the courage to ask her about her hair braids.

"How did you do that? It looks pretty. Complicated, I mean."

Claudette smiled. She turned her back toward him.

"Want me to show you how I do it?"

Before he could answer, Claudette undid the hair ties and pulled out the braids with her fingers. Once she'd straightened out the hair, she sectioned off two pieces near the top of her head. Several people pushed by them, but she worked as if the masses didn't bother her.

Her fingers moved quickly yet delicately as she folded strips of hair in and out of each other.

"I work on this right section first. When I get about halfway, I stop and move to the left side. Like this. Then, I bring them together. After a while, my fingers memorize the pattern. I've had a lot of practice."

Samuel watched her movements intently, and he was so close to her he could smell the sweetness of her hair. It made him wish he could grow his hair as long. He found himself grinning. He felt like she liked him, and the thought of her being attracted to him made his mouth go dry. A few months prior, he was resigned to a life of isolation and celibacy. But now, if the mayor stayed happy with his handlings of Zei, perhaps he really could live a normal life.

Claudette fastened her hair back and smiled.

Samuel clutched his coat shyly, pulling it tighter around his ribs. He wished it was a bit slimmer so it would feel more natural.

"Get away from me!" a stranger's voice screamed from behind them.

"It's your fault I lost my job! All because you're a lazy piece of deershit, and our whole crew had to pay the price for missing quota. Six guys with no job, Berkley! Six fucking guys!"

The crowd around Samuel and Claudette spread out, clearing out of range from the impending skirmish. The shifting bodies allowed Samuel to see where the commotion was coming from. A tall, middle-aged man with large muscles and a neck like a pine trunk cornered one young man who couldn't have been much older than he was. The young man was dressed in thick winter boots and a flannel shirt similar to what most of the loggers wore on a daily basis. His hands were raised up to his shoulders.

"Don't be stupid. You think I wanted this to happen?"

Samuel's muscles tightened. He remembered the sheriff's words and scanned around the perimeter, looking to see if he could spot any patrolmen. They were supposed to be scattered around the square. He saw none.

Claudette wrapped her arm around his, her face showing concern.

"Shouldn't you do something?"

Whispers and concerned chatter erupted around him, but no one seemed like they were going to make any sort of intervention. He didn't want to make himself a fool in front of Claudette, or anyone for that matter. But maybe he could stall until the other patrolmen arrived.

"Get the sheriff," he told Claudette. "Or another patrolman. Anyone else. Tell them to hurry."

Claudette squeezed his arm before moving around the large crowd forming. She ran in the direction of the tavern. Samuel took a long breath before stepping forward, his feet feeling like lead. His shoulder bumped into person after person as he forced his way closer and closer to the two men. He reached into his pocket and pulled out his hunting knife.

"Hey."

Samuel knew his voice wasn't loud enough. He had to try harder.

"Hey!"

The young man in duress backed himself into one of the game booths, his eyes frantically searching for the new voice. The angry attacker shifted his enormous body, his words mushed together and slurred. He squinted in Samuel's direction.

"Who are you?"

Samuel fought to keep his legs from shaking as he anchored the blade near his thigh. "I'm a patrolman. I am a patrolman commissioned by the mayor and the sheriff. I am ordering this fight to stop."

"You're doing what?"

Samuel paused. "Others will be coming."

The attacker reached a hand out and grabbed onto the young man's shirt, pointing the other at Samuel.

"Wait a minute. I know you. You're the cleric's bastard, aren't you? He's not a patrolman. He's a cleric. Look at him, boys! Not wearing a uniform either. What is that, a suit? The cleric's bastard is wearing a suit? He looks like a little bitch if you ask me."

Samuel swallowed. "Sir. I'm asking you to stop—"

"Hold on, now. Tell me this, little bitch. And be honest. Is it even legal for someone like you to be a patrolman? Aren't there laws about stuff like that?"

A crew of about five patrolmen came rushing to the scene. Their uniforms were neatly pressed, and their faces were hard as ice. Their weapons were readied. Half of them held firearms, the others, hatchets and machetes. The music coming from the stage stopped, the commotion too much for the band to ignore.

The angry man waved at the patrolmen.

"What? He's one of you now? You're on the bastard's side? My father was a patrolman in Haid for thirty years, until he got laid off to make room for younger recruits. Did that stop him? No. He busted his ass for his family. Kept us fed and warm. For what? So his son could grow up scraping for crumbs and have some religious nut's bastard telling him to play nice? This has nothing to do with him! It's my personal business, citizen business, so he can get the hell away from me!"

The patrolmen held their position, whispering things to one another. They glanced at Samuel and to the patrolman standing in the center. The one who seemed to be in charge of the others had wiry hair and a bulbous nose, a rifle draped over his shoulder. Their indifferent faces betrayed them. Samuel might have been hired as a patrolman, but he wasn't one of them. They weren't about to intervene on his behalf, especially not when their integrity had been called into question.

"I'm a whitelander," the drunk logger proclaimed. "Born and raised in this town. Like most of you."

Samuel's nerves caused his hand to tremble, but a new anger was festering. He hated being called a bastard, and he hated being called a cleric even more. He gritted his teeth, forcing himself to be like Zei. She was strong. He had to be strong like her or else everyone in Haid would continue to think of him as the cleric's weak bastard. Heat rose to his face as he gradually held up the knife.

He wasn't a cleric. He'd never been a cleric. He wouldn't become one now.

"This is your last warning. Sir. Leave him alone."

The man took his massive fist and shoved it into the young logger's face. He flailed back into the booth, knocking over several buckets and knickknacks in the process. The big man turned his back and reached after the young logger's limp body, dragging him out from the booth.

"Curse you, bastard. You're next."

In that moment, everything slowed for Samuel: his breathing, his body, his mind. He needed to think. He wasn't strong enough to stop the man, and it was clear he wasn't going to be reasoned out of his tirade. And none of the patrolmen were going to help him. He needed to get the man to stop. No matter what.

Samuel shifted his weight and narrowed his vision. He stood eight paces away, a moderate distance for throwing. He drew the knife up and behind his head, his hand remaining steady as he gripped the handle. He closed his eyes, pretending there was a carved X on the back of the attacker. His sight from the distance was a bit hazy, but he'd struck targets much farther away before. Before another thought could stop him, he launched his leg forward and threw the knife.

The blade sang as it whizzed through the air and sank deep into the man's left thigh. He dropped to his knees and grabbed at the knife, screaming and writhing in pain. His yells were deep and loud, the sound echoing across the entire square.

"What ... the ... ah!"

The crowd went ghostly silent. Samuel lowered his throwing

hand down by his side. He'd missed the target. His nerves must've still gotten the better of him. That or he'd only been practicing with the throwing knives, and the added weight of the hunting knife messed with his trajectory. Still, striking the thigh was better than somewhere that could've caused real damage. At least he wouldn't have to live with that guilt.

A loud boom erupted from behind.

"Damn animals!" the sheriff's voice slurred out as he rushed through the crowds, pulling Samuel to the side.

14

"O was scared."

Samuel fiddled with the pencil before writing down the word *knife*. He passed the sketchbook over to Zei. Her little hand took the pencil from his fingers and she scribbled the word over and over again.

Knife. Knife. Knife.

"You probably don't get scared. But I did. And I still did it."

He halfheartedly cocked his arm back and pretended to launch the blade. Feeling ridiculous for making the gesture, he folded his hands together. After the sheriff had put the burly man, whose name was Liam, in cuffs and hauled him off to the doctor, he gave Samuel an earful. "I told you to not be a damn hero. I said to let my guys handle it. Did you listen? No. It's like you enjoy being a pain in my ass!"

Samuel shrugged, knowing he had no good explanation to give. He'd never done anything that brash before.

The sheriff grunted before snorting a laugh. His anger turned to amusement.

"Still. Never thought you'd have the balls to do that. Loggers will be talking about this for a while."

The festival had returned to its previous bustle, but Samuel felt as though everyone's eyes were following his every move. If they hadn't been talking about the cleric's bastard before, they sure were now. Charles couldn't stop ranting about how amazing it was that Samuel had thrown the knife, complaining that he hadn't been there to witness it himself. The mayor praised Samuel's courageous actions. Samuel had wanted to stay out of the mayor's sight at the festival, but unfortunately the incident caught his notice. The mayor patted Samuel's shoulders as he loudly praised his new patrolman's courage in keeping the peace.

"A true northerner," he declared before cuing the band to pick back up their instruments and finish their music set.

Something about the mayor's hand on him made him uneasy. He made no mention of Zei, but he knew it was only a matter of time. And what would he say? Would he show him all of her sketches? Would he tell him that he was teaching her to read? Reason said his safest bet was to be completely open with the mayor about everything, but something about that didn't seem right.

Knife. Knife. Knife.

Zei wrote the word more than fifty times before sketching a knife on the bottom of the page. She drew a dual-edged blade with a leather-style handle and then added some sort of dripping liquid to the edge of the blade. Blood.

Samuel smirked.

"That's kind of gross. It wasn't a bloody mess or anything. At least, I don't think so. I mean, maybe when the doctor took it out."

Zei rubbed the scarred area on her leg where the trap had ripped into her.

"That must've been really painful," Samuel lamented.

Zei said nothing.

"I'm sorry about all of this. I don't think it's fair that you're stuck here. I wish I could help. But I can't. We'd both be in trouble."

She lifted her head, cracking several bones in her neck with the motion. Her long red hair fell down her back in a wave of curls. She pulled her head back up and pressed the sketchbook and the pencil in her hand, using what was left of her left arm to help balance the materials.

"Want to keep going?"

She gave a curt nod as she turned to a fresh page.

Samuel studied the blank page, trying to think of what new words they could learn. He leaned over, gathered the pencil from her hand, and scribbled the word *friend*. He said the word aloud several times before returning the pencil.

"You know what a friend is, right? It's someone you trust. Someone who cares about you. And you care about them. Like with family, only you're not related by blood. You accept each other. I'm your friend, right?"

Zei stopped writing. She flipped back through the sketchbook and stopped. The page was covered with the word *Sam*, and near the top corner, she'd drawn a picture of his face. He raised the sketchbook farther up into the light, forcing the shadows to move. The details were impeccable. From the way his cheeks contoured to the way his shaggy bangs covered his forehead, it looked as close to any reflection of himself as he'd seen before. On the page, he appeared relaxed, and his eyes nearly glistened with a gentle brightness he never noticed they had. Her drawing of him was nothing like the one she'd done of Charles. It seemed endearing. He scooted closer to Zei and touched the page.

"Is this what I look like?"

He expected her to ignore him, to look away or to simply take the sketchbook back. But Zei's green eyes glared at him unflinchingly, her stare petrifying. She took her hand and pressed it across Samuel's blushing cheek. Her skin was cold and soft. She didn't speak, but he knew she was trying to tell him something.

Before he could think of anything to say back, Zei pulled her hand away and reclined into the stone wall behind her as if nothing had happened.

The next morning, Samuel woke up to a harsh shaking on his shoulder.

"Get your ass up."

Samuel wiped his eyes in an attempt to clear the sleep. The sheriff walked by the doormat and tossed Samuel's boots onto his cot.

"One of my boys came in here to give me a message. There's an issue with a logging crew near the western wood."

Samuel's hands fumbled for his mother's dark frames. He slipped on his glasses and sat up. The wooden floors creaked as the sheriff gathered up the keys for the jeep and holstered his pistol. Samuel tried to shake off the sleep as he threw on one of his collared flannel shirts. He tucked the ends into his slacks and yawned. The sunlight was faintly refracting in the window. It must've only been morning for an hour or so.

"What is it?"

"Accident," the sheriff said as he shoved his feet into his boots.

"Some logger had a pine fall right on him. Still alive for now, but they're waiting for the doctor to get there before they try anything. These fellows can get a bit heated when things like this happen."

"But it's an accident."

"It's never an accident, kid. 'Accident' is a nice way of saying somebody fucked up."

Samuel laced his boots.

"I thought my only job was—"

"You're the one who decided to be some knife-throwing hero. You want to be a real patrolman? Fine. I'll show you what this job's really about."

They left the house, and the sheriff drove the jeep faster than he normally did. His eyes weren't as red as they normally were, and his breath didn't reek of booze. The wheels careened up and down as they moved through the square, past the mayor's estate, and onto one of the logging sites along the far end of the western woods. A large black truck was parked near the edge of the woods, the back of it stacked full of stripped pine trunks. Piles of chopped trees were lined up alongside the truck with various tools scattered all around it. There wasn't anyone near the equipment.

The sheriff hit the brakes and put the jeep in park. Samuel followed him out of the vehicle and into the woods. The earth below their feet had turned muddy and soft. Drops of water fell in spurts from the melting snow that hung on the branches above. Samuel looked up as a drop hit his lenses, and he noticed how the trees on this side of the woods were taller than the ones around his old cabin. Nearly all of the trees on the western end ran about twenty to thirty meters high, a lot bigger than the average on the east end. The trees' jagged branches only partially blocked the rising sunlight. Samuel trudged along after the sheriff. They walked along the premade path until they came upon the crew.

Twenty or so loggers were gathered around a large pine that had fallen directly in front of the path. Many of them stood there solemnly, a few of them talking quietly among themselves. Several patrolmen were there as well, including the one with the wiry hair. Samuel recognized him from the festival. The sheriff tilted his chin up to a balding man standing near the front of the tree, his hands fondling his gloves.

"Josiah, right?"

"Yes, sheriff." He bowed before motioning to the men behind him. "This is my crew."

None of the crew took any interest in acknowledging Samuel or the sheriff, their attention focused on other things. The sheriff paid no heed to their somber demeanor and spat into the ground, digging his thumbs into his belt. He waved at the wiry-haired patrolman.

"Doc here yet?"

"Over there." He kept his eyes away from Samuel. "Other side."

The sheriff gave a nod to Samuel, signaling him to follow. They moved past the clusters of men holding their tools and made a half circle around the pine. The doctor was on her knees, hunched over the fallen tree. The sheriff motioned for two loggers to move out of his path, and they did so without a word.

The doctor tucked a stray strand of her hair back behind her ear. Her head was bent down, and she was speaking softly to the man lying on the ground. His body was only visible from his chest up, the rest buried underneath the large pine. He was a bearded man with a square face, blood seeping out from the corner of his lips. Samuel had a hard time guessing how old the man was, partially due to his large amount of facial hair. His mouth was open, and his breaths were loud and forced. There was no need for the doctor to say anything. He'd seen enough of death to know the logger was near the end. Images of his father performing the rites engulfed his mind. He knew the routine by heart: the reading of the scriptures, the prayer of new life, and the shedding of blood. He remembered the old butcher. The thoughts prompted him to subtly scan the area for his father, but he wasn't there.

"What's the verdict?" the sheriff asked.

The doctor arched herself up, rubbing her thumb across her palm. She shook her head quietly. It was enough to confirm what Samuel already knew. The men around him knew it too, all of them at a loss as to what to say to their trapped crew member. One of them mustered up a weak encouragement about how Wilkens was the strongest worker he knew. The one logger's praise prompted another to speak up. He was a thinly fellow but still had brawny arms.

"This isn't fair."

The logger bent down and picked up a metal trap near his feet. The teeth were snapped shut, but there was visible blood on the pointed edges. He held the trap up over his head.

"The mayor had us bury all these traps in the middle of winter. For what? To catch some thief raiding his jewelry box?"

Most of the loggers grunted their agreements.

"And then, when the snow cleared, we're ordered go back to work in the western woods because 'it's the best lumber we have.' Did that prick forget he had us bury these traps in the snow, or did he just not care? And the mayor sits up there, in his cozy little mansion, while we bust our balls! Where is the justice in that?"

The man threw the trap angrily against a tree, forcing a loud thud. The loggers around him nodded, muttering swears and curses of their own.

The patrolmen on the other side stepped forward. "Careful. That is Haid's mayor you're talking about."

One of the loggers wrapped an affectionate arm around the

infuriated man, trying to calm his friend. It seemed to be enough for the moment. Samuel expected the sheriff to speak out a rebuke, but he didn't say anything.

"He's right," the doctor said. She reached in her bag and pulled out a black vial. "Tree was falling. The men cleared the way, but then he stepped on the trap, and ... "

Samuel wondered if the logger's legs were visible on the other side of the fallen tree, and if so, how he'd not seen them before. Those traps had been set to catch the mayor's thief. So far, they'd only caught Zei and this unfortunate logger.

The doctor uncorked the vial and put it next to the man's open lips.

"You're going to have to swallow this. It'll feel like you're drowning, but you have to force it down. It'll help with the pain. I promise."

The dying logger groaned, and Samuel's chest felt heavy as he imagined the weight of the tree on his own chest. The logger drank the doctor's medicine, nearly gagging as he managed to get down most of it. The doctor wiped the blood and spilled medicine from his cheeks and lips with a rag.

"Rites," the logger choked out. His red eyes welled with fresh tears. "I want the rites. Please."

Some of the loggers fidgeted uncomfortably once they heard the request of their dying friend, while others looked on with sympathetic gazes. Samuel wanted to be surprised as the other men were, but he couldn't be. As much as society despised the clergy and all their archaic practices, the dying were forced to deal with their mortality in a way that others didn't have to. Samuel had only seen the living rites performed a handful of times, but he'd seen enough to know that those near the end worried about only a handful of things: the lives they'd lived, their loved ones, their pain in death, and the afterlife.

The doctor peeked at the sheriff before turning back to the man. She made her voice sweet. "I'm sorry. There's not enough time."

The logger huffed harder, almost as if his chest were fighting to lift the tree. "Rites," he whined. "Please? Rites."

"Can't we just lift the tree, Elizabeth?" the logging supervisor asked as he came around the other side of the pine. He straightened his posture as his boots dug into the mud. "The sheriff can drive him to the cleric's place. Give the man what he wants."

"He's not going to make it."

The logger who'd thrown the bear trap came to Samuel.

"You're the cleric's son, aren't you?"

The sheriff turned, his heel sinking deeper into the ground.

"He's a patrolman."

Samuel pushed his glasses up his nose. He could feel the eyes of the loggers and the patrolmen on him.

"I'm not a cleric," Samuel said with a forced calm. "My father is. You have to be ordained and marked in order to perform the rites."

The logger clenched his arms together, shaking his limbs. He got closer to Samuel, their faces nearly touching. Samuel was forced to look at the man, and it made him feel helpless.

"Come on," the logger whispered. He bit his lip before continuing, making sure to keep his voice low enough so only the two of them could hear. "That's a good man dying down there. He's got a wife and three kids. Works hard every day. Even talks about the roots all the damn time like some religious do-gooder. Really good guy. And he never complains about the job. And he never asks for anything. Never. Which is more than I can say for most of us. For me. More than I can say for me."

Samuel arched his head into his left shoulder, trying to hide himself from the logger's desperation. It had been easy for him not to think much about his father the past few days, but death always reminded him. People often despised the clergy until they needed them, and his father always did his duties diligently. But he was not his father.

The logger kept on.

"I don't know you, kid. I don't care. But if you can, help Wilkens. Give him what he wants. Do it. Even if it's not real. Please. Do the rites."

"That's enough," the sheriff called out.

"Please," the man pleaded once more.

Samuel forced himself to look at the dying man. His breaths were slowing, his face growing more and more pale.

"I can't. I'm sorry. I'm not a cleric. It's against the law."

The sheriff waved his hand. The wiry-haired patrolman raised his firearm, and the others around him did the same.

"Tell your man to back away, Josiah. Or I'll have Jax here make this nasty."

Samuel's jaw twitched. He wished more than anything that

his father were there to perform the rites. For the first time in a long while, he would've been relieved to see his father holding the scriptures tightly. But the guilt of the dying man wasn't enough. He couldn't stomach the vision of reciting the old lines or slicing his hunting knife over his palm. He wasn't a cleric. He never had been. He would rather be the one under the fallen tree than be the one to conduct the rites.

"Back away, Gibbs," the logging supervisor called out.

The logger squinted his eyes, his nose wrinkling. He grunted loudly before stomping away, heading deep into the woods alone. The doctor petted the dying man's hair as he fought to stay alive. Several of the loggers started tearing up, while others remained stoic. The sheriff stood next to Samuel, both watching the man breathe his last breaths.

"I can't," Samuel said to himself weakly. His eyes turned wet. "I can't do it. I won't. I'm sorry."

The sheriff lifted his hand as if to put it on Samuel's shoulder, to give him some sort of reassurance, but put it down and shoved his thumb into his belt.

15

The rest of the day, Samuel felt frozen. He went to the jailhouse and did his duty with Zei. They shared a meal of boiled potatoes and half of a roasted chicken, but Samuel struggled to keep the food down. His stomach weighed heavy, each breath causing his ribs to twinge. He was nauseated and threw up twice. He didn't do any new lessons with Zei, content to only stand alongside her and watch her sketch pictures of whitelands mountains.

Ebauch Wilkens's funeral wouldn't take place until the next day. Samuel pictured the logger's bloodied mouth quivering as he made his request, his voice weak and desperate.

Rites.

Samuel blinked hard. How many dead bodies had Samuel encountered throughout his life? He never kept count. Wasn't it supposed to get easier? He wasn't merely haunted by the logger's ghost, but also by the nagging guilt of his refusal to offer a prayer. It was illegal for anyone not ordained by the clergy to perform the rites, and he wasn't a cleric. He needed the loggers and the other patrolmen to understand that, and they weren't going to learn if he performed the rites. He'd done the sensible thing, so why did he feel so dirty? A chilly wind pushed through the barred window, so Samuel gathered fresh wood and rekindled the fire. The warmth quickly took possession of the prison cell. He rolled up his jacket sleeves and looked on his arm. Against his own volition, he imagined inked roots starting from his elbow and creeping down in complex motions until they reached his wrist.

Samuel heard the chains rattling and turned. Zei stood beside him, the top of her head barely reaching his shoulders. She softly held her stub with her good hand as if she were nestling it safely across her side. She didn't say anything. She couldn't. But something about the way her slit-eyes were looking at him made him think she had an interest in his emotional disposition. He wasn't sure what to tell her, or if she even cared to know.

"I watched someone die. I didn't ... I couldn't help him."

Samuel fiddled with the ends of his shirt.

"Have you watched someone die?"

He regretted the question as soon as he asked it. He already knew the answer.

Zei's bare feet rapped across the dirt floor, the chains around her ankles following her as she made her way to the window. The breeze from outside caused her long red hair to sway in sporadic waves.

As usual, Samuel found himself trying to decipher what was going through her mind. Did she care about him at all? Did his question upset her? How much did she understand him, or was it that there was only so much she wanted him to know about her? Where had she come from? What happened to her missing arm? And, since she wasn't a demon, what was she?

The funeral took place outside, near the northwest corner of the woods, and those in attendance were mostly the loggers that worked for Josiah's crew. Samuel went by himself, choosing to stay on the outskirts of the procession. A few of the loggers gave him a nod of acknowledgement, but most of them ignored him completely. He spotted the logger who'd confronted him standing in the front of the casket next to a crying woman dressed in black. There were three children huddled around her; the oldest one couldn't have been more than seven or eight. The youngest one, a boy of about two, swayed back and forth as he kept a soft hold on his mother's dress.

The crew leader went beside the open casket and said a handful of good things about the dead worker, and later shared a funny story about how the logger had managed to save a coworker's life who was so busy taking a piss he didn't notice a falling tree.

"Wilkens ran up screaming and grabbed Cully, who still had his cock in his hand, and yanked that fool out the way. Got piss all over the both of them. We gave Cully so much shit for that. Wilkens too. But he didn't get mad or make a stink about it. 'Got to do the right thing,' he kept saying. That's the kind of guy Wilkens was. I wish one of us could've done the same thing for him."

Samuel fiddled with his fancy peacoat, still feeling inadequate in the garb. He'd come to the funeral in an effort to ease his conscience, but learning more about the dead logger only made him feel worse. He spotted his father coming out about a couple of miles past the square. Samuel squinted to focus his sight, and he could see how his father's footsteps were heavy and slow. He must've walked nearly eight miles just to get to the ceremony. His father waited patiently behind the coffin as other men sang their fallen coworker's praises.

When the loggers finished making their speeches, his father got beside the dead man's coffin. He took out the leather-bound scriptures from his jacket pocket and loudly read a passage Samuel recognized from the book of Iskriel, the same passage he'd read to the dying butcher.

"'We are but dirt. To the dirt we return. For Azhuel will draw out your flesh and pain, and in Him you will grow again, connected to the His roots. In Him, there is always life.'"

His father slit his palm open and squeezed until the blood dripped over the logger's stiff body. Could the dead man feel any peace from beyond the grave? Could he take any comfort in somehow knowing the rites had been performed for him?

Once the rites concluded, his father stepped back and wrapped his hand with a strip of cloth to stop the bleeding. He'd used one of the old hunting knives to make the cut, and Samuel remembered how dull some of those blades were. He must have had to press really hard to make the cut. Samuel lowered his hand into his pocket and fiddled with the three throwing knives he'd bought from the blacksmith months before.

Many of the attendees left as the body was lowered into the ground. Josiah's crew would have the rest of the day off to spend time with their families, but they would have to return to work the next morning or risk losing their jobs. That was the way the lumber trade was. Samuel's father edged himself back near the corner of the woods, allowing the people to make their exodus before he would make his leave.

Nearly everyone except the three loggers who'd elected to bury Wilkens was a far distance removed. Samuel swallowed. It wasn't as if it was against the law for a citizen to talk with a cleric. He took several steps toward his father but stopped. What if someone saw them conversing? Would they spread rumors that he was going back to the clergy? Would they keep treating him like the cleric's bastard? He looked around to see if the volunteer gravediggers were watching before continuing on the path to his father.

Samuel petted his hair, buying time for him to find words. He stopped a few meters to the side, making sure to push his back against one of the pines. He glanced out of his peripheral. His father's hand was far more bloodied than what was typical, the wet blood still dripping from the edge of his palm.

"It was a nice ceremony."

His father nodded with his usual stiff demeanor, his uncut hand squeezing tight on the scriptures.

"How are you, Son?"

The way that he said the word *son* nearly sent chills down his spine.

"Okay. Good."

"How is—"

"She's not a demon," he said sternly. He recalled the weight of his father's fist across his chest, forcing his words to have an edge he rarely spoke with. "She's really smart. And talented. And she's not the monster everyone thinks she is."

There was a long moment of silence shared between them. Samuel looked to his feet, kicking the dirt below. He didn't want to fight with his father, and he didn't come to discuss theology. He took a breath and reached into his pocket, carefully retrieving one of his throwing knives. He'd planned on practicing his throwing for a bit after the funeral, but the desire had left him. He held onto the thin handle, pinching it between his thumb and forefinger. He maneuvered his hold to the edge of the sharp blade and extended the knife forward.

"Here. I have two more. It's a small blade, but it cuts clean. For next time."

His father hesitated a bit before taking hold of the tiny knife. Samuel gave a quick bow before turning away. He jogged his way back into town, nearly catching up with the crowd that had left the funeral.

Over the next few weeks, Samuel got back to his normal routine. He resumed his writing lessons with Zei, who had learned well over fifty words. He knew that she enjoyed the lessons, because he was getting better at reading her. When she was happy, or relatively pleased, subtle divots would form in the center of her freckled cheeks, and her hand would move in gentle strokes. Every time he would show her a new word, she would hover over the page, her cheeks dimpled, and watch his writing as if it was the most exquisite art piece. She would delicately trace her finger in the air and mimic the motions of his pencil as he scripted the word.

Samuel became more strategic with the words he taught her. He showed her words like *hungry* and *tired*, poorly drawing his own depictions of the words and explaining them as well as he could. He wasn't sure if she would ever use words to communicate, but he was hopeful. He tried bribing her with the promise of a book at the conclusion of his lesson on greetings.

"If I tell you 'Hello' in the morning and you write back 'Hello,' then I'll buy you your own book. You'd be able to read something other than what I write. It'll be fun."

To his surprise, the bribe worked. He greeted her with a chipper "Hello," and she turned to a blank page and wrote "Hello." He told her how happy he was that she'd done it and raved about how smart she was. He went to the square later in the afternoon to special order a children's book from the dry-goods and specialty store. He browsed through the printed catalogues and picked a book titled *Winds of Mercy*. From the description he read, it was about a magical wolf that became an orphaned girl's guardian. The postman told him it would take a few weeks for the order to make it onto the train cart.

"Shipments come through here every three or four days," he said as he filled out an order form and took Samuel's payment. "But Medda's the closest city to us that has these things in stock, and for some reason it's taking them a long time to get their orders through. I heard some rumor about the greenlands being in some trouble, but that could be just a bunch of gossip."

Samuel nodded dumbly, deciding it was best not to mention the riots.

Zei wasn't the only person he spent time with. Every few days, Charles would drive by the jailhouse to hang out with Samuel, but he no longer moseyed into the building. Instead, Charles would bump the jeep's horn until Samuel came outside. They'd sit inside the jeep as Charles ranted about politics, complained about the weather, and bragged about the new garments he'd gotten shipped up from the south. He'd always insist that they go back to the estate, where they could relax, but Samuel made excuses why he couldn't go over. He was too tired, he had more work to do at the jailhouse, the sheriff was supposed to come by soon, and he'd be in trouble with him if he left. It wasn't that he didn't like being with Charles, it was just that he wanted to be close to Zei. It was his job, and it felt good to be around her.

One day, Charles asked Samuel to teach him how to throw knives. They stayed outside the jailhouse, and Samuel took him to a tree he'd already marked.

"My dad keeps talking about you," Charles muttered. "About how proud of you he is. I bet he wishes you were his son."

Samuel didn't know what to say. "I'm sorry."

Charles rolled his eyes. "It's not your fault."

"I know. But I'm still sorry."

He handed Charles another knife. Charles nibbled on his lip before clumsily throwing the blade forward. It landed several meters from the tree.

"It'd be better if we'd just go back to my place," Charles said, his face pouting in a way that reminded Samuel of a small child. "Smoke some tobacco, drink, do fun stuff. Not work. Don't you like hanging out with me?"

"Of course," Samuel said. "But I have responsibilities. This is my job. Your dad is my boss."

"I could pay you extra cash from my allowance if you need."

"No. We're friends. I can't do that. I won't."

"Friends," Charles said, kicking his loafers across the grass. "Sure."

"Maybe some other time?"

Things had been quiet since the mayor's return from the political assembly in Kairus, and Samuel hoped it would stay that way. The last thing he wanted to do was run into him at the estate. He didn't want to face the mayor unless he absolutely had to.

Samuel also made a habit of visiting the butcher's shop. If things weren't busy, he would stay and chat with Claudette. If she was too busy helping her mother with the work, he would buy a small item and leave. Claudette would always greet him with a warm smile, and his blood would always rise when she did. One day they talked for more than an hour, and Laura Litten burst out from behind the swinging doors to dryly pick on their flirtations.

"Are you of wedding age?" she asked as Claudette showed him more of the fancy ways she braided her hair.

"Not yet," Samuel said weakly. "Less than a year away."

"I look forward to the day you can ease my daughter's suffering."

Claudette rebuked her mother; her face flushed red. Samuel was so embarrassed he couldn't say anything the rest of his time there without stuttering.

"I think I've got it this time."

Samuel folded three sections of Zei's red hair over one another, the movements slow enough to ensure every lock was tidy. She sat still with her legs crossed together and kept her head up and straight. Samuel squatted lower, trying hard to make sure he was doing it right. Before he'd cross a new section over the center of the hair, he'd grab some additional strands on the side he was working on and include them in the crossover. By the time he'd reached the nape of her neck, all of her hair was wrapped into a tight braid. His insistence on watching Claudette rebraid her hair had paid off. Zei looked nothing like the wild creature she seemed to be the first time he'd met her. Her face and body were washed clean, she was wearing a white top and a fancy floral-patterned skirt that stopped right at her knees, and now her hair was fixed in a style that looked good enough for a politician's daughter to wear. She looked like a normal girl, except for her eyes. And her missing arm. And the scars. And the shackles around her ankles. But it didn't matter. She was beautiful.

"You look pretty." He tied the end of her braid together with an elastic band. "I can get the mirror. Do you want to see?"

Zei nodded.

Samuel left the inside of the cell and went over to the hope chest, fumbling around for the portable mirror. He'd brought it over to the jailhouse weeks ago but had forgotten about it. The mirror was stained and cracked, but he got it at a cheap price. He moved around some of the clothes until he felt the wooden handle. He made his way back to Zei, turning the mirror so that the glass faced her.

"Here."

Her little hand took the mirror's handle. She studied the glass, tilting her neck from left to right, her lips slightly parted. She watched her reflection studiously, blinking her long lashes in random spurts. She pulled the mirror back and petted her stub across her cheek, tracing it down her chin and back around to the other side. It was as if her own body fascinated her.

The sudden sound of a roaring engine followed by a harsh squeaking caught Samuel's attention. He went over to the barred window and got on his tiptoes. He looked around and spotted a jeep in the far corner, and a large man with balding hair stepped out of the vehicle. It was the mayor. His suit was black, and his tie appeared to be a silky shade of purple. Samuel's nerves caught fire. He extended his hand forward, motioning for the mirror. Zei handed it over without a fuss.

Samuel gathered up Zei's sketchbook and pencil as well, tucking them in between his arm and his chest. He had to move fast. He hurriedly put the supplies back inside the hope chest and slammed it shut. He didn't want to bring up Zei's writing or her sketches, not yet. Not if he didn't have to. He came back to the bars, pressing his face against the cold metal before slamming the gate shut.

"He's here," he said in a lower voice. "Please, I need your help. Do whatever I tell you to do. Okay? Just this one time?"

Zei said nothing, but something about her gaze made him believe she was willing to play along for the time being. Samuel straightened his posture. The wooden door into the cell room flew open, and the mayor sauntered inside, his smoking pipe hanging from his plump lips. He closed the door behind him and grinned as he removed his jacket, exposing his pressed, collared shirt and tight suspenders. Samuel carefully took the jacket from the mayor's hold, placing it on the coat rack in the corner of the room. The mayor removed his pipe, smiling as he extended his arms welcomingly. Samuel bowed low, noticing an awful twinkle of delight on the mayor's face. He stretched himself back up, and the sound of another engine echoed across the room. It had to be the sheriff.

"How can I serve?"

The mayor sucked on his tobacco.

"Formalities, boy. How are you? It's been a long time."

Samuel turned so that he could look at both the mayor and Zei.

"I am doing well, sir. Charles has been kind to me."

"Good. He needs good friends, that strange boy."

Samuel paused, unsure of how to respond next. He would hold onto Zei's secrets as much as he could, but he knew better than to play the mayor for a fool.

"She's doing well. Her leg is healed, as you can see. She's gotten much more comfortable with me."

Zei lowered her head slightly. Samuel cleared his throat.

"She is calm now. Peaceful. Compliant."

The sound of harsh yelling from the outside hallway made Samuel's muscles spasm. He heard the sheriff screaming obscenities, followed by a quick threat.

"Don't make me break your skull!"

The mayor removed his pipe, smiling more widely.

"Sorry. I forgot to mention that we have a guest."

The sheriff burst into the room, thrusting a bound man in after him. The man had to be in his forties or so, his lanky arms tied behind his back with a rope. A gag covered his mouth, his teeth gnawing into the white cloth. The man jerked his shoulders in resistance to his oppressor's sturdy grip, but the sheriff jostled him harder. He hurled the man down, his head smashing into the ground. The man winced as he struggled to lift his face, blood running down his eyebrows.

Samuel's breath stopped. He recognized the man. It was Claudette's father.

The sheriff spat on the ground, glancing at Samuel before handing his revolver to the mayor.

"I've done my job. Can I go now?"

The mayor nodded. "Thanks, Eugene."

With that, the sheriff stormed away as suddenly as he'd come.

Samuel pushed up his glasses, biting the inside of his mouth. Zei's chains rattled as she stood and unleashed a piercing stare at the mayor.

"I am sorry, dear lad, if this is upsetting to you."

The mayor pulled back the revolver and pointed it at Claudette's father.

"I am a very patient man. I get what I want and reclaim what is rightfully mine. Even if it takes a bit of waiting. Isn't that right, Harold? You thieving ingrate."

Claudette's father squirmed, his frantic eyes falling on Samuel as his teeth chomped into the cloth. The mayor took a step forward.

"And now it's time to see what demons can do."

16

Samuel stepped back, the heels of his boots crunching into the dirt floor. He readjusted his frames, his voice meek and vulnerable.

"I'm not sure I understand."

"This is my thief, boy. Caught him tampering with my safe. Found more than three hundred silvers stuffed in his socks."

Claudette's father writhed on the ground, the dark circles around his eyes making him seem like a woodlands critter. Zei stood erect, her eyes glowing. Samuel rubbed his palms across his thighs. Was the mayor telling the truth? Samuel remembered the festival, and his tongue swelled.

"Didn't he earn a bonus? For his hard work at the estate?"

The mayor's belly jiggled, and he shook the gun a bit.

"A bonus! I pay my employees fairly. Do I not?"

Claudette's father mumbled, but it was impossible to understand

him with the gag. The mayor gave him a swift kick in the ribs.

"Shut your mouth," the mayor hissed. "At least you could face your punishment like a true northerner, and not like some entitled greenlands bitch."

Zei shifted her weight, and the chains rattled. The mayor nodded in her direction, his mouth forming a casual grin.

"Greetings to you, demon child. It's been a long while." He turned to Samuel. "Oh my. That demon looks deceptively lovely. Did you dress it?"

"Sir? I mean. Yes, sir."

The mayor took a puff from his pipe.

"That is a bit concerning. Playing dress-up with a demon. It's unnatural for a man to spend his time on frivolous things, don't you think? Perhaps you're not as good of an influence on my son as I hoped."

Samuel stood silently as the mayor removed the pipe from his mouth and carefully laid it on the ground.

"Regardless. I've hired you for a job, boy. That job was to be this demon child's caretaker, to befriend it, to get it to trust you. Have you done your job to the best of your abilities?"

"I believe I have."

"You have a knife with you, correct?"

Samuel's skin burned intensely. What was the mayor planning? What was going to happen to Claudette's father? Could he do anything to help him?

"Yes."

"Get it."

Samuel went to the hope chest, the muscles in his chest constricting. He retrieved his hunting knife. The handle nearly slipped out of his grip as he unsheathed the blade.

"Good," the mayor said. He waved at Samuel to come closer. "Cut him loose, but leave the gag on."

Samuel moved toward Claudette's father and got on his knees, the knife outstretched. Claudette's father stared at him intently, his teeth chomping into the gag as he sat up and lifted his bound hands. Samuel wanted to ask questions, but he said nothing. He knew better. He carefully sawed into the rope until the strands broke free.

Claudette's father wriggled his wrists, curling his fingers up. His bloodshot eyes were damp. He could've reached up to pull off the gag, but he didn't. Samuel could tell by the positioning of his legs he thought about running, but the gun made it a risky choice. The mayor licked his bottom lip before speaking.

"I'm feeling generous," the mayor said leisurely. "No. That's not the right word. Equitable. Yes. I am feeling quite equitable. Look at that child there. Harold, I mean you. Look. That is a demon. Look at its eyes. Look!"

Claudette's father did as instructed, his cheeks paling. Samuel's palms perspired.

"I want to play a game," the mayor said. "Samuel, open the gate. Give the demon creature your knife."

Samuel had to make sense of everything. He couldn't stand in the way of the mayor's wishes, but maybe he could redirect them.

"Sir," he mumbled. "I think—"

"Enough whispers. Speak up, boy."

Samuel forced mucus down his throat.

"Sir. I wonder if this is the best course of action. I know how much this ... demon means to you, and I don't think she's in a place to be trusted with a weapon."

"Are you questioning me?" The mayor's voice got loud, his disposition immediately shifting to rage. "Open the gate. Give the demon the knife. Now!"

Samuel had never known fear like this before. This was something terrible, like a nightmare he couldn't wake up from. He shoved his glasses hard into his nose before getting the key for the cell and sliding back the gate. His teeth chattered as he made his way to her. She didn't move, but her eyes readjusted their focus onto him. He couldn't keep his hand steady, the knife twitching in his grip. He stopped a foot away from her, curling the blade end away. Zei stood still. He towered over her, but he felt so small next to her in that moment. He inched the knife closer. She didn't take it.

Samuel took her hand into his and opened it. He tried to shake his head, but he couldn't. The thought of showing any sort of disobedience to the mayor terrified him. He was a coward. But still, he didn't understand it. Why would the mayor do this? If Zei died, then it was all for nothing: the job, the lessons, everything. He lowered the knife into her palm, wrapping her fingers around the handle. He stepped back, for a moment imagining she would take the knife and plunge it into his guts.

The mayor waved the revolver at Claudette's father.

"Go on. You want absolution for your crimes? You'll have to earn it. Don't be fooled by its looks. That creature is not human."

Claudette's father gradually moved himself into the cell. Samuel wanted to tell him something, anything. Don't do it, he wanted to say. Please. Don't. He pointed his chin downward, refusing to look at Claudette's father as he skirted into the cell. The mayor switched the gun from one hand to the other, but the barrel never lost its target.

"I'd give you a weapon, Harold, but that creature is a bit on the small side. And, it is in shackles. And, you're the one who has committed the offense. I want to be fair. I am a fair man. Close the gate, lad, but stay inside. Stand near the demon."

Samuel slid the gate shut, the metal clinking as it locked into place. He rubbed his palms across his thighs as he made his way to Zei. She stood silent, her face unreadable. The knife's blade was pointed down to her feet, her hold on it loose. Claudette's father cautiously took several steps forward.

"What are you waiting for?"

Claudette's father took another step, but then froze. He carefully removed the gag.

"I can't do this," he whined. "I can't."

The mayor lifted the gun and fired a shot into the air, the boom so loud Samuel nearly fell. His ears rang harshly, and the mayor's voice sounded muffled as he spoke.

"Shame," the mayor said. "The least you can do is be a man and fight with some damn dignity."

Zei remained still.

"I deserve punishment," Claudette's father stammered. "I do. I'm a thief. I deserve whatever you see fit." He shook his head in short bursts. "But not this. No. This is wrong. This is evil. I won't. I could never face my family alive if I ... I can't do it. Just kill me, please. That's all I ask."

Samuel stared at Claudette's father in awe, searching for any sort of hope. Harold was a decent person. He knew he was. He probably only stole to help support his family. That didn't make him a killer. Zei wasn't a killer either, as much as the mayor kept saying she was. The sheriff too. They were wrong. He knew they were all wrong.

Claudette's father gave a nod to Samuel.

"Take care of my daughter. My girls. Please. Tell Laura that I'm sorry."

The mayor swung his arm forward and fired another shot in the direction of the cell, but the bullet struck the stone wall. Samuel covered his ears. The ringing morphed into pain. The mayor charged forward, shoving his belly against the bars.

"You think your wife and daughter won't share the responsibility of your crimes? Am I supposed to believe they knew nothing about your thievery? Does money rain from the sky? Do you take me for a simpleton?"

Samuel's teeth chattered. No, he couldn't. He wouldn't.

"They knew nothing," Claudette's father sputtered. "I swear to you on my life, they knew nothing."

"Your word is like your life," the mayor retorted. "It means nothing now. You want to guarantee sparing your family the wrath of all deserved justice, then you'll turn around and you'll do what I told you. Be a man and fight. Kill that demon. Fight it. Take the knife from its hands and eradicate it."

"I can't kill a child like this," he whimpered. "It's evil."

"It's not human! It's a monster! Defend yourself, coward!"

Samuel scooted back against the wall as Zei's fingers snaked tighter around the handle. She was stoic. This wasn't justice. Claudette's father shifted his body, his arms in a frantic state of motion.

"Mercy, please. Don't make me do this."

"This is mercy. Attack. Now!"

Claudette's father closed his eyes, his lips muttering something. He dropped to his knees. "I can't," he said. "I can't."

Zei came forward. Samuel saw something in her eyes that brought him terror. He watched her lick her lips and curl them back into a grin.

"No," Samuel mouthed.

Zei ignored him, her tiny feet gliding in rapid steps before she launched herself on top of her would-be attacker like a wildcat. Claudette's father rolled onto his back, his arms savagely shoving against her small body. She was unshaken by his desperate pushing and swept her legs into a straddle over his chest.

"Exceptional," the mayor called out.

Samuel was dumbstruck, absorbed in a horror that didn't seem real. Claudette's father screamed as he reached out and grabbed Zei's braid, yanking it down violently. Her neck snapped sideways from the pulling on her hair, but she otherwise seemed unfazed. Her eyes fell on Samuel as she curled the blade up, hovering it over her would-be attacker's chest. It was almost as if she was waiting for Samuel's response. But he couldn't say anything.

"What is this thing?" Claudette's father yelled.

The mayor shook the bars.

"Order the demon to kill him. Now, boy!"

Samuel was petrified.

Claudette's father pulled Zei's braid harder, forcing her head backward. Zei pushed her stub against his arm, guiding his elbow back until he lost his hold. Her hair strands were wild and out of place. Samuel couldn't give the order. He didn't need to. Zei was too lost in her own bloodlust to notice. She only needed the briefest opening to make her strike. Her hand aligned the blade over the man's stomach, and she thrust it down.

Claudette's father gagged in pain as the knife plunged into his bowels, his hollering muffled. Samuel stumbled back. How could this be real? How could this be the same girl he'd spent countless hours eating with and teaching to write?

Zei twisted the handle before wrenching the knife out. Claudette's father yelped in agony. She continued her assault indomitably, moving the blade up near the sternum and hammering the blade in and out of his chest again and again and again. Her red curls spilled out of the disheveled braid over her shoulder as the man's blood sputtered up to her face with each new hit, the droplets splattering all over her pale skin and white top. Some of it landed on Samuel. Claudette's father's writhing and screaming lessened with each jab until he went completely limp. Zei gave several more strikes before ceasing her attack. The chains around her ankles sang as she slowly rose to her feet. She was peppered with blood, her predator eyes glaring at the mayor through the prison bars. She walked until the slack of her chains had disappeared, holding the knife tightly.

The mayor's expression hardened. He pulled the revolver up in between the bars, aligning the barrel with Zei.

"Get the knife."

Samuel blinked repeatedly.

The mayor stomped his feet.

"Do your job, boy."

Samuel forced himself to find words. She'd killed him. No. She'd slaughtered him. He never needed to say a word. It's what she wanted to do. She liked it. He could tell she liked it a lot.

"Please," he stuttered. "Please put down the knife. Please."

Zei slid her thumb across the handle, stroking it methodically.

"Take the knife from her," the mayor ordered. "She would've hurt you by now if she saw you as a threat."

Samuel sucked through his nostrils as he approached Zei. He reached out an open hand, unsure of what she would do next. This wasn't the friend he'd come to know. This really was a monster.

Zei waited for a long minute, her expression unreadable. Before the mayor could scream out once more, she calmly gave the knife back to Samuel. The handle was soaked in red.

"Very impressive." The mayor shoved the gun into his trousers. He clapped his large hands together, the sound echoing across the room. "A bit gruesome for my taste, but you, my dear, will make me a fine soldier. Wait until they see what I've caught. The demon of the whitelands. I like the sound of that."

Zei whipped her head back. She strolled past the lifeless body in the cell, her left foot grazing the fresh pool of red.

"Come here, boy," the mayor said warmly. He spoke emphatically with his hands. "I did expect a bit more from you, but overall, I am quite pleased."

Samuel stepped out of the cell. He closed the gate. His arms were shaking. He was crying, even though he didn't want to. The mayor noticed.

"A man should never show his tears," the mayor rebuked. "You're a man. Aren't you?"

Samuel swallowed, finding the strength to choke back the tears. "Yes, sir. I'm sorry. It won't happen again."

"You see, boy. I want that demon free of its shackles. Like you. But, you're the one that's holding the key. Don't you see that? You are the key. Not only did the demon leave you untouched, it also submitted to your instructions. In the heat of conflict, it looked to you for orders. Do you realize the gift you've been given? You have surpassed your father immeasurably."

Samuel said nothing. A wave of nausea engulfed him, and his head ached. He dropped the blood-soaked knife, the metal clinking as it struck the floor. The mayor strolled over to Samuel's side. He reached down, picked up the knife, and cleaned it with his embroidered handkerchief. He handed the knife back to Samuel.

"Don't worry about the Litten women. They will be well taken care of. And as far as I'm concerned, you've earned yourself a permanent position on my payroll."

Samuel gave a sluggish nod. The mayor put his hands on his shoulders, forcing Samuel to look up.

"Boy," the mayor said harshly. "Look at me."

Samuel obeyed, but he locked his sights on the mayor's square forehead. Away from his eyes. He couldn't look into his eyes.

"I see the way that demon watches you. It longs for your guidance. You must be strong, Samuel. I need this creature to fight with us in the war to come. And make no mistake. War is coming. We must be ready to defend our homeland no matter the cost."

The mayor ranted on about state independence and northerners' preparations for possible invasion, but his words washed over Samuel. He kept seeing Zei driving the knife into Claudette's father, twisting it hard to ensure the wound couldn't close. It was messy, violent, savage. Nothing like any kill or death he'd witnessed before.

"You're a true northern citizen," the mayor said as he gave Samuel a light shake. "But I need to make sure you know where your loyalties lie. Understand?"

"Yes," Samuel said blandly, his nausea growing.

"Are you with me?"

"Yes."

When the mayor finally left, Samuel hunched over and vomited.

17

amuel tried to ignore the dead body as he dragged the water hose through the hallway and into the cell, his lips quivering but silent. He pressed his thumb across the nozzle's opening and systematically sprayed the cell, doing his best to guide the mixture of dirt, blood, and bits of entrails to the other side of the bars. He remained on the outside of the cell as he hosed down Zei. She stood erect as water struck her body, her arm pressed against the wall behind her and her eyes watching him in a way that made his skin crawl. He could hardly bear to look at her, but he had to clean the mess. The blood had stained her clothes.

After he finished hosing, he grabbed a large broom from outside the toolshed and swept the filthy concoction back down the hallway and outside of the jailhouse. Once the mess was cleared, he rolled up his sleeves. He didn't want to go inside the cell, but he had to. He

needed to get the body, and it wasn't as if anyone was going to help him.

Filthy liquid dripped from Zei's skirt and hair. He grabbed a black dress from the hope chest and reluctantly opened the gate. He swallowed as he threw the dress over to her. She did nothing to catch it, and it fell on the muddied ground. Samuel wiped the sweat forming on his neck with the collar of his shirt. He shoved the key for the cell in the lock, but his hands were wobbly, so it took him twice as long to unfasten the bolt. The gate screamed as it slid back. He reached into his pocket, his fingertips grazing the end of his hunting knife. Would she attack him? Would she tear into him like Claudette's father? He felt like he didn't know her at all.

"I'm coming in," he announced faintly.

Zei cocked her head, but otherwise kept her position against the wall. Samuel watched his feet as he scuttled over to the body. He bent down and took a long breath before fighting to drag the corpse out. He'd barely moved the carcass a couple of feet before he lost his grip and fell. His hands were too sweaty and his muscles far too weak to do this alone. He went back and took hold of the arms, but he accidentally caught sight of the gored torso. "Don't look," he told himself. He squeezed and gave the hardest tug he could muster. He'd managed to move the body another few feet before the same thing happened.

Samuel's eyes burned as he gritted his teeth, allowing his saliva to spill out as he clutched the body's tattered shirt. He got on his knees and fought to scoot Claudette's father out of the cell. He wouldn't give up. He wouldn't lose it. He had to get the body out of the cell. He'd gotten the corpse to move halfway to the gate before he lost his hold once more. He fell backward, his back and arms on fire. He sat on the wet floor and slapped his hands over his face, struggling to hold himself together.

"Come on," he said to himself, his blood rising. His words offered little motivation or encouragement. He'd never felt so lost in all of his life. He started crying again. He didn't want to, but he couldn't bring himself to keep it together. He wept uncontrollably for several minutes, his mouth tasting salt and snot. He hit the ground with his fists. He couldn't do this.

"What are you?" he asked, wiping his eyes repeatedly.

Zei watched him from the end of the cell, her body dripping wet. Her face was unreadable, an expressionless statue. Samuel had always been so patient with her, but he couldn't be any longer.

"Are you a demon? Tell me, Zei. If you're not a demon, what are you?"

He sprinted to the hope chest. He dug out Zei's sketchbook and pencil and then hustled back into the cell. His heart was beating so loud he could feel it hitting across his ribcage. He held out the pencil and notebook for her to take. She didn't move. He flipped to a blank page, dabbing the pencil's point on the paper.

"Write something. Draw something. I have to understand. You just killed someone, Zei, and I need to understand why. Is the mayor right? Are you scared of him? Were you trying to protect me?"

Zei stared blankly.

"Do you like it? You like killing? Are you a demon, Zei? Are you a girl? What are you? Are you anything?"

Zei took the pencil and paper as if she was contemplating what to do. She waited for a moment before scribbling two words.

They hungry.

Samuel frowned. "What?"

Zei did nothing.

"Who is they? Are you asking for food?"

Zei turned to the side. Samuel reached out and took hold of her hand. Her skin was smooth and cold as marble.

"Please. Try again. A picture."

He let go of her hand. Her fingers relaxed, and the pencil dropped to the floor. Why wouldn't she answer him? Why was she doing this? Hadn't he done enough for her? He wanted to yell at her, to throw the sketchbook across the room like he'd done with the scriptures months before. But he didn't. He picked up the pencil and put it and the notebook back inside the chest.

He somehow found the strength to drag Claudette's father out of the cell.

The sheriff sat by the kitchen table with an open green bottle and a drink glass half full of liquor. The whites in his eyes were lined with redness, and his cheeks were wrinkled. He wriggled the glass around in circles before bringing it to his lips.

"You're late," he said before taking a long sip.

Samuel stripped off his coat and hung it on the coat rack. He pulled out his hunting knife and placed it beside his cot.

"The body," he said with a scrunched face. "It's in the hallway at the jailhouse. I could only get it out of the cell room. I couldn't do any more."

The sheriff nodded as he downed the liquid in his glass. He poured a fresh serving of liquor and held it up near his nose. Instead of drinking it, he lowered the glass onto the table and scooted it to the other side. Samuel paused before taking a seat opposite the sheriff. He gingerly lifted the glass, twirling the liquid inside. He remembered how it tasted, and his jaw stiffened. The sheriff picked up the green bottle and held it up high.

"To the mayor of Haid," he said before swigging from the bottle. "Asshole."

Samuel took a drink as well, the liquid sliding into his throat. It burned hard.

"What do I do now?" Samuel asked.

The sheriff reclined into his chair and wiped his peppered mustache. "You do your job."

Samuel gulped down another sip, the second more bitter than the first. He rubbed his tongue against his teeth, trying to neutralize the sting of the alcohol.

"I couldn't help him. I tried. What am I supposed to tell them?

Claudette and ... "

The sheriff lowered his arms onto the table and slouched forward, his hands open.

"Look, kid. You like that Litten girl, don't you?"

Samuel nodded.

"How do you think she's going to feel if she hears how you stood there and watched her father die? I'll tell you. Every time she looks at you, she's going to think about her dead daddy. Regardless of whether or not you did anything wrong. Hey. Samuel. I need you to understand. You did nothing wrong. You did your job, and that's exactly what you had to do." The sheriff scratched his neck. "This world is not all black and white. It's a lot of gray. Sometimes ... how do I say this, maybe it's best to not volunteer facts. Sometimes, ignorance is the best option."

Samuel blinked heavily before taking another sip. He wanted his mind to go quiet. He wanted the pain to go away.

"What do I say to her? When she asks me questions?"

The sheriff lowered his shoulder, groaning.

"Fuck. Kid. Lie, okay?" He waved his hand as if it were a fluttering bird. "You were never there. You got called away. You didn't see anything. Put it all on me. I don't give a shit. Everybody in this town hates me anyway."

Samuel cupped the glass with both hands. He put it back to his lips and forced himself to drink the rest of the liquor. He coughed a bit before sliding the glass back onto the table. His skin tingled, and his breaths loosened. The sheriff poured him more.

"I can't move the body outside. Not by myself." He swallowed, forcing himself not to cry. "I'm not strong enough."

"I'll help in the morning. Just make sure to keep that little monster locked up good."

They drank together silently for about twenty minutes. Samuel started feeling lightheaded soon after. His body swayed slightly. He readjusted his frames.

"She killed him. She was so fast. Like it was nothing."

The sheriff snorted.

"Of course it did. You think I'm stupid? Did you think I was lying to you?" He propped up his elbows, his fingers forming into the shape of claws. "Landon. Ripped him to bits. It dug its fingers into his chest and ripped him open. You hear me? No person could do that. I won't sleep a good night's rest until that thing has a bullet between the eyes." He shot an imaginary gun and laughed. "Well. Maybe we *should* call on your old man. Do that thing. What's it called again?"

"Exorcism."

The sheriff snapped his fingers. "That's it. Exorcism." He said each syllable slowly. "A demon. Whatever it is, it ain't human. That's for damn sure."

"Not human," Samuel echoed.

The sheriff snorted as he stood up, his feet so unsteady he held the table for balance. His heavy eyes looked at Samuel. He leaned forward. "I'm gonna show you something. Something the mayor hasn't seen. And if you so much as utter a word to anyone, I swear to your father's god—"

"You'll beat my ass?"

"Good lad. It's a deal?"

Samuel pursed his lips, unsure if he wanted to make such an agreement, but the sheriff didn't wait for a response. He staggered to the bedroom, his arms outstretched to help his balance. Samuel rubbed his hair, his senses dulled and his skin tingling. He felt as if his muscles were jelly. He needed sleep, but his mind probably wouldn't allow him the opportunity. He took another sip of liquor and heard the sheriff's rustling footsteps behind him.

"Here," the sheriff said with a grunt. He dropped something on the table.

Samuel's sight was hazy, so he readjusted his frames to bring the item into focus. It was some sort of mechanical device, the browning metal and rusted bolts giving away its old age. The top portion contained a two-pronged claw with multiple spur gears inside of it. Three rusted pipes extended from the claw down to a tattered leather holster. The holster had two straps: one that buckled tightly around the base and the other that hooped several inches over it. The entire contraption couldn't have been more than a foot in length.

"Around the harness," the sheriff said while twirling his finger. "Look right there. Do you see it?"

Samuel picked up the device, surprised by its weight. He needed both hands to secure it. He lifted it to the candlelight, examining the straps. Sewn into the leather appeared to be miniature glass-like tubes and wires, the technology resembling an expensive relic the mayor could have mounted to the wall of his estate.

"What is it?"

"Are you serious?" the sheriff asked as he sank back into his chair. "I guess you're not as smart as I thought you were. It's a prosthetic. A fake arm. Military grade, from the looks of it. Pre-blackout. Forbidden technology."

Samuel tightened his grip. The hooked claws reminded him of Zei's hand when she tore into Claudette's father. "Is it hers?"

"Anybody else you know have need for a machine arm?" The sheriff kicked his feet onto the table, his arms crossing over his chest. "After we left the scene, one of my boys found it underneath the snow next to the trap. My guess is Landon must've been able to rip it off of the little bitch before it got the best of him."

Samuel pictured the device attached to Zei's stub, imagining what she would look like with a mechanical arm. "Why keep this a secret? Why not show the mayor?"

The sheriff laughed.

"Tell me this, kid. Who would have access to the forbidden technologies? And … why would they give it to a monster like that? It's like it was custom made for it." The sheriff sucked air through his teeth. "No. I'm not showing this to the mayor. Last thing that power hungry asshole needs is a loaded weapon."

Samuel put the prosthetic arm on the table and slid it over to the sheriff. "If you hate the mayor so much, why are you his sheriff?"

The sheriff huffed. "Same reason you're an overpaid babysitter. We do what we have to. If you wanted to live by some moral code of right and wrong and good and evil, then you should've stayed with the cleric."

Samuel stood beside Claudette throughout the funeral's procession. She locked her arms around his. She wore a lavender dress, her hair tied back into a tight bun. She cried in little spurts, but she never lost her composure. Laura was much more reserved, her expression blank. The mortician had covered the body with a sheet up to the neck, covering the gored torso. No one had any words to share, not even Claudette or Laura. There was no point in singing the praises of a criminal.

"Idiot," was the only thing Laura said aloud during the entirety of the service.

Samuel's father went up to the coffin, and Laura stared at her feet. Samuel brushed his bangs to the side as his father read from the scriptures, sharing a passage about the mercy of Azhuel extending to all people. When he finished his prayer, his father pulled out the throwing knife Samuel had given him. He slid the blade across his palm. Blood leaked through his fingers.

Samuel looked away. Part of this was his fault; he knew it was. If he hadn't been so trusting of Zei, if he had found a way to persuade the mayor out of his cruel test, perhaps Claudette's father would still be alive. Maybe Zei wouldn't have butchered him.

He reached into his peacoat's inner pocket, checking to make sure the paper was still there. He'd have to find a way to pass it along without drawing any attention. The rites concluded, and Samuel helped Laura and several loggers who'd volunteered to assist with the burial. They carried the coffin over to the graveyard near the southeast corner of the neighborhoods. The only markings for the graves were thin sticks that had been shoved into the earth on top of the coffins. However, when the snowstorms came, many of the sticks would be knocked out of place. It mattered little to northerners. It was their way of symbolizing how everyone was the same in death. Politicians and other men of higher status, however, could be buried wherever their surviving loved ones wanted. Samuel knew all the past members of the Thompson family were buried behind the mayor's estate, but he'd never seen if their graves were marked any different.

After they lowered the casket into the plot, Samuel turned back to check on his father. He was already walking away, his path a straight shot to the eastern woods. Samuel apologized as he told everyone he had to use the restroom but would be back quickly. He saw his father disappear into the woods and dashed after him, looking back frequently to see if anyone was paying him any mind.

Once he got into the woods, he called out for him.

"Father."

He shuffled around the pine trees and hard dirt. A group of squirrels darted up the trunk of a tree as he came up toward them. He stopped, looking around a bit. His father had to cut across back onto the path they'd made. He knew he couldn't be too far from it, but he needed to hurry.

"Father," he said a little louder.

He rounded several more trees and heard the bustling of the wildlife around him. He spotted a doe from about a hundred meters away, but the creature darted off as soon as Samuel noticed her. He moved deeper into the woods, and his feet found the path. His father was nearly out of sight, but he saw the back of his long coat. He ran as hard as he could, and his father turned to face the noise. He stopped, his mouth slightly agape.

Samuel reached him and took a couple of deep breaths. His father towered over him, his eyes watching with concern. Samuel dug into his pocket and handed the paper over.

"She drew this," he said with rushed breaths.

His father unfolded the sketch of Azhuel's roots, his stone face studying the drawing intensely while his other hand squeezed the scriptures.

"Maybe you're right about an exorcism. I can leave the door unlocked. Keep the cell open too."

"Do you have faith?" his father asked.

Samuel kicked the snow. "I don't know. I just ... I want to help her. Else. I don't know what will happen next."

"I made a promise to your mother," his father said in a low voice. He looked away from the sketch, his fingers crinkling the paper as they morphed into a fist. "To keep you safe. And I've failed her. I've failed you. I'm sorry, Samuel."

"You never talk about her." A pit welled in Samuel's stomach. "All I have is her name and that photograph. I don't know anything.

Why won't you tell me about her? Who she was. What she was like."

"Your mother loved you." His father looked up, his eyes gazing at him with a softness Samuel wasn't accustomed to. "I'll tell you everything. The next time we meet. You have my word. But you need to go now, or someone might become suspicious."

"Will you do it? Will you try to save her?"

Samuel stood in place as his father turned away and headed deeper into the woods. He thought about the photograph and the way his mother's lips parted in the smallest smile. He wanted so badly to remember her voice, and the way her skin felt as she rocked him in her arms. But he was only a baby, and no matter how hard he tried, he couldn't will the memories to life.

Samuel slid the glasses farther up his nose before heading back to the gravesite. The volunteers were working to cover the body with fresh earth, and he helped put the final layers of dirt over the coffin. Claudette positioned the stick near the center of the grave, burying it as deeply as she could with her bare hands.

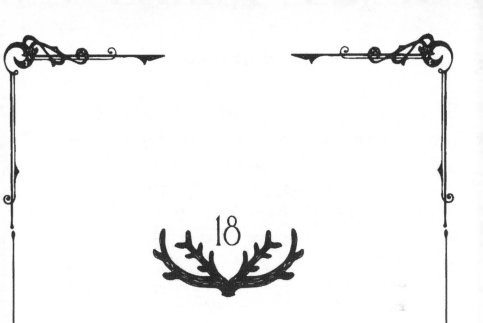

18

The sun was starting to rise as Samuel took a detour stroll through the woods. He kept his gloved hands by his side, his breath turning to vapor as soon as it left his mouth. The temperature was dropping, each new day a bit chillier than the last. Even for the whitelands, the sudden shift to cold was a bit odd. The almanacs had predicted five more weeks of summer, but the shortening sunlight and graying sky forebode something else. The animals knew it too. Already the birds were joining together in flocks and migrating down south, and the squirrels and foxes were busily foraging for extra food. It wouldn't be much longer before the first snowfall.

The sheriff offered to give Samuel a ride to the jailhouse, but he declined. He needed time alone. He was grieving the loss of Zei, of who he thought she was. The Litten women were grieving the loss of Harold, but they both dealt with his passing differently. Laura

threw herself into her work, unwilling to let herself show any grief. The mayor ultimately forgave the Littens of the debt, but the loss of an additional income made it all the more important for the shop to succeed. Claudette wasn't as hard as her mother. The brightness in her smile had diminished, and she didn't speak with the same joyous lilt. Her pain made it all the worse for Samuel. He blamed himself. He couldn't rid himself of the guilt.

As he neared the jailhouse, he came out from the pines and trekked to the front entrance. He grabbed onto the door's handle and turned it. He'd made sure to leave it unlocked the evening before. He went inside, plodding down the hallway and into the cell room. The gate was slightly cracked, just as he'd left it. Zei sat cross-legged in the back-left corner of the cell, her index finger tracing in the dirt. Within a matter of days, her once tamed hair had morphed back into an erratic mess of entangled knots and wild curls. The embers inside of the firepit were barely glowing, the room nearly as frigid as the outside. Samuel said nothing as he rekindled the fire. He wasn't so much afraid to be near her. He didn't want to be.

Once the fire was set, Samuel stripped off his coat and gloves and prepared a meal. He didn't feel like cooking anything, so he made her a plate of raw cabbage and a bit of almonds. He wasn't hungry, and he wasn't going to force down food.

Samuel slid the plate over to her and got out of the cell, choosing instead to sit far away in the chair by the coat rack. He arched his back as he toyed with one of his throwing knives, twirling it in between his fingers. She took no interest in the food, instead entertaining herself with her dirt sketching. She wasn't only drawing. While he was working on the firepit, Samuel noticed her tracing out some of the words he'd taught her: bird, deer, knife, snow, and Sam.

Zei wanted the sketchbook. He knew she did. But he wasn't going to give it to her. He was acting childish, but he didn't care. He'd been ignorant enough to believe in her. He was absolutely certain she wasn't a demon or a killer or any of the horrible things everyone else thought her to be. He didn't know what to think about her now. Had her good behavior with him all been a ruse? Had she been playing him for a fool, gaining his trust so that she could manipulate him into gaining her freedom? If she had her mechanical arm, would she be able to break through the chains and tear into him the same way she had Landon Swen and Claudette's father? He didn't trust her anymore. If the mayor wanted her to be his demon, to be some sort of mindless and violent creature, then he could have her.

Samuel slipped the knife back into his pocket. That wasn't true. There was a small part of him that had misplaced faith in Zei's redemption. What if his father had been right, and she was under the control of an evil spirit? What if an exorcism was the only thing that could save her soul? If she were normal, maybe the mayor would cut her loose. What good would she be to the mayor if she lost her strength and bloodlust? There was also the chance that the mayor would simply kill her. Knowing the mayor, that was the probable outcome. But even so, maybe Zei's death would be better than the alternative. At least she could die with her dignity, and a small part of him liked the idea of the mayor not getting what he wanted.

He knew the set of events he'd conjured up in his head were all unlikely possibilities. First, he needed his father to sneak over to the jailhouse and perform the exorcism, and there was no guarantee he would come. Second, and the most unlikely scenario, the exorcism would actually work. If that happened, he would somehow need to test and prove that Zei was indeed free from demonic oppression. It was all a fantasy. But for the first time in a long while, he wanted to believe in the power of Azhuel and His roots.

The sound of a wailing horn from outside the jailhouse awoke Samuel with a jerk. He'd nearly fallen out of the chair, his hands reaching out like wings as he regained his balance. He must've dozed off. He hadn't been able to sleep much at night. He adjusted his glasses and looked around. Zei was up on her feet, her attention veering to the barred window.

The sheriff must've come to pick Samuel up, even though he'd told him not to. Samuel yawned. He gathered his belongings before moving to the gate. He stared at Zei for a brief second before sliding the gate, but he made sure not to close it all the way. Her food was untouched.

"Goodnight," he found himself saying.

It was the first thing he'd said to her in days. He exited the jailhouse. Charles sat in the driver's seat of his father's jeep, his arms cradled over the steering wheel. Samuel was a bit relieved. It would've been harder to fake securing the front door if it was the sheriff. Charles gave him a wave. Samuel waved back as he took out the jailhouse keys and pretended to fasten the front door's lock.

"What were you doing in there?" Charles asked as Samuel got into the passenger's seat. "Took you long enough."

"Sorry," Samuel said as he rubbed his gloved hands together. The jeep was warmer than the inside of the jailhouse, so much so that his lenses began to fog. "Why are you here?"

Charles put the vehicle in reverse, turning the jeep back and around.

"What's wrong? You getting sick or something?"

"I'm fine." Samuel pulled off his glasses and wiped the lenses with the tail end of his coat. "I'm tired."

The jeep edged its way to the square. Charles barely tapped on the accelerator.

"I got some big news," he said. "Swear you won't tell anyone?"

Samuel gave a half-hearted nod.

"I mean it," Charles said with more force. "Not even the butcher girl."

"I won't say anything."

Charles squeezed the steering wheel. "My dad is heading to Tallow tomorrow. All the whitelands mayors are voting on whether or not we're going to secede from the states. The riots in the greenlands are only getting worse, and it's affecting the trade routes. Governor Bloom is calling for total northern independence. Cutting off trade and everything. He's already trying to reestablish trade with the Others."

"Others?"

"I forget. You've lived in these woods too long. The Others. You know, those living across the seas?"

Samuel put back on his glasses. He knew about people living on other bodies of land across the water, but the Laevis Creed forbade any contact with foreigners. That was one way to prevent the wars. Were the whitelands going to forsake the Creed? The states had been firmly united since the blackout. Why was it changing now?

"That sounds dangerous. What if the citizens don't want that?"

"They're working out the details," Charles said with a shrug. "People have to trust our politicians. They have every citizen's interest at heart. Right?"

"I guess."

Haid was a logging town. Lumber trade was essential to its survival. It wasn't like there were a plethora of crops that could grow in their hard soil, and there definitely wasn't enough wildlife around to adequately feed every family in town. He supposed the citizens would go along with the politicians, so long as the lumber trade didn't take a hit.

Charles reached over Samuel and popped open the compartment underneath the dashboard. He retrieved a briarwood smoking pipe, a can full of tobacco, and a pack of matches.

"It gets better." He peppered the pipe's bowl with tobacco. "If we disconnect from the greenlands, there's no way we can rely on the redlands to fight for us. And some whiteland cities are going to be commissioned to train their own militia, in case those riots try coming up here. And guess which mayor volunteered his services?"

Several weeks had passed since his conversation with Charles about whitelands independence, but life in Haid continued as it always had. The loggers worked in the western woods hacking away at pine, the shop workers were busy with their daily routines of commerce and stocking, and the children were out enjoying the tail end of their summer play. The sheriff seemed oblivious to the news of secession, that or he wasn't bothered enough to comment on it.

The sheriff and Samuel were spending more time together than they had before. When Samuel would come in for the evening, the sheriff would be sitting at the kitchen table with an extra glass of liquor poured and ready. Samuel wasn't fond of drinking, especially after the night he got so drunk he passed out on the side of his cot in a pool of his own vomit. But he would have a glass or two with the sheriff anyway. Sometimes the sheriff would talk about random things: how getting older was making it harder for him to move, his disdain for the cold weather, his peacekeeping tactics, and how it'd been years since he'd had a good lay. Other nights the sheriff wouldn't say much of anything as they sipped on their alcohol and stared into nothingness.

Before heading to the jailhouse, Samuel visited the butcher's shop. The bell above the door dinged as he stepped inside. No one was in the front room, so Samuel went by the display counter and waited. A few seconds passed before the swinging doors popped open and Claudette walked out. When she saw Samuel, she went over to him and hugged his neck.

"Hey," she said in a sweet but low voice.

"Hey."

Claudette released her hold and went behind the counter, wiping her forehead. "Did you need something?" she asked as she tossed off her bloodied apron.

"No. I just ... I missed you. Wanted to see how you and your mom were doing. See if there's anything I can do to help."

A seemingly forced grin escaped her lips. "There's nothing you can do."

"He could help with the shipment," Laura called out from the back room. "The train should be arriving in the next twenty minutes."

"Sure. I don't mind."

Claudette turned on her heels to face the door. "He won't know what to do or where to pick up the shipment or—"

"Go with him, then."

Samuel put his gloved hands inside of his pockets, unsure what to do.

Claudette thudded back behind the double doors and returned with her jacket and a tiny leather purse. They left the shop and made their way over to the rail depot. The building was nearly as big as the mayor's estate, but its only decoration was a large black sign hanging above the pavilion that had *Haid* painted in fading white letters. Claudette sat on the empty bench, her eyes looking south along the railroad tracks. There was a crew of loggers waiting by their parked truck, their boisterous conversations nearly audible from the far distance. Samuel squinted as he scanned down the track. There didn't appear to be anything approaching.

"Must be running behind today," Claudette said. "I'm sorry." She kicked her legs back and forth, the ends of her dress flowing. "I don't want to take you away from your important job."

Samuel shrugged. "You're more important to me."

"No, I'm not." She pulled her braid over her shoulder. "I don't like you working there. I don't like what patrolmen do to people."

"I'm sorry."

"What happened to him, Sam? What did they do to him? Why didn't you stop them?"

Samuel rubbed his throat. "I'm sorry. I couldn't. I—"

Claudette's eyes watered, and she wiped them aggressively. "You would've stopped them, right? If you could have? I know that he was stealing, but he didn't deserve to die. He was only trying to help us. I saw his body, Sam."

Samuel nodded stiffly. He hated that she was in pain, and he hated lying to her. He hated how Zei had turned into the mayor's butcher. He hated the mayor for making her that way. Most of all, he hated himself.

Claudette dug her fingernails into the wood underneath her.

"My mom is going on like nothing happened. All she talks about is work. And how now we've got to figure out better ways to cut down on spending. I don't understand her. Why is she so heartless? Doesn't she feel anything?"

"My dad was like that too. About my mom." Samuel slouched back into the hard bench, his stomach bubbling. "My whole life. He never wanted to talk about her death. She was executed because of me. Because she had a child with a cleric. I wanted him to explain it to me. Tell me what happened to her. How she died. If he tried to save her. If he even cared. But he never told me anything."

Claudette looked at him. "That's terrible."

Samuel breathed deeply. He wanted to see his father again and hold him to the promise he'd made in the woods. His father was never one to break his word. If he said he was going to do something, he'd do it. Every night Samuel went to sleep imagining what information his father might share. He didn't know if the truth about his mother would bring him any fulfillment, but he wanted to know more than anything. It's what he'd always wanted.

And yet he was holding back the truth from Claudette because he didn't think he could bear the weight of her pain anymore. He couldn't risk losing her. Fear had strangled him to silence, and the guilt continued to swallow him whole.

"Maybe that's all he could do," he mumbled. "Try to forget. Maybe it's the same for your mom."

Claudette nodded.

The bench underneath them began to tremor, and soon after, the entire structure around them was quaking. They both turned their heads to the south, noticing the faint black machine chugging its way toward them. The railway worker came out from his station, joining them on the platform. He was a tall gentleman dressed in a black coat and corduroys. He was the only other person in Haid Samuel had met who wore glasses, but his frames were much thinner.

The railway worker leaned out to face the oncoming train and cupped his hands over his head, shielding his eyes from the sunlight. "I'm hoping this will be a big one. Our shipments have been delayed for a while now."

Claudette stood, and Samuel followed suit. As the train drew closer, the wooden deck underneath his feet shook more rapidly, and the squealing of the metal wheels running along the track was enough to force Samuel to cover his ears. The circular steel front of the locomotive churned down the track like a sluggish bullet, the smokestack pushing out gray clouds and the bell behind it dinging loudly. The squealing grew as it got closer to the depot. The train was slowing. The crew of loggers made their way alongside the tracks, their heads watching the carts pass by. One of the loggers turned back and waved for the loading trucks stacked full of lumber to move closer.

When the train came to a halt, the conductor popped out of the cab and trudged out onto the platform. He was an elderly man with gray hair, a thick beard, and bare arms stained with soot and dirt.

The railway worker walked over to the conductor, who was now up on the pavilion. "Shipments have been late. Not to mention the carts keep getting smaller and smaller. Anything to do with those riots I keep hearing about?"

The conductor shook his head, wiping his hands with a filthy rag he'd stashed in his back pocket. He wasn't wearing a jacket, but perhaps the furnace from the train's engine kept him warm enough.

"I just drive the thing," he said in a cracking voice. "It's chaos down there, if that's what you're asking. Damn near got raided by a crew of starving greenies in Borem. Getting too old for this."

"Aren't we all?" the railway worker countered as he received the necessary paperwork. He looked at Claudette. "Yours is on two. One crate of chickens and a goat."

The conductor guided the crew of loggers to the empty carts near the rear of the train, warning them he wouldn't be able to fit the usual haul. Before Samuel and Claudette could make their way to collect the shipment, another man emerged from the cab of the locomotive. The man was shorter than most northerners. He was dressed in dark pants, black boots, and a tan shirt that fell to his knees. His hair was black, like Samuel's, and his bangs fell down his cheeks. His body was lean yet exceptionally toned, and despite a smaller stature, his gait commanded a certain level of respect. Claudette scooted herself a bit closer to Samuel as the man marched up the wooden steps, stopping directly in front of them.

"Greetings," the man said in a warm voice. He bowed low, but he held out one of his arms as if he were extending a gift. Samuel and Claudette bowed in response. When he came up, he poked out his chest slightly. He was handsome, and his high cheekbones made it hard for Samuel to approximate his age.

"My name is Mikael. Would either of you be able to offer assistance?"

He spoke in an accent that Samuel had never heard before. It was almost as if every syllable he spoke was smoother, more drawled and rhythmic than what he was accustomed to hearing. His olive-toned skin left Samuel with the assumption that the man was from the redlands. Claudette said nothing, perhaps waiting for Samuel to respond. He was too enamored of the stranger to speak. He'd never met someone from the redlands before, and his skin reminded him of his mother's photograph.

The stranger sighed. "The rumors are true. Whitelanders are cold."

Samuel pushed up his glasses. "Sorry. Forgive me. How can I serve?"

"I am looking for the mayor of this town," he said. "It seems he is too busy to provide an escort for his guest."

19

The town square was packed to the brim. The loggers had been sent away from their work sites, some of them still lugging around their hatchets and gear. A few men griped about having their day interrupted, but most seemed relieved to have the unexpected break. The blacksmith had been commissioned to set up the makeshift stage in the center of the square, and a few bored loggers helped him haul out the broken pieces and reconnect them with temporary nails. Shop owners gathered directly outside their businesses, as all work in Haid had been canceled for the rest of the day. Patrolmen had been posted around the congregants and near the stage, their weapons exposed in case of any unruly activities.

Samuel rested his back against the butcher's shop, scanning for the sheriff. The large crowd reminded him of the festival, and this time he had no intentions of policing anything. Claudette and her mother stood beside him. Their deep breaths turned to fog the moment they left their mouths.

"Must be important," Laura commented.

"Do you think it's about the foreigner?" Claudette asked.

Samuel put his hands up to his mouth, blowing hard. He had some ideas about what the mayor might announce. He would probably give news about the greenland riots and share how the whitelands were, in all likelihood, breaking alliance with the other states. But what would he tell the citizens about their livelihood? Would he guarantee the loggers that their income would remain unaffected and that the politicians had already reestablished trade with those across the seas? Or would he only make a declaration of independence?

"I don't know," Samuel said dolefully.

Before helping Claudette unload the crate of chickens, he had directed the foreigner in the direction of the mayor's estate. The foreigner thanked him for his assistance and strolled off to the mayor's house. Who the man was, and why he had been personally summoned by the mayor, was beyond Samuel's reasoning.

Another hour passed before the stage was ready. More families had made their way out from the neighborhoods, most of them women and children searching for their husbands and fathers. Samuel listened to the conversations around him. Some worried about the severity of the news, since it required an immediate announcement, while others were annoyed that it was taking so long for the mayor to arrive.

"Do you have any answers?"

Samuel turned. The doctor maneuvered around a few shuffling children, her hands tucked underneath her armpits. She got closer to the butcher's shop, giving a nod to Samuel.

"You're a patrolman, aren't you? Why aren't you gathered with your posse?"

Laura Litten patted her bloodied apron, her nose pointed out as she watched the stage. "He knows as much as we do."

The doctor tucked a wild strand of silver hair behind her ear. "Figures."

The hardness in the doctor's expression made Samuel uneasy. She was there the day he'd refused to pray for the dying logger. And she was the only citizen who knew about Zei. What did she think of Zei? Of him?

"Damn it, people," the sheriff's distinguishable voice yelled out into the masses. Samuel spotted his balding head near the front of the stage. "You all need to move back. Come on, now. Move it!"

Heads and bodies turned as people stepped backward, their bodies pushing against one another. The mayor's jeep rolled through the path made by the citizens. The vehicle parked next to the stage, and the mayor stepped out from the driver's side. He blew into his smoking pipe as he strolled up to the wooden steps. The side door swung open, and the foreigner came out. He followed the mayor, his gait long and relaxed. Charles exited last, but he seemed unsure about where he was supposed to go. He awkwardly moved to the end of the platform, choosing to stick beside the sheriff. The patrolmen eased their positions, and the crowds quieted of their own accord, nearly every head facing the stage.

The mayor surveyed the citizens, his hands by his side. He stepped to the front of the platform, his pipe writhing back and forth. He eventually removed his pipe and spoke loudly, his voice reverberating across the shop buildings.

"Citizens. I want to thank you for gathering here today. I realize that this is an inconvenience to your schedules, but I have important news regarding the welfare of our town, of our whitelands state, and of the future."

Samuel reached inside his pockets, allowing his fingers to graze the end of his knife.

"I'm certain many of you have heard of the southern unrest. Some of you may have even heard that ruling greenlands politicians, men who've long aided in maintaining the stability of our alliances, have been savagely overthrown by a crew of mad dogs. In light of this, Governor Bloom and the ruling whitelands mayors have decided it most appropriate to begin terminating our relations with the greenlands. Soon we will cut off all trade and commerce with them. We have voted, and decided, that secession from the states is the best option for our citizens."

Low whispers buzzed from the citizens, but none dared to project their concerns. The patrolmen held straight faces, their eyes scanning the crowds. The foreigner seemed almost bored by the mayor's proclamations, his weight shifting from one foot to the other.

"The heinous actions of those greenlands criminals will not be condoned by this great state, and we will do everything to ensure we have no more affiliation with those animals."

"I have a sister in the greenlands," the doctor muttered. "Is she an animal?"

The mayor paced the stage. "Now, let me ease your fears. As your mayor, I have and will continue to make your wellbeing my highest concern. Trade with the greenlands will be phased out in a reasonable timeframe, as we work to build new alliances with the Others. Our aim is to leave your daily lives as undisturbed as possible."

The doctor rolled her eyes.

"Deershit. There's more to it than that."

Samuel gave a curt nod, allowing his disdain for the mayor to slip out.

"I also realize that any adjustments with trade will inevitably cut profits in the beginning, but fortunately Governor Bloom has commissioned Haid as one of the towns responsible for training our own militia. Additional state funds are being allocated to help with military supplies, training, and of course, additional pay. This is an opportunity for ordinary citizens of the whitelands to serve our state in extraordinary ways. We do not want a war. But if those greenie dogs think they can bring their greed north, they are sorely mistaken."

The mayor gave a nod and took a step back. The foreigner brushed his hair back, and he lackadaisically made his way to the front of the platform. The murmurs from the crowd were growing, but the foreigner spoke as if he were unbothered by their confusion.

"I am no politician," the man called out emphatically, his accent thick. "I am a soldier. I've been hired by your mayor to train every willing and able-bodied man to serve in the whitelands' new militia. I know most of you lack basic understandings of military tactics and combat weaponry. I don't expect any of you men to become experts of war. But, under my tutelage, you and your families can be ready and armed to face an untrained mob."

Once the mayor had returned to the estate with the foreigner, the citizens discussed the news with one another. Most seemed to support the mayor and the actions of the governing politicians, especially since he'd promised their livelihoods wouldn't be affected. "A job is a job," was a phrase uttered over and over again. A small group of citizens did voice their concerns. Those who griped seemed averse to any sort of change, and a few shared their fears about being a part of any sort of war.

Samuel stood by the butcher's shop, quietly observing the masses discuss politics and the future of the whitelands. Claudette and Laura had gone inside to continue their work, but he opted to stay put. He held his bunched hands up near his lips, blowing warm air onto his fingers. The children seemed oblivious to the discussions of their parents, many of them finding ways to play chase amid the masses. The other patrolmen held their positions throughout the square, observing the crowd and waiting for further instructions.

The blacksmith worked to dismantle the stage, removing nails and dragging parts back inside of his shop.

The sheriff dismissed the assembly. He stood near the disassembled stage and yelled at the citizens to return to their homes. "Go on! Everybody get out of here. Talk it out over your own dinner tables, not in the streets."

Crews of patrolmen waved citizens along, and most of them obeyed without a fuss. But when the square had nearly emptied, a disgruntled group of four loggers made their way to the sheriff. "What is all this riot talk, Eugene?" an older logger asked. "You know, some of us got family in the greenlands. What's happening down there? These politicians tell us only what they want us to know."

Another logger spoke up as well. "We need answers."

The sheriff gritted his teeth. "Look, be glad you're getting the chance to make up any losses with that militia, okay? Stop your whining. Take the work you're given and move on."

One of the loggers, who Samuel recognized from Josiah's crew, pushed past several of his cohorts to get in front of the sheriff. He was the man who'd pleaded for Samuel to perform the rights. His brawny arms were level by his side, but his hands were clenched.

"We don't want to be soldiers, sheriff. Haven't enough people died?"

The sheriff spat onto the ground beside the man's boot, his hand hovering over his revolver.

"You're arguing with the wrong man. Now get out of my way before I beat your ass."

The man held his ground, his face reddening.

"You're a drunk. To hell with you and the mayor. I can't speak for everyone else, but I'm done being yanked around like some puppet."

The sheriff didn't have to move. Six patrolmen swarmed the disgruntled logger and brought him to the ground. Samuel's muscles tightened, and his hand grazed the knife's handle inside his pocket. The other loggers backed away as their friend struggled to free himself, his arms flailing wildly. One of the patrolmen anchored his knee deep into the logger's back and struck his head with the back of a rifle. The logger's body instantly went limp.

"Don't kill him," the sheriff barked. "Pull him up!"

Samuel inhaled as he went over to the sheriff, his fingers rapping across the sides of his coat. The remaining citizens watched as the patrolmen lifted the unconscious logger.

"Get him out of here," the sheriff said to the other loggers. "Tell him next time it'll be much worse than a bump on the head."

Samuel pushed up his glasses. The sun was lowering over the western sky, its light refracting through the jumbled trunks and branches of pine. The sheriff straightened his back, his hand cradling his revolver.

"Is everything going to be okay?"

"People fear change," the sheriff said in annoyance. "It's natural."

The blacksmith took hold of one of the stage's side compartments, draping it over his broad shoulder. "They're scared, sheriff. Talk of war makes people remember their history. Some traumas don't leave people, no matter how many generations removed. Leaving the states. Forgoing the Laevis Creed. I don't think that's something most of us are ready for."

"Do the politicians really think rioters are going to come north?" Samuel asked.

The sheriff cocked his head.

"Enough. Let the politicians plays their games. Whitelands. Greenlands. Redlands. It's all the same. An assembly of power-hungry men ruling over their towns and a fat governor keeping them all happy. The rest of us are along for the ride. But unlike some of you morons, I keep my head down and mind my own damn business."

A crew of patrolmen stood outside the jailhouse. One of them, with greasy hair and a hooked nose, sat against the front door, his legs crossed and a rifle by his side. Jax, the wiry-haired patrolman, stood beside another patrolman near the toolshed. Samuel dug his hands deeper into his pockets, wishing more than anything that the sheriff had dropped him off. He hadn't the faintest idea what the men were doing at the jailhouse. He tucked the package farther inside his coat.

When the patrolman on the ground saw Samuel coming, he sprang up to his feet and scooped up his rifle. Samuel stopped. Jax looked to Samuel and gave his fellow patrolmen a wave of reassurance. "The mayor sent us here," he explained. He wiped his sleeve. "Wants us standing guard outside the jailhouse at all times."

"Does the sheriff know?" Samuel asked. "Why didn't he tell—"

"The sheriff is busy," Jax said curtly. "He might be our boss. But the mayor is law. We've been directly ordered to keep surveillance outside the jailhouse. That's all you need to know."

Samuel nodded, hoping to avoid any more conversation. He went to the door, placing his hand on the fastened lock. The patrolman who was sitting beside the door pointed to the chains. "It wasn't locked up, so I fastened it for you. You should be careful, kid."

Samuel bowed. "Yes. My mistake."

The patrolman nodded toward the jailhouse. "What do you do in there all day? How do you not go mad with boredom?"

"Ignore him," Jax interjected. "Move along."

Samuel gave another polite nod. He unfastened the lock with his keys and moved the rusted chain away from the bolt. Had his father visited Zei the night before? If not, he hoped his father was aware enough not to approach the jailhouse while patrolmen stood guard. His father wasn't a fool. Besides, there was no guarantee he would come. Perhaps he'd found Samuel's plea for an exorcism risky. Regret made Samuel's mouth dry. He never should have asked his father for it in the first place. He opened the door and shuffled inside, closing it quickly. He pressed his back against the door, taking a moment to collect his nerves. He made his way down the hallway onto the cell room.

Zei sat underneath the barred window. Her knees were drawn up to her chest, her chin resting on her bare knees. Most of her face was covered by the tangled, chaotic nest that had become her ungroomed hair. Zei's arms wrapped around her legs.

Samuel looked away. He searched the room for evidence that his father had come but found nothing. The gate to the cell was just as he'd left it. Slightly cracked. He took off his coat and pulled out the wrapped package. It was nearly the size of Zei's sketchbook, only smaller. His hand squeezed the paper wrapping.

Zei waited silently.

Samuel breathed deep. How long could he punish her? How much of that day had been her fault? What if she was only acting in the way of her nature? How much of his pain was his own fault? He was the one who'd created the fantasy where Zei was just some misunderstood girl. In his mind, Zei had been a mysterious kid with a quiet longing to connect with the world around her. Like him. But he was wrong. Was she even a girl? Even human? She'd never answered those questions before, no matter how many times he asked.

Samuel held the package out as he went to the gate and slid it back. Could he ever trust her as he once did? He stopped a foot away from her and bent down, lowering the package on the ground.

Zei remained still.

"Take it," Samuel said as he backed away.

A long minute passed before Zei lowered her knees, the shackles around her feet clanking as her heels slid farther down into the dirt. Her tiny hand reached out and took the package. She tucked it between her thighs. She held the package in place with her stump as her hand tore back the paper wrapping. She pulled out the hardbound book and guided it up into the light, examining the cover. It was a brown leather printing of a little girl lying across the chest of a large wolf. The title, *Winds of Mercy*, was craftily etched into the spine.

"It's a book for kids," Samuel said. He stood up, and his joints popped. His legs were tired from the constant walking.

Zei propped the book back down onto her legs and opened the book. She turned page after page, her eyes fixated on the large printed words and the cartoonish pictures.

"You're not ready to read it yet. I haven't taught you enough words."

Samuel allowed his back to recline against the metal bars of the gate. "I don't think I can teach you anymore. I'm scared of you, Zei. You hurt people. And with the mayor ... the way things are ... I don't know if I'll ever not be afraid of you."

Zei turned another page, her focus solely on the book.

"I saw your arm," Samuel said. "The mechanical one."

Zei looked up, her pupils wide.

"How did you get something like that?"

Zei remained stoic.

"I don't know if you're a demon. But I know you're a murderer. And. To me. That is just as bad. Do you feel bad for him? He was ... my friend's father. How am I supposed to forget what I saw? I see his body every time I close my eyes."

Zei allowed the book to slip out from her lap. She reached across the ground and traced a word.

F R I E N D.

Zei's index finger came up from the dirt. She pointed to Samuel.

Samuel pushed his glasses farther up the bridge of his nose. He shook his head.

"I don't know. I don't think we can be."

Samuel turned away. He stepped outside of the cell and sealed the gate shut. He opened his mouth, his insides longing to force more words. But nothing came up. Zei waited for a moment before lowering her head, lifting the book, and turning to another page.

20

Samuel stirred, his fingers digging into his cot. Light escaped from the window, the morning rays leaking out from the small gap left by the curtain. He cracked open his eyelids for a second but quickly closed them shut again. His retinas burned, and his head felt as though a large rock had struck it. He'd made the mistake of having more than a couple glasses of whiskey with the sheriff. He wanted to stop when his muscles felt loose, but the sheriff taunted him for being a little girl with a weak constitution.

It took Samuel several minutes to sit up from the bed. When he did, a sudden nausea swept over him. He clenched down on his teeth, tasting acidic vomit as it ran up his burning throat. He staggered for the kitchen counter and puked. He convulsed as the contents of his stomach splattered into the sink. The queasiness subsided slightly when he'd finished. He wiped his mouth as he looked around

the room, squinting. His insides were always so sensitive. He half expected to see the sheriff standing by the table, ready to mock him, but the house was empty. It wasn't like the sheriff to be gone so early in the morning. Not unless he had to be.

Samuel put on his glasses before heading to his drawer. He got dressed slowly, careful not to make too many sudden movements. He scratched his arms before tucking his shirt into his pants, still feeling awkward in his uniform. Perhaps it would always feel that way. He laced his boots and stood. His eyes were watering heavily, so he blinked hard. He wanted to stop by the butcher's shop before heading to the jailhouse.

He buttoned up his coat before stepping outside. He placed a hand on his forehead, taking a brief moment to get his bearings in the daylight. He turned west, scanning down the square. The streets were empty, save for several patrolmen who'd been positioned outside the blacksmith's shop, the large wooden doors sealed shut. It was the same three patrolmen who'd stood guard outside the jailhouse the day before. Samuel slogged down the square, thinking it odd that the blacksmith's doors were closed. He usually worked with his doors open because the furnace got so warm. Jax eyed Samuel, his rifle stiff by his side.

It made Samuel uncomfortable, so he moved to the other side of the square and did his best not to look over there again.

Before reaching the butcher's shop, he stopped to briefly survey the happenings over by the western woods. A large number of loggers, several hundred at least, were lined up in rows with their limbs by their sides. He could hear the faint yelling of the foreigner, ordering the men to take steps forward, then quickly commanding them to stop. It was odd seeing burly loggers marching in awkward steps and taking commands from a man shorter than most of them. Gibbs and a few other loggers might have had reservations about joining a militia army, but the prospect of earning additional income swayed the majority. The mayor was getting what he wanted, and the loggers were earning coins in the process. Samuel hoped the militia would turn out to be an unnecessary undertaking. Governor Bloom would reestablish trade with the Others across the seas while phasing out trade with the south, and in the meantime, the citizens of Haid wouldn't go hungry as they spent some of their time training for a temporary army.

Samuel put his hand on the butcher shop's front door. The notion of loggers serving as a militia seemed silly to him. What weapons were the loggers supposed to use? Axes and hatchets and chains and knives? The sheriff barely had enough resources to arm the patrolmen he employed. Less than half of them carried firearms. Samuel wondered if the militia was merely a distraction, a way of keeping everyone busy while they waited for trade to reopen.

The bell dinged as Samuel pulled the door back. He went over to the glass counter. Claudette was rearranging the meat display, adding fresh cuts of steak to the lower portion of the shelf. She popped her head up and wiped her hands across her apron. Her face seemed to whiten as she looked at Samuel.

"Hi," she said feebly.

"Hi."

Claudette jostled behind the counter, grabbing a pair of metal tongs. Her movements were jerky and rushed.

"I'm sorry. I'm really busy today. I can't talk much. Did you need something?"

"Are you okay?"

She nodded. "I'm fine. Just busy."

Samuel tucked his thumbs into his palms. There was always plenty of work at the butcher's shop to keep Claudette busy. He knew that. But something was different with her. He could feel it.

"I was going to get some more chuck. And talk. But I can come back later."

Claudette shook her head. "No. It's fine." She grabbed a sheet of packing paper and shakily laid it on top of the counter. "How much do you want?"

"Half a pound is good. Have you seen the sheriff around? He left early this morning."

Claudette froze for a second before shaking her head stiffly. She reached underneath the counter and grabbed a handful of the meat.

Samuel swallowed. "Claudette. What's wrong? Are you okay?"

Claudette dropped the meat on the paper and quickly bundled it up, keeping her eyes down. "Damn it."

The swinging doors from the back room swung open. Laura Litten held a filthy rag, wiping it in between the crevices of her hand. She gave a quick glance to Claudette before staring at Samuel. Something about the way her cheeks were bunched up made him feel more suspicious.

"I'm sorry, Sam," Claudette said. She looked to her mother. "You have to tell him. I can't lie to him. Tell him, or I will."

Samuel interlocked his fingers, his brain somehow forcing out the remnants of his hangover. "Tell me what?"

Laura glared at Claudette but relented immediately. She turned to Samuel.

"I've been up a few hours before sunrise, working. I was by the front, seeing what cuts we needed to replenish. I heard some voices outside, so I went to the window." She paused. "The sheriff and some patrolmen were making a commotion over by the blacksmith's shop." She clutched the rag. "Your father. They had him tied up. They brought him inside."

"What?"

Samuel's heart dropped into his stomach, the nausea from before making a strong return.

"I'm sorry," Laura said.

Samuel stepped back, his head turning to face the window.

"Do you know what they'd want with him?" Claudette asked.

Samuel shook his head, his breathing feeling constricted. He pushed up his glasses as he looked at the patrolmen standing outside of the blacksmith's shop. They must have caught his father trying to get inside the jailhouse. This was his fault. He'd done this. What would they do to him? Would he be tortured until he confessed his crime? Would they give him a harsh beating and let him go? Would they even believe him? Would the mayor simply order Zei to butcher his father like he'd done with Harold?

"I have to go," Samuel said as he went for the exit.

"Sam, don't," Claudette pleaded. "Please stay."

He ignored her. The bell above the door dinged as he burst outside. The patrolmen who'd gathered outside of the blacksmith's shed were together. Jax held out a firm hand to Samuel, his rifle dangling from the strap over his shoulder. "We can't let you in."

"Where's the mayor?" Samuel asked. "I need to talk to him. If he's inside—"

"He's not."

"Then let me in."

"No. Sheriff's orders."

Samuel stopped. He clenched his hands. He knew the sheriff wasn't as cold and hard as he pretended to be. Maybe he could help if Samuel pleaded his case. But he'd have to get inside, to see him face-to-face, to try and reason with him. There was no way he could force his way in. And alone, he was no match for three armed patrolmen.

"Can you get the sheriff, then? I'll wait."

Jax moved his thumb down, flicking off the rifle's safety. "No. You need to leave, boy. Now. Go home."

Samuel forced his arms by his side. There was no point in fighting. He needed to try something else.

"Sheriff!" Samuel screamed, his voice cracking. "I need to talk to you!"

The patrolmen watched Samuel apprehensively, unsure if they should do something to silence his yelling. Samuel eyed the door eagerly.

"Sheriff!" he somehow screamed louder. "Eugene! Eugene Black!"

Jax gave a nod to the other two patrolmen, and they both moved toward Samuel. The one with the hooked nose reached for Samuel first, but he was easily able to dart to the left and avoid his grip. He wasn't as strong as they were, but he was faster. He dashed to the back of the blacksmith's shop. He furiously pounded his fists on the back wall. "I know you're in there! Sheriff! Where is he?"

Samuel backed up. He scanned the walls, noticing the small glass window in the center. It was too high up for Samuel to see through it, but if he stood on his toes, he'd probably be able to peek through.

A pair of arms wrapped around Samuel's torso before he could try to see. He felt the arms lift his legs from the ground. He fell hard. His head recoiled as it hit the dried earth, and his glasses fell from his nose. The patrolmen forced Samuel's arms around his back, bending his wrists in a way that immobilized his hands.

Samuel coughed. He still had breath in his lungs, and he wouldn't stop screaming until they gagged him.

"I'm your patrolman! I guard your jailhouse! I work for you, sheriff!"

Samuel felt a knee crash into his skull, pushing his face down, further constricting the movements of his head. His cheeks burned. He heard what sounded like slamming doors and thunderous steps.

"What is this?"

The sheriff shoved the patrolman off Samuel.

"You want the whole town to hear this?" he asked, charging forward. "Don't beat him. Just shut him up. He's only a stupid kid."

Samuel could make out what appeared to be Jax's boots.

"He is a stupid kid," Jax agreed. "A stupid kid who took down a three hundred pound logger like that." Jax snapped his fingers. "Are we supposed to go easy on him because he's scrawny?"

"Pick him up."

Samuel was lifted to his feet, each of his arms held by a patrolman. His blurry sight was eventually made clear when one of the patrolmen clumsily put his glasses back on his face. The first thing Samuel saw was Jax tightening his grip on the strap of his rifle and the sheriff gnawing on his own lip in annoyance.

"I know he's in there," Samuel said. "I know—"

"Enough." The sheriff shoved his thumbs inside his belt loops. "Shut up and listen. We're still trying to sort everything out. Ain't gonna do no good to have you out here squealing like a mad dog. Making a scene—"

"It's my fault. I told my father—"

The sheriff's hand struck Samuel's cheek so hard he nearly fell back into the patrolmen holding his arms. His face burned with pain, the blood rushing. Samuel reached for his cheek. His eyes watered.

"Shut your mouth!" The sheriff grabbed Samuel by the hair and pulled his face close, mushing their noses. "You're out here calling yourself a patrolman, but you're acting like a little whiney bitch. My patrolmen know how to act. My patrolmen know how to follow orders. My patrolmen know to shut their mouths when told to do so!"

Samuel's lips quivered. He couldn't find words.

"Leave. That's an order. My patrolmen follow orders. You hear me? One more word and I will personally bash your pretty little face in. Go."

The sheriff shoved Samuel to the ground, storming past him. "Get him out of here. Now!"

Samuel's feet dragged as the patrolmen picked him up once more. They carried him off to the edge of the square and then threw him forward.

Samuel wiped his face, trying to move away the spit and the tears.

"I don't care if you think you are the sheriff's pet," Jax said. He smirked. "I'm a man really good at following orders."

Samuel's jaw clenched as he stared back at the patrolmen.

"Go on," Jax commanded. "Move."

Samuel forced his eyelids closed. He turned away, his breathing rushed and his heart pounding. He was weak and pathetic. He couldn't do anything here. But he couldn't do nothing. He had to do something.

The mayor's estate was a mile's walk from the square. Samuel trudged forward, his cheek still tingling from the sheriff's slap. Arguing with the sheriff was a pointless endeavor. He needed to plead his case to the mayor. He'd done so much for the man. Maybe he could somehow dissuade the mayor's anger, convince him to show mercy. Samuel had no more pride. He would beg like a child if he had to, swear to do whatever the mayor wanted him to do with Zei. He would be better, work harder. He only wanted his father alive.

Samuel walked past the militia training grounds but stayed two hundred yards back from their combat drills. "You must put your dominant foot forward," the foreigner's voice called out to the crew of loggers. The redlands native marched through the rows of men, directing them how to plant themselves when facing an unruly mob. "Like this. Ankle to ankle. You have to stay together. As close as you can. A man alone is one soldier. But together, you can become a force to be reckoned with."

The loggers mimicked the foreigner's motions, their bodies attempting to unify. The foreigner nodded in approval before gazing past his recruits and glaring at Samuel. He did so for a moment before directing his attention back to the loggers. "Always hold your ground together," he yelled out. "Side to side. Never leave your brothers. Separation is annihilation."

When Samuel finally reached the estate, he jogged up the stone steps and rapped on the door. Thelma answered the door, bowing as she greeted him.

"I'm looking for the mayor."

Thelma shook her head. "He's away. But Charles is here."

"Can I see him, then?"

"Wait here," she said before closing the door.

Samuel did as Thelma instructed. The clouds above were dark

and moving in a way that predicted rain or snow. He wasn't sure which it would be. He drummed his fingers against his legs.

A minute later, Charles opened the door. He smiled wide, his teeth showing.

"Look who finally ditched work! Come in! It's cold out there."

Samuel walked inside, holding his arms by his side as they moved into the living room. The radio was blaring loudly, and the announcer discussed the finer details of reestablishing trade over the Great Sea.

"The trouble," the announcer drawled, "is making sure we have enough ships that are large enough to cart back and forth our goods. It's been so long since we've needed to haul supplies over open water. It'll be a gradual process, the governor assures us, but that doesn't make it a cheap one."

Charles turned the knob on the radio, silencing it.

"It's all so crazy." Charles plopped into one of the cushioned chairs. "I'm so lucky I finished school before this whole thing started."

Samuel's toes scrunched. "I need your help."

Charles waved a hand before digging inside his pocket. He pulled out a smoking pipe. "Sure. Sit down. What's up?"

"My father. They've got him locked up."

"The cleric?"

Samuel bit into his lip. There was no one else for him to confide in.

"It's my fault. I told him to come to the jailhouse. I told him to come, to try and do the exorcism. He must've gotten caught."

"Why did you do that?"

"I don't know. I'm stupid. It took a while, but I saw what you and everyone else did. She … I guess I still wanted to help her. I didn't think it'd work, but I wanted to try. It was dumb."

"Yeah," Charles said with a snort. "I thought you said all that faith stuff was deershit?"

Samuel shook his head, as if to empty the noise inside.

"I don't know. I'm telling you this because your father is the only one who can protect mine. I want you to tell him that it was my fault my dad was there. It was me who wanted the exorcism. Okay?"

Charles shifted his legs, tucking his feet underneath the chair. "Look, Sam. I don't think that's a good idea."

"I don't care. I've done everything the mayor has asked me to. If I've got to be punished, I understand. My dad too. Just don't let him die. Mercy. That's all I want. I'm asking for mercy."

Charles ran his fingers through his oily blond hair. "I don't know. My dad's not one to forget stuff like that. I think you should wait it out. Sit back. See what happens."

Samuel clenched his teeth, the agitation inside him festering.

"He's your father. If you talk with him, maybe he'll listen."

"That's not how it works, Sam. Try to calm down. I'll get Thelma to make us something to eat. Maybe we can figure something else out."

"What do you mean?"

Charles rubbed his hair. "Look. Maybe you're making a big fuss about this over nothing. Maybe they're just going to rough him up a bit. He does deserve punishment. He broke the law."

"I helped you," Samuel said, his frustration spewing out in his tone. "When Zei ... when the monster was hurt and dying, I helped you. It was your fault her leg was bleeding again. I'm supposed to believe you were trying to help her? It makes no sense. Why does she hate you so much? What did you do, Charles?"

"Come on." Charles sighed, dusting his pants. "I already thanked you for that. And that demon? It's just a crazy, mindless animal—"

"What did you do to her?"

"Nothing."

"Liar," Samuel said, his fury surprising even him. "You're lying."

Charles squirmed as he rolled up his sleeves. He stood up, his eyes at his feet.

"My dad," he said dryly. "He's always on my case about girls. About ... not being into them like he was at my age. And then, when they caught that monster ... " Charles looked up, as if trying to choose his words carefully. "My dad said it was a demon. I was like you, at first. I called deershit on the whole thing. It made no sense, right? I thought the guy had lost his mind. Like he was suddenly going to flip open the scriptures and sign up for the clergy."

"What did you do?"

"Let me finish," Charles said sternly, looking down at Samuel. He turned to the side, shoving his hands in his pockets. "The day before that patrolman's funeral, my dad put me in charge of watching the demon, or whatever the hell that thing is. But, at the time, it looked just like a normal girl. The demon chained up. Quiet. Didn't seem to be bothered by me. I talked to it a lot, but it doesn't speak, so that was a waste of time. But it stayed docile. Relaxed. Calm. I thought it was just a girl who wasn't right in the head, you know? Maybe it wasn't all there. So, I went in. I sat next to it. Just like you. It was just sitting there. Staring at nothing. I touched it, and—"

Samuel's belly churned. "You tried to—"

"No!" Charles yelled. He looked around as if he was paranoid someone else was listening. "I didn't! I guess … I just thought I should try." He held up his hands. "He hates me, Sam. And I hate him. But, I thought, if I could try … " He swallowed. "But I didn't do anything. I wouldn't have. Couldn't have. That thing went crazy, and I barely made it out alive. I know better now."

Samuel's teeth chattered, the muscles in his neck tight and hard. "What?"

Charles groaned. He looked away.

"Forget it. I thought you'd understand. Don't you understand? You're like me, Sam. Aren't you … different?"

Samuel's breaths were quick and hard.

"You shouldn't have done that."

"It's not a real girl," Charles snapped back, his tone sharpening. "Doesn't even have lady bits, remember? That thing is a monster. You said it yourself, didn't you? You're not thinking, Sam. About the cleric. You told me you didn't want to be a cleric, that all of that roots stuff was nonsense. You told me your father was a little crazy with this faith. Why do you care what happens to him?"

The words struck Samuel hard, and for a moment he couldn't think of anything to say. He'd harbored so much resentment toward his father and his passion for Azhuel and the holy roots. He longed for his father to be warm and kind, and not a cold man who showed more love to a god he couldn't see than his own son. He hated that he was a bastard and that his mother was dead. But that didn't mean he hated him.

In spite of himself, and his father's faults, he loved him. He couldn't let another person die. Not because of him. He couldn't bear the weight of his father's death. And now, the people he thought cared about him were turning their backs on him. He was alone. He knew that now.

"You're not going to help me," Samuel said. "Are you?"

"Don't put it like that." Charles put a nervous hand on Samuel's shoulder. "Come on. I mean, haven't I done enough for you?"

Samuel shrugged away Charles's hand. "I thought you were different. But you're like the mayor. You only care about yourself."

Charles stood there dumbfounded, his lips slightly agape.

Samuel turned away, shoving his fingernails deep inside his palm. He pushed his fingers harder, nearly breaking into the skin. Without looking back, he stormed out of the estate, unsure of where to go next.

21

Two hours after sunset, the sheriff returned home. Samuel sat on the kitchen counter, his back reclined against the cabinets. A fresh bottle of liquor was right beside him. He stared at the sheriff as he entered the room.

The sheriff gazed at Samuel briefly before turning back to close the door.

"What have they done to him, sheriff?"

The sheriff unfastened his belt, grunting as he lowered his gun onto the table. He made his way to the bottle and scooped it up, careful not to get too close to Samuel. His steps were unsteady, and his breath already reeked of booze.

"What are they going to do to my father?"

The sheriff grabbed an empty glass by the sink and filled it with liquor. He downed the entire glass and refilled it.

"Answer me!"

"Can you stop with the yelling?" The sheriff's words were slurred. He licked his mustache. "You sound like a spoiled brat."

Samuel said nothing but held his ground, eyeing the sheriff.

The sheriff labored a long breath. He took another sip of liquor. "Got a call in the middle of the night. Surprised you didn't hear it, but you were out cold. The mayor. He'd stationed some of my men at the jailhouse. Prick told me he did it to keep you safe, but you and I know that's deershit. I think he was feeling the need to protect that monster. What from? Hell if I know. Whatever. Looks like the mayor was right."

Samuel's muscles tingled, like his nerves were on fire. He couldn't stop his hands from shaking. Why were they shaking so much?

The sheriff sucked his teeth before continuing. "One of my men ran all the way here, in the dead of night, to tell me they caught the cleric sneaking around the jailhouse. They'd beat him senseless before recognizing him. That idiot patrolman was standing right there, right outside my door, in the middle of the damn night, telling me he'd touched a cleric and he didn't want to be punished for it. It's like half of these idiots have no clue how the world works."

Samuel understood what the sheriff was hinting at. If a cleric broke the law, he was no longer a cleric, but a traitor of the state. "Is he alive? Tell me."

The sheriff nodded, taking another swig before he continued.

"I went over there. I cuffed him, put him in the back of my jeep, and brought him over to the blacksmith's shop. I didn't want to bring him in the jailhouse." He paused. "Didn't want to give the mayor any more ideas. You're welcome for that."

"What's going to happen to him?" Samuel asked, his voice rising. He hopped off the counter, his feet slamming onto the floor.

"You need to calm down."

The sheriff plopped himself into a chair, wiping his damp mustache. "He's bloodied up, but alive. The mayor hasn't made a decision yet, says he wants to know more information first."

Samuel swiped the bottle of liquor away from the sheriff. "How bad? How bad is he hurt?"

The sheriff took the liquor bottle back, jerking it to his chest. "Give him more credit than that. Your old man is hard as stone. Won't say anything, no matter how many times they hit him. He's a self-righteous moron. But damn. The man can take a licking."

"It's my fault," Samuel said instinctively. "I told him to go the jailhouse. I wanted him to try the exorcism."

The sheriff groaned.

"My mistake for thinking you'd turned rational." He took a swig from the bottle, then slammed it onto the table. "Exorcism? An exorcism? Are you actually buying into that? What? You thought some prayer was gonna do what? That useless god your father prays to isn't going to turn that thing into some sweet child. And that god isn't going to save your father."

"What are you—"

"No," the sheriff slurred. He jammed a finger into Samuel's forehead. "You need to listen up. There is no god. There's no roots or demons or anyone out there watching over us. There's just us. Just this!" He lifted his arms, flailing them wildly. "No one is there watching out for your dad. Nobody cares. Why can't you see you that?"

Samuel swallowed. He tried to calm his nerves. "You are right. It's just me. And I'm the only one who cares." He looked away. "No. I think you do care. That's why you're drunk and alone."

The sheriff shoved his knee into the table, forcing a loud thud. "Damn it, kid. Now you're just pissing me off. Let me tell you what happens next. I'm going to finish my drink, sleep, and then wake up and do my job. If you'd done yours, none of this would have happened. This is on you, you little shit. Man up and accept the truth. You messed this up real bad. And there's no fixing it!"

"You're the monster," Samuel said. "You're worse than she is."

The sheriff rose in a fit of blind rage. He tried to grab Samuel but couldn't keep his own footing. He fell to the ground, moaning as he staggered back up to his knees.

Samuel walked past the sheriff, glaring at him defiantly. "You're right. This is my fault. And I'll fix it. Do nothing. Like you always do."

Samuel slipped on his black coat, pulling the fur hood over his head.

The sheriff used the table for leverage. He took his seat, and grabbed the bottle of liquor, cradling it near his collarbone. "I'm your boss. Don't forget that."

Samuel turned the doorknob.

"Hey!"

The sheriff's scream made Samuel's skin rise. He turned.

"What?"

"Where are you going?"

"Out," Samuel said. "Away from you."

The sheriff threw his bottle across the room, the glass bursting with a loud crack. "Stay away from that shop. It's guarded. Heavily. To keep idiots like you out. Stay away from the jailhouse too. You're not allowed in there until further notice. You hear me? That's an order."

"Are you going to beat my ass?"

"Please," The sheriff tsked, brushing the air. "You're so soft. I mean, if it wasn't for that little girlfriend of yours, I'd be sure you were playing tunnel buddies with that little mayor." He spat on the ground. "You want to die, kid? Fine. Go wherever you want. And you can pack up your shit in the morning and get out of my house. I'm done with you. Knock that Litten girl up and live with her. Or go stroke that little mayor's cock. Suck him off until he gets his daddy to buy you your own house. I don't give a shit. You know what? You are a real—"

Samuel slammed the door behind him.

Samuel ambled around the outskirts of the square, keeping his distance from the blacksmith's shop. From far away, he could count four patrolmen guarding the front door.

Samuel drifted farther toward the eastern woods. His eyes were heavy, worn down from the constant tears and stinging cold. He didn't know how late it was. The darkened sky had all but snuffed out the starlight, and the moon was barely visible through the thick waves of gray clouds. A cold wind was gusting, gaining bite, and the animals had all retreated into their burrows and nests. Random snowflakes fell, foreboding a larger storm on its way. Summer had made an early exit. Winter was here now.

Samuel's muscles scrunched from the sting of the wind. He wanted to go to the jailhouse, to tell Zei about his father, to tell her what he had to do next. Seeing her there, he might have even set her free from the shackles, giving her the one thing she wanted most. Freedom. But more patrolmen guarded the jailhouse than before. He couldn't risk getting caught there. Not if he had any chance of making his plan work.

Samuel pictured Zei curled up by the barred window in her cell. How would she do without him? Who would tend to her? He liked to think the mayor would be bold enough to waltz into her cell. He wouldn't mind if Zei tore him to bits. She probably hated the mayor as much as he did.

The wind whistled as it pulled Samuel's hood from his head. He yanked it back up. He couldn't stop his hands from shaking. What if he got caught? Would he only make things worse? What if he did it, but then they got caught on the way to the border? Even if they made it, what would prevent the mayor and his rage from coming into the greenlands? Besides, why would any citizen willingly aid and abet a refugee cleric and his bastard son?

Samuel picked up speed, crunching his leather boots harder into the dead grass. He knew his plan wasn't the best and that he might be making things worse. But he knew the mayor, and he knew what Charles and the sheriff wouldn't admit. His father was a dead man if he didn't get him out of that shop.

He thought of Claudette and what it would mean to leave her behind. He cared for her. A big part of him wanted to marry her, to live with her, to kiss her and touch her in ways he never thought he would be able to touch anyone before. But he knew he could never do that. Not after what had happened to Harold. Samuel watched her father die. He wouldn't make the same mistake with his father.

For so long he'd been terrified of becoming like his father, but now, more than anything, he didn't want to be like the sheriff. If being hard meant that he had to sit back while people died, then he'd rather be soft. And if being a patrolman in Haid meant turning into an apathetic drunk, he'd rather take his chances elsewhere.

The pine trees creaked, their bristles rustling in the darkness. Samuel stopped near the edge of the woods. He bent his neck down, his glasses lowering. He looked to the hard and dying grass, which was now peppered with white flakes.

"I don't know if you're there."

Samuel's breath fogged.

"Because you've never been there before. Not for me. But, if you're there, I need you. If not for me, then for my father." He paused. "He's done nothing but serve you. He's a good man. You know that. Help him. Please. Help me."

Samuel looked up, despite himself, pushing his glasses into the space between his eyes. He needed to move.

He returned to the sheriff's house. He opened the door quickly yet quietly. He scanned the room before stepping fully inside. The sheriff was passed out by the kitchen table, his head buried in his arms, his snores muted.

Samuel tiptoed to the dresser and began packing things into his backpack. First, he put in all the money he'd saved. It was a little over four hundred coins, enough to help them make do for a while. He put in an extra pair of jeans and a shirt, as well as the peacoat Charles had given him. He made sure to leave all his uniforms. He never liked them anyway.

He snuck into the sheriff's room, which was littered with unwashed clothes and empty bottles of liquor. He watched his footsteps as he rummaged through the sheriff's things, looking under the mattress and inside the closet until he found the prosthetic arm hiding underneath a spare pile of bedsheets. The mechanical arm jingled as he lifted it. He cradled it tight against his chest to mute the noise. He wrapped an extra shirt around the prosthetic, covering it, before packing it inside his bag. Samuel draped the backpack over his shoulder and slipped on his gloves. He felt his coat pockets, making sure he had his two throwing knives and his hunting knife. His feet treaded lightly as he went to the door and eased the handle back. The sheriff never stirred. A small wave of white powder forced its way inside the house as he took his exit. In a matter of minutes, the snowfall turned aggressive. He crept to the square, careful not to make too much noise with his footsteps. His nostrils burned as he sucked in freezing air and bits of snow. He wasn't bothered. The snow, while a nuisance, would give him more cover in the darkness. What if Azhuel had heard his prayer?

He went to the back end of the main row's shops, making sure to avoid the sight of the nearby patrolmen. As Samuel suspected, they had only posted guards in front of the main entrance.

Samuel wiped his glasses, cleaning off the snow. He squinted, but he didn't see any figures. He approached the window, and when he was directly underneath it, he got on his knees. He hoped it wasn't locked. He got on his tiptoes and gently put his nose on the cold glass, gazing inside. Everything was blurred and distorted. The flames inside the blacksmith's furnace danced wildly, but he saw no moving figures. He could make out some of the metal tools mounted on the walls. In the center of the shop, he spotted what appeared to be the blacksmith's main table.

Samuel pressed his face against the window, peering harder. In the left corner, a human-sized shape was hunched near the glowing fire. It was hard to be completely sure, but the figure seemed to be dressed in nothing but black.

Samuel held his gloved hands against the window, and when he tugged up, the glass moved with his palms. Everything inside became clearer. He scanned the room hastily, and thankfully found that the figure in black was his father sleeping in the left corner, his head drooped against the wall. His arms and legs were bound with rope, and his face and beard were caked with dried blood. His jacket was nowhere to be seen, and the sleeves of his shirt appeared to have been ripped off, the ragged edges crooked and torn.

Samuel tightened the straps of his backpack. He pushed his glasses farther up his nose before lifting himself through the open window. He slowly writhed his way inside, his backpack gently scraping across the top frame. Samuel got low, eased out his hunting knife, and crept to his father. He tapped his shoulder softly.

His father stirred, his eyelids fluttering. Samuel grabbed his father's bound wrists, aligning the blade over the strands. He'd made it this far, and his risky plan seemed to be paying off. His courage grew. He was going to sneak his father out of the shop, and they'd be a few miles deep in the woods before anyone noticed he'd gone missing. They'd keep moving, not stopping until they'd crossed over into the greenlands. They could start new lives down south, perhaps in a smaller town where the riots weren't as prevalent. Or maybe only he would start a new life. Samuel had learned enough to be a butcher, and he wasn't opposed to becoming a farmer or some unskilled laborer. Anything but a patrolman. He couldn't imagine his father willingly choosing any other profession than the clergy. Maybe they would separate as soon as they made it to safety, never to cross paths again. His father would more than likely want to go and plead sanctuary with a sympathizing cleric. Perhaps their destinies were always meant to be apart, but at least that one didn't involve death.

His father groaned as he woke. He stared at Samuel, the confusion visible on his face. Samuel sliced into the ropes binding his father. "It's okay," he whispered. "I'm gonna get you out of here."

"You're not very good at stealth, are you?"

The hairs on Samuel's body jolted up. He tightened his hold on the knife's handle, drawing it away from the nearly broken strands. He turned to face the voice behind him.

The redlands foreigner was tucked near the back-right corner of the room. He had his right hand pressed against his cheek. He nearly looked humored, his dark eyes gazing like a spectator. "To your credit, you did manage to slip past the guards outside."

Samuel rose to his feet, the knife level by his side.

"No," his father uttered, his large body shuffling. His voice was deep and choked.

The foreigner arched his shoulder back. Hatchets and knives dangled from the wall behind him, their handles fastened with strings and kept in place by nails. The light from the furnace flickered, forcing the shadows in the room to dance.

"I've been bored since I've arrived. The people in this state are too stiff. Too dull. Too cold." He nodded to Samuel. "But I like you. You have spirit. Aren't you the lad from the train station? I do suggest you put that weapon down. Else you're going to have to kill me."

"No," his father said again, fighting to get himself up on his knees. "Samuel."

Samuel gripped the knife harder. His father was too weak to be of any help, and it was up to him to make a decision. He wasn't strong, but he was quick. He'd learned that much. His jaw twinged as he pressed the knife's side across his thigh, hoping to force his hand to remain steady. He'd come this far, and there was no turning back. He had one shot, and it had to be perfect. He whipped the knife behind his back and flung it forward, aiming it at the foreigner's heart.

The foreigner, as if expecting the blade all along, dropped low and spun to the side, dodging the knife as it whizzed by him and stuck into the wall. Samuel lost his breath for a moment, unable to recover from the shock. His aim had been perfect. He'd felt it in the release. He couldn't think about it. He had to move. He rushed his hands inside his pockets, fumbling for the other throwing knives he still had.

The foreigner darted across the room and pounced on Samuel, knocking him onto his back. The air left his lungs with a violent thud.

Samuel couldn't see his father, but he could hear him trying to scuffle to his feet. The foreigner remained steady, his knee pressed onto Samuel's sternum. He reached out and shoved his father back hard. His father fell with a thud, his bound ankles crippling him from having any sort of balance. The foreigner snaked his hand underneath Samuel's back and flipped him over. Samuel's face smacked into the dirt, his glasses plunging hard into his nose. The foreigner worked Samuel's arms back into his backpack, turning his wrists up in the same way the patrolmen had done before.

"Intruders!"

Samuel forced his neck to turn. One of his lenses had cracked. A jagged line squiggled across the center of the left lens, splitting Samuel's view from that eye into two parts. The doors to the shed swung open, and in rushed four patrolmen. Two of them darted over to Samuel's father, ramming him harder into the wall. One of them punched him in the jaw, forcing his head to ricochet.

"No!" Samuel cried.

"Get more rope," the foreigner ordered as he rummaged through Samuel's pockets. He took out the knives, tossing them away. "By the anvil. Move."

One of the patrolmen went to get the rope, but the other stayed close by, hovering over Samuel. He looked up and was able to make out the man's face. Jax left his mouth open, exposing his crooked teeth. He bent down, glaring at him with wide eyes.

"You have some balls," he said stiffly. "I was there that day in the woods. I heard what you told that logger. You said you weren't a cleric. But here you are. With him."

Jax spat on Samuel's cheek. Samuel cringed as foreign saliva dripped near his lips. He grunted and writhed his body as he felt rope being tied around his wrists.

"We knew better than the sheriff and the mayor. We knew we couldn't trust you."

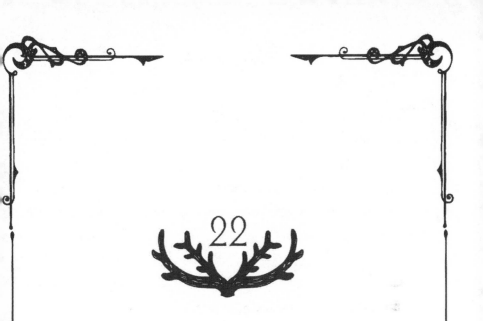

The furnace burned steadily, the heat causing Samuel's body to sweat underneath his coat. It might have been snowing outside, but it mattered little in the confines of the blacksmith's shop. The foreigner sat with crossed legs near the furnace, unfazed by the excessive warmth. He twirled one of Samuel's throwing knives around his fingers jovially, his motions fluid and natural. Patrolmen stood guard outside of the shop's doors, and Jax had elected to stay inside. He fondled the blacksmith's tools, grabbing a pair of tongs and snapping them open and closed.

Samuel sat beside his father, his legs and wrists bound tightly together. For so long he'd been the spectator of the captive, but now he was the one trapped. His father's broad shoulders touched his left side.

"You shouldn't have come," his father said. He sounded so weak.

Samuel sucked in more air, his ribs aching. He'd failed, and all he could do was wait for the mayor's judgment. He wasn't sure if he'd be executed. How much did the mayor value his services with Zei? He continually spoke of her needing to be controlled, but so far, he'd never released her from the confines of the prison. Would he merely be content to unleash her? Would he try and unleash her on him and his father?

The foreigner yawned loudly before rising. He pointed the knife at Samuel's father. "You're the boy's father, are you not?"

His father lowered his head.

"He's a bastard," Jax said matter-of-factly. He tossed the tongs aside and took up one of the hammers, examining the craftsmanship.

"How interesting."

The furnace flames crackled. Samuel closed his eyes, wishing to slip away into the darkness. He listened to his father's unsteady breaths, regretting everything. A part of him didn't care if the mayor would have him killed. Maybe he could sleep in peace.

"I'd been ordained," his father said feebly. "Stationed in the redlands by the high council. I worked in Charos. A small town near the outskirts of Vayler."

Samuel opened his eyes, looking at his father through the cracked lens. Drool and blood leaked from the corners of his lips, and his face was so swollen it was hardly recognizable. What was he doing?

"A redlands town," the foreigner repeated. He smiled. "Quaint little place along the coast. Clear ocean. Beautiful sand."

His father craned his neck, his bloodshot eyes falling on Samuel.

"I was a man barely grown. A few years older than you. Charos was a quiet place. Small population, so death wasn't a frequent visitor. My hut was a mile away from the town, in between a row of dunes. I spent many days alone in prayer."

"Quiet," Jax said. He playfully struck the hammer on the anvil. "Or I'll gag you."

"I first saw her," his father continued, "when I was returning from the sea with my catch of fish. She stood by my hut, her hair flowing in the wind. She wore glasses, but you could still see the beauty in her dark eyes from a hundred meters away."

Samuel pulled his bound hands farther into his gut. He'd fantasized this moment as long as he could remember, the day his father would explain the young woman in the photograph. He wanted to ask questions, but was afraid any interruption could halt the story. He remembered the last time they spoke. His father was a man of his word.

"She ... had this little leather bag with her. She came up to me, unafraid. Told me she was a runaway. She needed a place to stay. She told me she would pay whatever I wanted. She also told me she kept a hidden blade with her at all times, that she'd already killed a man the day before, and she would gut me if I tried anything."

"That's enough," Jax ordered. He slammed the hammer down harder, the sound of striking metal ricocheting across the walls. "No one wants to hear your sobbing love confession."

"I told her I was a cleric. I showed her my mark. I told her I couldn't help her. But she was relentless. 'Are you a man of faith?' she asked me. 'If you are, what would your god have you do? Ignore the request of a young woman in need?' She fascinated me."

Jax draped the hammer over his shoulder as he leisurely moved to Samuel's father. Samuel balled his hands into fists. He didn't have much strength, but he wouldn't allow his father to take another blow. He couldn't.

"Let the man be," the foreigner said. He lifted a knee to his chest, his fingers continuing to dance the knife between them. "I want to hear his story."

Jax turned. "I don't."

"Then go outside. You really are an unpleasant fellow."

Jax scrunched his large nose. His eyes reflected aggravation, but he didn't care enough to do more. He tossed the hammer onto the table and toyed with the blacksmith's handcrafted knives.

Samuel's father coughed violently, his voice dry. The foreigner meandered over. He gave his father a drink from his thermos. His father coughed once more, but the liquid had cooled the itch.

The foreigner took his seat. "What was her name?"

Samuel knew the answer.

"Atia."

"Lovely summer name."

"We stayed together. We were alone. I lived far away from the citizens, and the town was small. I was rarely called to perform the rites."

Samuel kept his face down. He couldn't look at his father.

"She was a better fisherman than I was. I was a greenlands orphan.

The clergy picked me when I was thirteen, said I had an aptitude for learning. But she ... she was much smarter than I ever was. She knew politics and science and music. She was a wonderful singer. She'd come from a wealthy family, I could tell. But she refused to talk about it. 'That is my old life,' she'd tell me. She said she only wanted to stay in the present. With me."

Samuel bit into his cheek. He shifted his bound wrists, the rope dragging across his tender skin.

"We were happy," his father said. "I was happy. She wasn't afraid of me. One day, when I'd snagged my hand on a fishhook, she cleaned the cut and bandaged it. She touched me as if it was natural. I loved her for it. I forsook my vows. I wanted only to be with her. To ... not be alone. She became pregnant."

Jax spat on the ground as he rummaged through more tools, the iron dinging.

"A citizen, someone near the town, must have seen her wandering the beaches. They followed her to our home. I was away. I was out ... " His father looked up, almost as if he was searching for the right words. He pursed his lips, his eyes going wet. "The sheriff of Charos came. He took her. Took the child. Hours later, a group of patrolmen found me, threw me in a cell with her. We were judged the next day."

Samuel wanted to touch his father. But he couldn't. His hands were tied, and he didn't know how to embrace a man he'd always regarded as stone.

"All men are slaves," the foreigner said, his tone compassionate. "Slaves to the law, the earth, their own hearts. No one is free." He paused. "Please. Continue."

Samuel's father scratched his chin across his shirt. "Her father attended the hearing, Fernado Kuramo. He'd brought his younger daughter with him. She looked like a younger clone of her sister. She couldn't have been older than six or seven."

"Interesting," the foreigner interjected. "I think I recall that name. Yes. General Kuramo. Famed swordsman and brilliant military strategist, if I'm not mistaken."

His father nodded. "I listened to him advocate for the execution of his oldest daughter. By running away to escape her engagement to the son of a well-connected politician, she had disgraced her birthright. I remember him saying something like that to all the clergymen and politicians. He kept his younger daughter beside him the entire time. He made her sister watch."

"Pride is a man's legacy," the foreigner said.

"Damn that man's pride," his father said. He turned to Samuel. "Damn my pride. I'm sorry. I'm sorry I didn't fight for her. For you. I've failed you both. And I'm sorry."

Samuel nibbled on his cheek. His mother was the daughter of a general? She risked her life to run into the arms of a cleric? His eyes swelled. "Why? Why did she have to die?"

"She didn't," his father said. "I deserved to die. She didn't."

"Don't say that," Samuel mumbled. "You don't. I love you. No one deserved to die. You're my father. And you're a good father."

His father sighed. "You've always been a gentle soul. You're her son. Our son. I wish you could have met her."

The front doors to the blacksmith's shop swung open. Samuel jumped up, his head nearly hitting the post behind him. Several hours had passed since his father wept himself back into unconsciousness. He must have fallen asleep shortly after. He was more exhausted than he realized.

Mayor Thompson marched inside the shop, the stem of his pipe writhing in his teeth. His eyes darted back and forth wildly. Snow continued to fall outside, and an inch or so had accumulated on the ground outside. The other patrolmen kept their stations outside but peeked in until the mayor turned and slammed the wooden doors closed. He came forward, his feet smashing into the floor like hard bricks. He clenched his jaw tighter, the pipe sticking up.

"Get out," the mayor said with a snarl. He turned to Jax. "Wait outside. You as well, Mikael. I need to speak with the accused. Alone."

The foreigner bowed lowly, giving Samuel and his father a subtle nod before taking his exit. The mayor rubbed his chin excessively, his ears reddening. Samuel's father squared his shoulders, the dampness from his eyes all but dried up. Samuel watched the shadows dance around the mayor as if they fed on his rage.

"I told you," the mayor said behind closed teeth, "that I needed you with me, boy. I told you to make sure your loyalty was with me. Have I done anything to you that would give you reason to doubt my graces?"

Samuel couldn't force the conviction. "No."

The mayor inhaled on his pipe, rolling his fingers on the table's surface. He plucked the stem from his mouth before speaking. "The work you're doing with that demon. Do you realize the potential? If that creature were trained enough to be brought onto a battlefield and comply with orders, can you image the power we would have? Greenland simpletons would run in fear once they heard tales of the demon in the whitelands. Northern lives would be saved. The whitelands can rise from the chaos. We can become the greatest nation these lands have ever known."

Samuel said nothing. His father kept silent as well, but he watched Samuel.

The mayor came closer to them, jamming his hands into his pockets. "I am going to be frank. With the both of you. I have no idea if that child is a demon or possessed or some other form of altered human. It doesn't matter. What I know is that it likes you, Samuel. And it has been more responsive to you than anyone or anything else. Keeping that creature chained up in a jail cell isn't enough. Men must see it. They must witness its uncanny viciousness with their own eyes."

The mayor raised his right arm.

"Don't you understand?"

"I don't, sir," Samuel said.

The mayor stepped back. "What?"

Samuel nudged up his glasses, gazing at the mayor through the cracked lens. "I don't see it. I don't see the demon becoming your weapon. She can't be controlled."

The mayor's belly rose and fell, his breaths deep and intentional. "Are you saying you are incapable of doing your job?"

Samuel paused. "Yes. No one can do what you want. She can't be tamed."

Samuel's father shook his head. "Forgive him, mayor. The boy is upset. He doesn't mean to be obstinate."

The mayor popped the pipe back into his mouth. "I agree with you, cleric."

His pupils widened. "But. I do think the boy needs to learn about respect."

Samuel sat beside his father, watching as the half-asleep blacksmith entered his shop. The large man pulled his coat tighter to his chest, covering his stained nightshirt and woolly pants that were bunched up near his ankles. He surveyed his shop, seeing the foreigner, Jax, four patrolmen, Samuel, and his father. There was hardly much room to move.

The blacksmith bowed to the mayor.

"Mayor Thompson. How might I serve?"

The mayor grinned. "Tybel, you've always been a true citizen of our northern state. You work hard and fast."

"Thank you, sir," the blacksmith said, his demeanor reserved.

Samuel tilted to his right side, his elbow grazing his father's arm. His father's swollen eyelids made it look like they'd been burned with smoke.

The mayor puffed on his pipe before waving a hand at Jax and another patrolman. The men stepped back, giving the mayor more space to maneuver. He sauntered over to the wall adorned with crafted knives varying in size and shape. His round belly jiggled as he grabbed a knife with stylistic line designs carved into both the wooden handle and the blade. He pulled it closer to his nose.

"Your care and attention for detail is beyond compare."

The blacksmith bowed low once more.

"You are too kind."

Bumps rose on Samuel's skin. Something about the way the mayor held the knife made his chest tight. The foreigner stood by the furnace, his olive skin glowing in the light. He leaned his head back, forcing some of the bones in his neck to crack.

The mayor dug inside of his suit pocket and pulled out a handful of coins. He motioned for the blacksmith to come, jingling the money in his hands.

"Thank you, sir," he said as the coins fell into his palms. "But this is far too generous. I can't accept—"

"I have a special job for you." The mayor tapped the knife against his leg before turning to the foreigner. "Grab the lad. Bring him here."

Samuel's throat swelled closed.

The foreigner trekked to Samuel, his lips no longer grinning. He extended his hands. Samuel waited for a moment before lifting his bound wrists up. The foreigner helped him to his feet.

"Please, mayor." Samuel's father rose to his knees. "I am the criminal. He's only a child. He has acted childishly."

Samuel followed the guidance of the foreigner, his blood racing as he came to the mayor. He was somehow able to keep his composure, but he didn't know how much longer he could.

"Restrain the cleric," the mayor said. "Now."

Jax got to Samuel's father first and shoved him. His father bounced into the wall, but he immediately rolled back and dove into Jax. The other two patrolmen ran to aid their struggling comrade, all three of them taking hold of Samuel's father. Jax got back to his feet, kicking his father in the ribs. His father doubled over, gagging for air.

"No," Samuel cried. "Stop."

The patrolmen tugged on his father's arms, lifting him up.

"Do what you must," the mayor said sternly. "The old law doesn't protect a traitorous criminal."

Without restraint, the patrolmen launched their assault, layering Samuel's father with a barrage of kicks and punches. His father fought back, his body finding the strength to push itself up.

"Stay down!" one of the patrolmen yelled as he rammed his elbow into Samuel's father. The hit forced Samuel's father to drop to his face, his nose smashing into the dirt ground. Blood leaked out from his nose down his thick beard.

The foreigner tugged on Samuel's restraints.

"Don't watch, lad," the foreigner whispered. "They'll only hurt him worse if you fuss."

Samuel closed his eyes, trying to ignore the violence behind him. His father was strong. He needed to hold on, bide his time until he could think of how to escape.

"Put his arm here," the mayor yelled. "Pull back his sleeve. Palm side up. You might have to unfasten his hands. One of you back there. Come here. Surely it won't take four of you to handle a half-dead cleric. Help Mikael. Do whatever he tells you."

Samuel was guided to his knees, and he felt the foreigner untie the ropes binding his wrists together. He tried regulating his breaths to show the mayor that he would cooperate. There was no point in resisting. Not now.

The jacket sleeve covering Samuel's right arm was rolled up past his elbow. When his skin touched the cold iron of the metal, his hand involuntarily twitched. He decided he could no longer keep his eyes closed. He forced his chin down, staring at his own naked arm.

The mayor stepped forward as one of the patrolmen came alongside him. "Old loyalties cloud your judgment," he said in Samuel's ear. "Today will forever be a reminder of what happens when you disobey my law."

Samuel dug his fingernails into his palms, keeping quiet.

The mayor put his hand on the blacksmith's shoulder. "You have an eye for artistry and the skills to match it. I want you to give the boy the mark of the clergy. Use the cleric's arm as a frame of reference. Make it clean. Make it deep."

"No," his father's voice choked out behind him.

"Shut his mouth," Jax screamed. "Get a gag. Now."

"This is what happens to those who are servants of Azhuel," the mayor said to Samuel. "Is it not? I think you've forgotten what liberties have been afforded to you on my behalf. I hope that now you'll never forget."

Samuel could no longer contain himself. His breaths morphed into desperate heaves. He stared at the exposed skin through his broken lens, remembering all the times he'd imagined the inked roots on it. It was too much to fathom. He couldn't grasp reality, his mind morphing into waves of panic. He instinctively tried to pull his arm away, but the foreigner had it pressed down in a way that immobilized him.

The blacksmith stepped in front of Samuel.

Samuel looked up, whimpering.

The blacksmith swallowed hard. The veins underneath his dark skin were poking up slightly. "Sir. I am no artist with skin and ink. That job is better suited for clergymen."

The mayor straightened his back. "Use your own methods, Tybel."

"But, sir," the blacksmith objected. "I carve my designs into smoldering metal. With chisels and heated picks. I don't know how to replicate that sort of technique on skin. I could kill him."

The mayor chewed on the stem of his pipe. "You can practice on yourself, if you'd like. But you will do the job I've commissioned you for."

Samuel's teeth chattered, his ribs pushing farther into the end of the anvil. Tears fell down his cheeks, and he tasted salt. He forced out words.

"I'm sorry, mayor. Please. I'm sorry."

The foreigner sighed. He motioned to the blacksmith.

"Get one of the picks. I've witnessed branding before. Heat the tip of the rod in the fire. You'll put the point on the skin, press, then lift."

The mayor snapped his fingers at the patrolman standing closest to him. "Do as he says."

"Hold the lad," Mikael ordered the patrolman. "Wrap your arms around him, like a tight embrace. Keep the other arm pinned. He will shake."

The patrolman obeyed, coiling his limbs around Samuel. His father's muffled screams echoed behind him, and the sound of loud poundings followed.

"He's one man," the mayor said with a growl. "And there are three of you. How hard is it to do your job? Get him here so the blacksmith can see his arm."

"Strike the back of the head," the foreigner called out. "The bulge in the skull. Make him sleep. It will be easier that way."

The mayor nodded, and Samuel heard a hard thud. He bit hard into his lip and drew blood. His father's muffled objections were silenced, and the patrolmen dragged his limp body next to the blacksmith. Jax pulled his father's arm to the side.

"Good," the mayor said.

The foreigner leaned his lips into Samuel's ear. "If you move, you will make it worse. Do you understand?"

Samuel couldn't stop crying, snot dripping to his lips.

He forced a nod. "Okay."

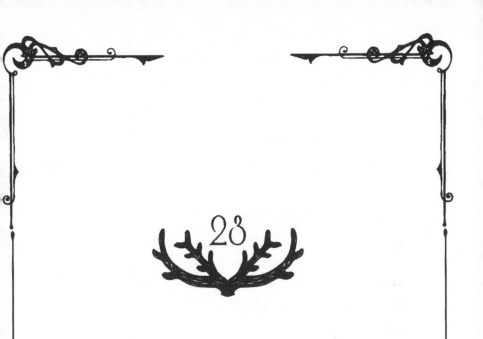

28

Samuel screamed.

The blacksmith etched the intricate lines of the roots. After a few minutes, the metal pick lost its molten glow. The foreigner waved at Jax, getting him to retrieve another heated pick from the edge of the furnace. The blacksmith exchanged the cooled rod for a fresh one, continuing his work. Samuel's unconscious father was outstretched beside him, and the blacksmith would occasionally glance at his arm for reference.

After an hour of agony, Samuel knew the blacksmith still had much more work to do. The areas where the pick had grazed Samuel's skin were dark red and blistered. But the design was clean. Lines thick and thin, entangling themselves into one another. The holy roots. It nearly looked identical to his father's mark.

The foreigner never lost control of Samuel's arm, his sweaty hands holding the limb steady.

"We'll have to rotate the arm," he told the others. "But we'll need to cool the skin first. One of you. Go out and gather fresh snow. His pulse is too elevated. I can feel it. He'll need a break soon or else his heart might stop."

"You truly are a gifted soldier," the mayor said. He stood back, watching, smoking his pipe. "Your experience is invaluable."

The foreigner smiled wide. "I hope your pocketbook shows that."

Samuel quaked, but he was powerless to do anything. He was having so much trouble breathing. The patrolman behind him squeezed so tight it made inhaling all the more difficult, and there were a few times when everything went black. As his eyes rolled back, the foreigner would strike him across the cheek, forcing him to stay awake. Other moments, he could smell his own flesh roasting. He would've done anything to stop the pain.

When the palm side of Samuel's arm was complete, the foreigner had the patrolmen pile fresh snow onto the etched roots. The cooling brought instant relief, and Samuel's muscles relaxed slightly. He tried to slow his breathing, imagining the moment when all of this would be over. The blacksmith drank some water, wiping sweat off his brows. He offered Samuel a drink from his cup, but Samuel refused.

"You need to drink," the foreigner said. "I don't want to force you. But I will."

The blacksmith edged the cup closer to Samuel's mouth, and he drank. The water cooled his burning throat, and some spilled over his chapped lips. He hated them all. The patrolmen. The blacksmith. The foreigner. All of them like the sheriff. All of them following orders. All of them. Evil.

"Continue," the mayor said. "I'm tired and would like to be done with this soon."

The foreigner lifted Samuel's arm and dusted away the snow. He gently laid the burnt half of Samuel's arm onto the anvil, putting a loose hold on his wrist. Samuel's raw skin stuck to the anvil, and he groaned.

"Try not to move as much," the foreigner said. "If you must squirm, try pushing the arm up. Like this." The foreigner locked his elbow, stretching his arm out and back. "It will hurt much worse if I have to press the old burns onto the anvil. Understand?"

"Yes," Samuel whimpered.

The blacksmith got the tools ready, and when he came back to the anvil, he gave a consoling nod. Samuel took a deep breath before the smoldering pick touched his skin. He thought he'd be more prepared the second time around, but he wasn't. He gagged on his own tongue, the hurt engulfing everything. *It'll be over soon*, he tried encouraging himself after each new pressing. *It'll be over soon. It'll be over soon. It'll be over soon.*

But it wasn't over. Time only slowed, minutes crawling like hours. He couldn't take any more. "Stop," he screamed as his flesh cooked. "Stop. Stop. Stop. Stop."

Samuel's father stirred once more, his shoulders arching. Jax didn't wait. He raised the butt of his rifle and swiped it across his father's skull.

The sound of his father's harsh gagging followed. His wheezing morphed into hard chokes, and his battered body began to tremor.

The blacksmith pulled the pick to his side. "The cleric. He's seizing."

His father's limbs shook, and bloodied spit oozed from his mouth.

"Help!" Samuel yelled as his father's body thrashed on the ground.

Everyone in the room went still. The foreigner arched his head back.

"I said he's seizing. Lift up the man's skull and hold the tongue back! Else he might choke on it."

Jax ambled over to Samuel's father, reaching down to help him.

"Leave him," the mayor said.

Jax obeyed. The foreigner glanced at the mayor for a moment, but then put his eyes back on Samuel's arm.

Samuel pulled back, digging his heels into the ground, his arm writhing as all of the muscles stretched. He strained to free himself from his captives, but couldn't break away. He watched in horror as his father's face went to blue. He couldn't breathe. He needed to breathe.

"Help him! Somebody. Please!"

This wasn't fair. Samuel needed his father to know that he was sorry for everything: for his mother, for leaving him, for sending him to the jailhouse on a fool's quest, for putting him here. He needed to ask him about the exorcism and tell him about Zei. He couldn't let him die like this. Tears blanketed his eyes, and his sight became more hazed.

"Father, please! Stop. Can you hear me? You have to stop. Breathe. Please."

His father's shaking grew more and more extreme, his body and limbs hitting the ground like bullets being fired into the dirt. Samuel wrenched his limbs back and forth, trying to break free. He couldn't get loose. His captors wouldn't let him go. His father's convulsions continued for another minute before they ceased entirely, and he went limp.

"Let me go," he begged, drool oozing. "Please."

"His body has taken too much," the foreigner said in a hushed tone. "He can't come back from this. I'm sorry, lad."

"Is he dead?" the blacksmith asked.

The mayor clicked his shoes together, knocking up a cloud of dirt. "Enough talk. Get back to work."

The foreigner closed his eyes, his brows furrowing. He seemed to be lost in thought. When he opened his eyes, his demeanor instantly brightened. "How would you all like to hear a song? I do not mean to boast, but I am quite a gifted singer. There's one particular ditty I'm quite fond of."

Samuel curled into himself, angered by the foreigner's levity. He imagined that he was back inside his father's cabin, sitting beside the fireplace reading the scriptures. Only this time, he was passionate about the ancient writings and longed for more insight into Azhuel's character; the desire to be anything other than a cleric was gone. If only he could've been happy with his destiny and not plagued by doubts and insecurities. He wouldn't be here. His father wouldn't be dying. He wasn't able to dwell on the thought long. When the blacksmith burned the roots near the side of his arm, the pain increased. Samuel rocked backward into the patrolman, pretending he was able to pull his arm away.

"Fine," the mayor said coldly. "Let's hear it."

The foreigner's grip tightened, and he cleared his throat before beginning.

> *Upon the shores of Briston Rock*
> *I came upon a lass*
> *With hair as black as ravens' wings*
> *And eyes as clear as glass*
> *I dropped down on a bended knee*
> *And asked her for her hand*
> *For I'd never seen a finer beauty*
> *In all the southern land*

The blacksmith switched picks, his hand remaining steady as he carved more roots into Samuel. The redlands soldier bobbed his head to the melody as he sang.

> *She embraced me with tender arms*
> *And with regret she said,*
> *"I can't give you my heart, dear lad,*
> *For another I must wed*
> *My betrothed is a wicked man*
> *Whose hands deliver strife*
> *He's paid my father handsomely*
> *To take me as his wife"*

"I can't," Samuel cried. He needed the pain to stop.

> *My body ached with maddening rage*
> *That I could not control*
> *I said, "Fear not, my dearest one*
> *I'll rescue your sweet soul"*
> *I waited 'til the dead of night*
> *Before I made my move*
> *I visited this villain's house*
> *My love I had to prove*

"Please," Samuel begged. He was sure he was going to die. "Stop."
The foreigner continued, his voice loud and boisterous.

> *I crept into his chambers*
> *And while he was asleep*
> *My blade cut through his fleshy throat*
> *He never made a peep*
> *My heart sung with joy*
> *For my beauty I had freed*
> *And although I'd killed a sleeping man*
> *I regretted not my deed*

Samuel's arm jolted, and he began to mouth his pleas. More
and more the mark was beginning to resemble his father's, only his
was being crafted with burns. He couldn't stare at his arm for long;

looking made the pain worse.

The patrolman holding Samuel squeezed hard. "My muscles," he said as he shifted his knees. "I don't know how long I can keep holding him."

Jax rushed over, interjecting his hand. "Move, then. I've got him."

"It's coming together quite nicely," the mayor said. "The holy roots."

Samuel sobbed as Jax took hold of him. He couldn't do it anymore. It had to stop. It was too much. "Kill me. Please. I can't. I can't."

The foreigner sang louder:

> *But soon the word had spread of how*
> *I'd murdered that cruel beast*
> *The soldiers came upon the shores*
> *And plucked me from the east*
> *They put my wrists in iron chains*
> *To Zian I was sent*
> *And found guilty for my crime*
> *Yet I would not repent*

Samuel's cries weren't enough to interrupt the song. The foreigner's voice was unfazed. It was as if his song had taken him away to another place.

> *The guillotine was raised for me*
> *My neck under the blade*

And so I met my end
My life and love did fade
Now lads, please heed this simple truth
Love glistens more than gold
But it makes fools of us all
No matter young or old

Daylight broke as Samuel lay beside his father's lifeless body. His red eyes were as swollen as his burned arm. A pool of saliva had fallen from his lips down to the dirt floor, the dribbled mud still touching his cheek. He wasn't sure how long he'd been lying there, his mind both alert and vacant. It was as if he were suspended from his own skin, a spirit hovering over the scene. Out of the corner of his eye, he saw the dark-pink lines twisting around his forearm. He stared at the mark mindlessly.

The shop was silent. All the patrolmen, except for Jax, had gone back into the neighborhoods to rest. The mayor had ordered a fresh set of patrolmen to stand guard outside of the shop. Jax slept beside the blacksmith's tool table, his rifle resting in his lap. The foreigner sat on top of the large table, his legs swinging as he twirled Samuel's hunting knife between his fingers.

Samuel wanted to sleep, but he worried of nightmares. He

grimaced as he moved his bound wrists. The foreigner had given Samuel a bucket filled with snow to cool his skin. After a while, it stopped helping.

"Some things never leave you," the foreigner said as he twirled the knife effortlessly. "I served for fifteen years. Retired with honors. But I got tired of it all. I wanted to work on my own terms."

Samuel flexed his arm, and pain shot up. He tried ignoring his father's corpse.

"But the problem," the foreigner continued, "is that I was really only ever good at one thing. I went to work as a private contractor. I am a soldier for hire. Of course, I'm not permitted to murder law-abiding citizens. But if a criminal has a bounty on their head, I can do whatever I see fit. Killing isn't all I do. Sometimes I'm hired to give my protection. But I've never had a job like this. Training an entire town of loggers to be soldiers. Odd request, but the money was right, and I couldn't refuse. Don't you agree?"

Samuel imagined himself as Zei.

The foreigner cleaned his fingernails with the blade. "A lot of people, redlands soldiers mind you, are afraid to travel through greenlands territory. Riots and murders in the streets. Me? I have no fear of mobs."

Samuel said nothing.

The foreigner clicked his tongue. "Thing is, I'm not afraid of the common man. I'm including myself in that realm, of course. I know how I think, and I know that most others think and feel and rationalize along the same scale. We all have the same needs: food, shelter, pleasure. In the end, we merely want to go through life with as little pain as possible."

The foreigner pointed his knife to the front door. "But the politicians? Those who are elite either by station or birth? Those are the men I fear. It's not their privilege or their influence. It's what's inside their minds. Their education is the real power. They access knowledge that we, as common citizens, cannot. They will always have that over us. They're human. I can discover their intentions or decipher whether or not they're telling the truth. But I'll never be able to truly know what they know."

"Why are you saying this?" Samuel whispered. He couldn't keep quiet any longer. "Why can't you leave me alone?"

The foreigner threw the knife into the air and caught it between his fingers as it fell. "I'm trying to comfort you. Your father died, but it was an honorable death. And you learned that you've got the blood of a master swordsman running through your veins. Isn't that something? I knew I liked you, boy. We share a kinship. You and I."

Samuel ignored him.

"You are right to question the mayor's intentions. I see the disdain you hold for the man. It's all over your face. You see what many others here don't; that mayor thinks he's playing us all for fools. If I was a different sort of man, I would cut you free. I would pack up my belongings, and leave this town, and never look back." He paused. "But, the mayor has money. And I need money. Adapt or die. That is the redlander way."

Samuel swallowed. He forced himself to sit up, his chest rising.

He motioned to his backpack. The bag had been shoved in the corner near the disposal pail, and no one had paid it any mind.

"I have money."

The foreigner giggled. "Oh, lad. Not enough. I'm sure."

But the mysterious prospect must have piqued the foreigner's curiosity. He rose and snatched up Samuel's bag. He walked across the room, sitting in front of Samuel. The foreigner guided the bag's zipper down. He eased open the flaps.

The foreigner turned to the side, assuring himself that Jax was unconscious. He pulled the bag up to his face. His eyebrows rose. "Oh. Now this is interesting. Banned technology. How did someone like you find something like this?"

Samuel said nothing.

"Do you know who this belongs to?"

Samuel shook his head.

"You're lying," the foreigner said as he coiled the bag behind him. "This is military-grade. Pre-blackout. Do you know what someone might pay for this?"

Samuel looked up. "Will you help me?"

"You're a criminal and a thief. Why would I help you? You're a bound captive. I can take it myself, and no one will be the wiser."

Samuel tightened his fists and his burned arm felt new pains. He winced before speaking. "I'll scream. I'll tell the patrolmen you stole it."

"Another lie," the foreigner said with a smirk. "Your eyes shift when you speak. And you're throwing out toothless threats. Speak truths, lad. Besides, what would you do if you somehow managed to escape here? You're too weak. You wouldn't last more than a day in your condition."

Samuel nursed his arm mindlessly. The foreigner was right. He was weak in every way: physically, mentally, emotionally. Weak.

The foreigner ran his hand through his dark hair, his cheeks forming dimples. He zipped the bag shut and returned it to its previous location, only he tucked it farther behind the disposal pail. Jax shifted his shoulder, but his eyes remained shut. The foreigner lifted his index finger to Samuel and drew it across his own lips before sitting back down. Was he letting him in on a silent agreement?

A fist rapped on the door.

"Jax?"

Samuel awoke abruptly, his skin and eyes burning.

"What?"

"The loggers are gathering for their training," the faceless voice called out from behind the closed doors. "The mayor is there too. He's asking for Mikael."

Jax tapped the sleeping Mikael with the heel of his boot. "Get up."

"Coming," the foreigner said with a yawn.

Both the foreigner and Jax took their time rising to their feet. They shuffled around the shop, lazily gathering their belongings. Samuel's bag remained right where the foreigner had left it.

"I'm going home," Jax said. "Do you need an escort?"

"I can find my own way."

"Good." Jax draped the rifle over his shoulder, his hands steadying

296

it behind his back. "I'll send a few more patrolmen this way after I track down the sheriff."

"Don't bother," the foreigner said as he dusted his pants. He put Samuel's throwing knife down on the table. "Sending men inside the shop, I mean. The cleric's bastard is not going anywhere."

"You don't know that."

"I do."

A loud scream from outside made Samuel jerk. Both the foreigner and Jax froze, their eyes looking to one another. The scream was followed by more screams, and the sound of banging from the outside walls filled the shop. It was almost as if someone was repeatedly punching the doors. Several shots were fired. Samuel's lips opened, but he didn't move. The foreigner pointed a finger at Jax, signaling him to move back.

"What is that?" Jax asked. He took up his rifle, cocking back the hammer.

Samuel dragged himself into a sitting position, bumps growing over his skin. He wasn't sure what was happening, but the foreigner's face looked troubled. The banging stopped, but Samuel could hear distant yells. Had someone been attacked outside? He put his hands to his chest, the burn on his arm tingling.

"Greenland natives?" Jax asked. "Are they here? Is this real?"

The foreigner's eyes widened, his stare authoritative. His fierce gaze was enough to silence Jax immediately.

They waited silently, watching the wooden doors. Nothing happened.

The foreigner gave Jax a nod.

Jax walked forward, his face full of apprehension as he approached the door. He looked back at the foreigner. The foreigner nodded again. Jax threw the door open, and the morning light entered the shop. He aimed his rifle up and down, his motions jerky. The snow had stopped, but an inch or so of white powder covered the ground.

Samuel edged his busted frames farther up his nose, allowing his eyes to dilate. He saw a splash of red over the white powder. Could the mayor be right about war? Had greenland citizens infiltrated the north? How could they have moved up so fast? And why would they do this? What could they gain from attacking a town like Haid?

"What do you see?" the foreigner asked. He stepped past the furnace and into the center of the room.

Jax cautiously stepped outside the shed. He lifted his rifle to the roof before turning it back in front of him. "Blood. And ... no. They're dead. Three patrolmen. I see three of them. They're dead."

"Nothing else?"

"No!" He craned his neck. "I can't see the western woods well enough. But the loggers are running. This is bad."

Samuel rounded his shoulders and tucked his hands into his chest. He didn't care if he died in the shop, if foreigners sprinted inside and gunned him down. But he remembered Claudette and Laura. Were they all right, safe inside the butcher's shop? Was it war? Where was the sheriff?

The foreigner leaned forward. "What else do you see?"

Jax took another step, turning from left to right. "The square is empty. No one is in the street. No. Wait. I see a girl."

"A child?" the foreigner asked.

"She's bleeding. She's coming."

Before Jax could say anything else, a figure darted across the doorway and pounced on him. Red hair danced behind the intruder as she pressed her knees into Jax's chest. She slammed a hatchet between his eyes, his skull splitting as the blade sank.

Samuel curled into his body. It couldn't be. He was immobile, his muscles having turned to liquid.

Zei got up slowly, her bare feet anchored to the snow-covered ground. Blood covered her legs and arms and face, her black dress stained red, hem swaying in the wind. She yanked the hatchet from Jax's limp head and looked around the shed. She ignored Samuel, instead locking eyes with the foreigner. She had become the demon once more, and he was terrified.

The foreigner didn't move, but an uneasy smile crept over his lips. He studied Zei carefully as he edged his blades up. "You must be the owner. Coming to reclaim what is theirs?"

Zei gritted her teeth.

"I knew it!" the foreigner said in excitement. "And those eyes! So this is what that silly mayor has been up to. Quite interesting. It's a shame you will not leave this place alive. No one will believe me when I tell this tale."

"Don't," Samuel said. "Please. Don't fight."

"What was the name?" the foreigner asked Zei. "Of your kind. I can't recall. Many souls. One host. The forbidden ones." The foreigner's smile widened. "Halyre."

Zei remained motionless, saying nothing.

Samuel winced in pain. He forced himself to watch. He couldn't comprehend the set of events that had led up to Zei's arrival. How had she gotten out of the prison cell? Was she killing patrolmen and loggers, and if so, why? He nearly pinched his own leg, wanting to be sure this wasn't a hallucination or nightmare. He looked down, seeing his father's body on the floor. He wanted this to be a dream, but the throbbing pain in his arm reminded him it wasn't.

"You are missing an arm," the foreigner noted. "Without that prosthetic, you're much more vulnerable. While I am not one to take handicaps, I will make an exception for you. I am not like the men you've cut down. I am a warrior. Many enemies have died by my hands. I will not die today."

Samuel tried to stand but couldn't secure his footing. "Please. Leave her alone. She'll kill you."

"She?" The foreigner laughed. "This is neither male nor female. Only an abomination." The foreigner crouched lower, his body positioned to attack. "Hungry, are you not? Then please. Let me whet your appetite."

Zei flicked the hatchet slightly, the blade nearly touching her toes. Her expression was mostly unreadable, but Samuel could sense Zei's annoyance with the foreigner. She raised her stub to him, almost as if it were a loaded weapon.

"Don't," Samuel pleaded, although he wasn't sure whom he was talking to. Perhaps both of them. He opened his hands, holding them out in surrender. He hated seeing her like this, because this was how the mayor wanted her. "Zei. You're not a demon. I know you're not."

"Demon?" the foreigner forced out. He glanced at Samuel's father. "What nonsense has that holy man—"

Zei rushed to the foreigner and made the first swing. The foreigner jumped back, knocking the blade away with one of the knives. He spun around and took a swipe at her legs, but she was well out of the blade's reach. Zei hopped on top of the blacksmith's table. She hurled the hatchet at the foreigner's chest, but he knocked it away.

"Stop!" Samuel yelled. "Don't do this!"

The foreigner lunged at his attacker with both blades. Zei leaped off the table. She swiped a pick from underneath the table and slammed it through the foreigner's boot. He yelled as he rolled away, into Samuel's father.

"You are fast," the foreigner labored to say. He pulled the pick out from his foot, wincing and grunting. "How many human lives have you taken, Halyre?"

"Stop it!" Samuel managed to get to his feet. He took two quick steps, then tripped, falling back to the ground. "Zei. He's going to help me. You don't have to kill him."

Zei darted out from under the table as the foreigner got to his feet. When she came up, she took one of Samuel's throwing knives and held it. The foreigner lunged toward her, swinging both knives in a way that would cut anything to shreds. She was too fast, hopping backward and to the side after every swipe. She darted behind the foreigner, dropped down, and swiped the blade across the back of his ankles. The foreigner yelped as he fell to the ground. He dropped one blade and swung the other madly, warding her off as long as he could.

Zei stayed back, spinning the knife around, then tossing it into the foreigner's belly. The foreigner grunted as he halted his defense, dropping his weapon as he struggled to remove the one inside him. Zei casually scooped the hatchet back up. The foreigner plucked the knife from his gut and threw it at her. The blade sank deep into her right shoulder near the collarbone.

Zei twisted her neck, her eyes examining the new injury. She reached up with her good arm but couldn't secure her grasp of the knife's handle. Blood spilled down her shoulder onto her black dress.

"Stop." Samuel got to his knees. Using the wall behind him for support, he rose to his feet. "You don't have to fight!"

The foreigner grabbed one of the blacksmith's spare knives next to him, and he rolled himself up to his feet. He cocked his legs back as his knees bent, preparing himself for a vicious launch at Zei. Before he could leap toward her, Samuel grabbed the back of his shirt and pulled him back. Together, Samuel and the foreigner crashed to the floor.

Zei came forward. Without time to prepare for the next attack, the foreigner made a desperate swing to his right, but Zei brushed it aside. He made another swipe left, but he was too slow. Samuel scurried to the wall as Zei jumped on top of the foreigner. Without hesitation, she pulled back and smashed the hatchet into his neck. His body went limp as the blood splashed out.

Zei sat still over the foreigner's body, the blood touching her knees. She looked to Samuel, her eyes hungry.

Samuel pressed himself against the wall. Zei was no longer a captive prisoner limited by shackles. Some way or another, she'd gained her freedom, and she'd shown no restraint. He hoped she wouldn't harm him, but a part of him felt he deserved it. He was pathetic, weak, and unable to protect those he cared for. He was the reason his father was dead. She'd proven herself much stronger than he could ever hope to be. He wasn't fit for this world.

Zei stood up. She turned her bloodstained face to Samuel. He tremored, his lips searching for words. He pressed himself closer to his father's body. He was going mad. He knew he was. The foreigner called her something. Halyre. Forbidden ones. A legion. A "they," as if she were more than one entity.

Zei came closer, her hand fumbling to get the small knife out of her shoulder. Samuel's breath halted, his lungs unwilling to give him air. Perhaps it'd be best for him to die here. He could close his eyes, and Zei could take his life. Make the pain stop.

"In the bag," he said. "Near the corner by the pail. It's your machine arm. I found it in the sheriff's house."

Zei stopped before making her way to the bag. She got on her knees as she unzipped it. Her head tilted with amusement as she pulled out the mechanical arm. She lifted it and grimaced. She went back to Samuel and extended the claw portion of the arm forward.

Samuel's body shook as he took hold of the prosthetic. Zei slid her stub inside. A humming noise rose from the metal arm, and its visible gears began to rotate. Zei strapped the first buckle around the base of the holster, then draped the larger strap over her left shoulder.

She leaned down and lowered her body.

Samuel's hands quivered as he tightened the strap over her shoulder and buckled it. The two hooks that formed the claw moved in and out, the motion causing a light squeak. Samuel moved his hands to her right collarbone, his fingers touching the knife's handle. As gently as he could, he pulled his throwing knife from her flesh. More blood gushed from the open wound, black liquid bubbling down her flat chest.

Zei loomed over Samuel. He put the knife in her hand.

"Do it."

He really did want to die. He knew that now. He didn't want to live in a world where he was the reason his father was dead. He didn't want to have a burned mark on his arm. He didn't want to face the mayor or the sheriff ever again. He wanted to be nothing. Like her.

"I know that you want to. Maybe you can't even control it. So it's okay. I want you to do it. Just do it, Zei."

Zei squeezed the knife's handle, pulling it up to Samuel's neck. He swallowed, waiting for the press of the blade.

"I'm sorry." It was the only thing left to say. He closed his eyes.

He waited in darkness, but nothing happened. He heard what sounded like the soft shifting of dirt next to him. When he opened his eyes, he saw Zei turn to the open door. More people were yelling outside the shed, the volume of their voices growing. She looked back at Samuel, her green eyes studying him. He couldn't make out what they were trying to tell him, but he knew it wasn't the answer he wanted. And then, as if nothing had happened, Zei dropped the knife into Samuel's lap and ran out of the shop.

Samuel remained motionless for a long while, passively observing the chaos from outside the shop's open door. Men were screaming, beckoning their friends and comrades to follow them to safety. The bodies Zei had left behind were enough to break apart Haid's newly founded militia. No one was fighting or giving orders to advance. They were terrified, even the patrolmen. "They're here!" one voice cackled. "I don't see anyone!" another yelled back. "Stay inside. Everyone stay inside!"

Samuel lowered his head and gawked at the floor by his feet.

FRIEND

Zei had scribbled the letters into the dirt before leaving him the knife and running outside. He didn't understand. She was wild and violent. She was savage in her killings, and her slit pupils seemed to widen with joy every time she drew blood. He told her they weren't

friends. They couldn't be. Not after what she'd done to Claudette's father. He told her to kill him. Isn't that what she wanted? Wasn't that her nature?

Samuel glanced at the foreigner's body. The side of his neck was torn open as if it had been nothing more than paper. He repeated the word *demon* as if it were the most absurd idea, but he spoke to Zei in full confidence. He called them they. Legion. Halyre. What did the redlands soldier know? If Zei wasn't a demon, wasn't possessed by a demon, wasn't a boy or a girl or human, then what were they? Were there others out there? Others like Zei?

It was pointless to wonder now. Samuel couldn't get answers from a corpse.

The patrolmen and loggers outside were confused, running for cover and screaming at others to do the same. Most were heading for the neighborhoods, and a few panicked patrolmen followed them. No one was able to understand who or what had caused the carnage. There was no leadership or direction. The once-disciplined gathering of loggers had turned into a panicky mob, and the patrolmen ordered to keep the peace were of no help. The only true soldier in Haid was dead now. So were Jax and the other patrolmen guarding the shed. So was his father.

A small crew of patrolmen dashed past the blacksmith's shop. Samuel heard someone screaming at the patrolmen, ordering them to come back immediately. He recognized the mayor's voice. "That demon is my property! Stop running like cowards and get it back! It went into the woods! Go! You fucking useless patrolmen! Fucking mindless loggers!"

Hearing the mayor's voice made his stomach churn. He clutched his father's lifeless arm, his blood boiling. For a long while, it was easy to put most of the blame on Zei. Then he blamed himself for the horrors: the execution of Claudette's father, his burned mark, his father's death.

But Zei and death and everything else revolved around the mayor. He was the one who'd forced Zei to be a prisoner instead of killing her. He was the one who wanted her as some sort of savage pet. He was the one who forced the loggers to work in unsafe conditions, jeopardizing their lives with his greed. He had arranged the test with Claudette's father. He was the one who had stationed the patrolmen outside of the jailhouse. He was the one who made them all do whatever he commanded. He was the one who made the blacksmith carve the roots into his arm. He was the one who refused to let the patrolmen help his dying father. He was the reason his father was dead.

His teeth chattered. He wanted Zei to find the mayor and kill him. He wanted her to take a blade and plunge it into his belly, gutting him like some fat pig for slaughter. A darkness he could not explain clouded over him. He didn't know if he craved revenge or justice, or if he'd become drunk on bloodlust himself. But he wanted to watch the mayor die.

He couldn't stand back and do nothing. He couldn't leave it to chance. Not anymore. This was bigger than him. It was for Claudette's father, for the dead loggers and patrolmen, for his father, for Charles, and for every citizen of Haid.

The door creaked as a gust of wind tried to shove it closed, but Jax's body prevented it from moving any farther. Samuel wiped his forehead with his arm. He huffed as he bent down and reached for the throwing knife Zei had left him, straining to hold it with his bound hands. Once he had it, he edged the handle into his mouth and bit down hard. He drew his wrists over the blade and sawed into the rope. The strands were thick and knotted well, refusing to break easily. He had to pause several times for fear of rupturing his teeth. His jaw ached. He ignored the pain, chomping onto the handle harder and rubbing the cords across the little blade. His wrists grew raw with each up-and-down motion. He felt the surface layer of flesh underneath the rope wearing away, and with it came fresh blood. The strands were cutting into his skin, the burn nearly identical to the throbbing of his arm.

But he wouldn't stop. One of the cords had snapped, but there were several more remaining. Either he was going to break free or the ropes were going to sever off his hands. His eyes were wet and red, but he continued. He was going to be strong for once in his pathetic life. He sawed faster, harder, faster until a few of the cords eventually snapped and his bondage slackened.

He opened his mouth, allowing the knife to fall. His jaw throbbed, his teeth aching as though he'd been chewing on stone. The slack was all he needed. He wriggled his hands and mashed his fingers underneath the ropes. With a few more tugs, he was free. He could see the raw markings the cords had made, patches of his skin cracked and bleeding. He stretched out his fingers, giving them time to regain their dexterity. He grabbed the knife, the handle damp with saliva. After rubbing away the spit, he aligned the blade over the ropes binding his ankles and cut himself free.

He stood too quickly. His legs shook, his muscles needing time to adjust. His arm burned with fresh pain. He reclined into the wall, pressing his palms into the wood. The bunched-up sleeves of his jacket fell, the woolly cloth scraping across his burns. He scowled as he stood without the wall's assistance.

"Come back here!" the mayor's voice bellowed, the volume increasing. The sound of a gunshot cracked through the air. "We need that demon! It belongs to me!"

Samuel stretched his calves for a moment, trying to regain his mobility. As he pulled his heels forward, he looked back on his father's body. His jaw trembled as he forced himself to turn away. He wanted to cry, but he wouldn't. His father shouldn't have died. He staggered to the blacksmith's table and retrieved his other throwing knife, dropping both inside his pocket. He rummaged through the shop slowly, trying to locate the hunting knife. He remembered the foreigner taking it, but he wasn't sure where he'd put it. He scanned around the furnace, unable to find it.

He surveyed the wall of mounted knives. In the bottom portion of the arranged display was a pair of twin knives, both comparable to his hunting knife in blade length and handle design. Both blades were double-edged and smoothly finished, but one was silver in color and the other black as obsidian. He took both knives, allowing his weary fingers to curl around the wooden handles. The weight of the blades felt good, nearly identical to that of his hunting knife. He turned, forcing himself not to look back at the foreigner or his father. He went to the open door, stepped over Jax's body, and walked out into the square.

The daylight was blinding, the gray clouds from the night before having all but left the sky. The streets were vacant of nearly everyone, but a few men were still in sight as they ran down into the neighborhoods. There were several more bodies outside of the blacksmith's shop and one in front of the post office. Samuel's broken lens skewed his sight, but he was able to recognize the dead logger as Josiah.

Samuel adjusted his frames, scanning the square. No one seemed to be inside the front portion of the butcher's shop. The lights were off. Nothing seemed out of place. It was as if the shop had never opened. It was a relief. Hopefully Claudette and Laura had never left the confines of their home. They were safe. They had to be.

He glanced at the other shops in a bit of disbelief. Every shop seemed undisturbed, as if no one had come to open any of them. As he came farther up, he noticed the mayor's jeep parked near the edge of the square. He went to the vehicle, peering inside. It was empty. He took a few steps back. He was too late. Everyone had run off, and Zei was nowhere to be seen. She must have run away into the woods.

He loosened his hold on the knives slightly. His mind pestered him with doubts and fears. His renewed strength was leaving him. He needed to find shelter as well. He could go and check on Claudette and her mother. He could make sure they were safe. He took a breath before squinting his eyes tightly, scanning over toward the logging sites one last time. When he did, he noticed a faint figure drudging through the small layer of snow and heading toward the pines. Samuel's heart raced, and the rage inside of him returned. The figure was round and wearing a suit.

The burns on his marked arm twinged. He ignored the aching, tightened his grip on the handles once more, and sprinted after the mayor.

26

Samuel trudged through the snow, heading to the western woods. He'd heard the bustle of swaying branches and the chirping of a lone bird, but nothing else. He breathed through his nostrils, and the hairs on his neck rose. The trees above blocked most of the sunlight, and his eyes had to readjust. He wasn't sure what he would do if he found the mayor. Did he have the guts to kill him?

He went deeper inside, careful not to brush his arms against any trunks. A gust of cold wind shook the branches, causing bits of snow to fall. He almost called out for Zei. He didn't. He wanted her to be far away from this place. The mayor's secret possession had escaped. She came to Samuel and spared his life. She left him a knife. Their time together had meant something to her.

Samuel pressed his heels deeper into the ground. He put a hand on the pine tree beside him. He imagined the holy roots crawling

around the earth below, able to see the things he couldn't. He knew better than to ask Azhuel for help. The last prayer he'd made hadn't done any good. His father was dead.

"Where are you? Come back!"

Samuel stopped, listening for the direction of the voice.

"I'm not going to hurt you, demon. I only want to talk!"

Samuel squeezed the knives' handles and headed northeast, following the sound. He treaded lightly and could feel his heart pounding against his ribs.

"You have my word as the mayor of Haid!"

A loud boom echoed through the woods, and several birds took flight. Samuel's ears rang. The gunshot was close. He kept moving. He could smell everything: the frozen snow, the sap seeping off the pine needles, the stench of wildlife. As he treaded farther down, he caught sight of the mayor. He was dressed in a fine suit, but his thinning hair was wild and ungroomed. His chin was shoved into his neck, and he pointed his silver handgun at the trees.

"I mean you no harm," the mayor called out to no one.

Samuel slid his glasses farther up his nose, his right eye straining to see through the cracked lens. His hands shook. He was no soldier. He was the weak, bastard son of a dead cleric. What did he expect himself to do?

"We can provide better accommodations for you! More freedom! More time with the boy! You like him, don't you?"

The mayor waved the gun over his head as he circled around the same pines. When he moved, he spotted Samuel. His lips parted, and his brows rose. He lowered the gun down to his side.

"Samuel," he said uneasily. His forehead wrinkled. "I didn't hear you. What are you doing here? How did you get free?" He paused. "That's not important. I need your help." He waved his free hand while keeping the gun's barrel pointed at the ground. "I guess you heard all of the commotion. It got free. Someone must've let it free. And when I find out who did it, justice will be served."

Samuel was stoic. Was he going to try and kill the mayor? Should he run? The mayor scanned the area once more.

"Come, boy! You're the only one it trusts. The only brave soul in Haid. I need you. Help me get it back, and I will give you anything you want. Half of my income and reserves. Ask, and it's yours. We can bury the past. You have my word."

"He's dead," Samuel said.

The mayor's expression went grave, his eyes going wide. "I am sorry." He jiggled the gun across his leg. "But you heard Mikael. There was nothing else to be done."

Samuel tightened his grip on the knives. He knew everything the mayor said was to serve his own interests. He wanted Samuel's help in finding Zei, and he wouldn't give him that. He wouldn't give him anything.

The mayor gritted his teeth. "You should think before you act, boy."

"You killed him."

"I never touched him. How dare you accuse me of murder! I am the law. And what gives you the audacity to question my authority?

You and the cleric are criminals. And, in my graciousness, I am giving you a chance to earn back my favor. Will you throw that away?"

Samuel didn't want to hear another word. The burn mark sang as he cocked back his throwing arm. He ignored the pain, envisioning a carved X across the mayor's large chest. He squinted, trying to judge the distance through the cracked frames. Before the mayor could aim the pistol, Samuel arched his wrist back, pivoted his foot, leaned forward, and released. The silver-bladed knife sailed past the rows of pine and plummeted into the mayor's stomach.

The mayor hunched over. He groaned as he plucked the blade from his gut and allowed it to fall from his hand. Samuel stepped back. Blood leaked onto the mayor's suit as he straightened his back. He pulled the gun up.

Samuel ran. He scurried behind a large pine. Bark and wood splintered next to him as several shots rang out. He tried tucking his body completely behind the pine but couldn't. The trunk was too narrow. Another shot was fired, and Samuel felt fresh pain in his left leg. He nearly dropped to his knees. It was like molten fire had been injected into his calf. It felt like the burning of his arm. He forced his feet closer together. His eyes watered, and his limbs shivered.

Four more shots were fired, but none connected. Next came the sound of metal clinking.

"Damn it!" the mayor screamed.

Samuel sank down. He grazed his leg with his fingers and whimpered as he felt the sticky liquid. More pain. How much could he take?

"Don't think I won't find you, boy. I will put a bounty on your head so high every man, woman, and child in Haid will be searching these woods by nightfall."

Samuel curled his arms around his chest. He'd failed. He was a fool for letting his anger get the best of him. He should've run to Claudette and Laura the moment he escaped the blacksmith's shop. He never should've come into the woods. He wouldn't be able to flee Haid, not with a bullet in his leg.

"I will have you gutted and hanged in the square as a traitor," the mayor screamed. "I will keep your body there for days, weeks, and the wolves and wild dogs will eat your bones. I will hang your father's body next to yours. Do you hear me?"

Samuel twitched his head. His father was dead because of the mayor. He clenched the knife in his left hand. No. He wouldn't die waiting here. He huffed as his fingers clawed into the tree behind him, and he stood up. He tried putting weight on the leg but couldn't. The pain was excruciating, and his muscles wouldn't hold. He bit into his lip. He had to move, but he didn't know how. He took a long breath and somehow forced himself to limp out from behind the tree.

The mayor stumbled eastward. His large body staggered pathetically, his arms cradling his gut. He was bleeding. He was in pain too. Samuel took several steps forward, nearly dropping with each one. He dragged the tip of his left foot across the snow, fighting to keep very little weight on it. He tracked after the mayor, but it was pointless. He wouldn't be able to catch up with him. He was too far ahead. Samuel didn't have the strength to throw another knife. Not accurately. Not this far away.

A thunderous snap filled the woods, the sound reverberating against the trees.

Clamp.

The mayor dropped flat on his back and screamed, his arms flailing. Samuel squinted through his broken frames, trying hard to see what had happened. As he doddered ahead, he saw the iron jaws of a bear trap snapped around the mayor's shin. The metal teeth squeezed into his leg as if it were a tasty meal, fresh blood spilling over into the snow.

The mayor wailed as he dragged his leg farther up, his hands frantically clawing at the trap. Samuel paused, hovering his wounded leg in the air.

"No," the mayor cried. He tried prying open the trap. He tugged with everything he had but couldn't get it free. "No. No. No."

Samuel tried swallowing, but his throat was sealed shut. The mayor yelled as more blood squirted out from the jagged teeth. He rolled onto his side and tried crawling away, but the trap had been anchored deep into the earth. The mayor bawled in agony. The pool of blood around him was growing.

Samuel waited.

The mayor's thrashing and whining reminded him of the wounded deer snagged in one of the old traps. The fingers on his left hand curled over the knife's handle, his thumb falling on top of the middle one. He teetered closer, making sure to not put much pressure on his injured leg.

"Stop," the mayor choked out, his breathing hard and rushed.

Samuel came beside the mayor and lowered himself to his knees. "Don't move."

The mayor recoiled as he reached out his hand. "Get away from me."

"Stop moving. You're only making it worse."

The mayor struggled for another minute before heeding Samuel's advice. He rolled onto his back, defenseless, his belly rising and falling dramatically. Samuel dragged himself forward. He climbed on top of the mayor, straddling his large torso.

"What are you doing?" The mayor pushed his belly up, raising his arms against Samuel. "Get off of me, boy!"

"It's okay," Samuel said softly.

He dug his knees deeper into the mayor's side, pinned him underneath his legs. The mayor squealed.

"It's okay."

Samuel allowed his weight to fall on the mayor's stomach.

"Get off me, boy!"

Samuel swatted back the mayor's feeble and desperate arms. He remembered his father's lesson about not letting a creature suffer needlessly. The mayor was an evil man, deserving wrath and darkness. But he was also a creature in pain. No one was coming to rescue him. With the wounds in his stomach and leg, the mayor would bleed out eventually.

Mercy.

"You're in pain," Samuel said airily, his head buzzing. He wished someone would ease his own pain. He leaned into the mayor, switching the knife to his right hand. The mayor tried thrashing his body out from underneath him but was unable to get free. Samuel had done this before; he knew how to secure a trapped beast. The metal trap rattled as the mayor kicked out in desperation.

This was mercy.

"I will kill you!"

"It's okay."

Samuel guided the dark blade over the mayor's jowl, aligning it over the neck. A deer, a pig, a human. It didn't matter. They all had the same artery. The mayor cursed as Samuel closed his eyes and slit into his meaty throat. The mayor convulsed for several seconds as the blood came rushing out onto the snow, but then he stopped moving. Samuel opened his eyes, looking down at the mayor through his cracked lens. The mayor's mouth was agape, the blood from the open cut on his neck now leaking onto Samuel's jeans.

He crawled off the mayor and moved over to the nearest pine. He sat and propped his back against the trunk. He tried cleaning the blade with snow but couldn't focus. A part of him expected Zei to emerge from the trees. She seemed drawn to blood and carnage. But she was gone, and he was alone with another corpse.

He sniffled and tucked the blacksmith's fancily crafted knife inside his pocket. He closed his wet eyes. His lips quivered. He saw nothing but black. His shoulders arched as he rested his head against the tree. He allowed his body and mind to sink into the darkness.

The harsh stinging of his skin forced him awake. His dry lips cracked, and he tasted blood. He heard voices around him. He tried opening his eyes but couldn't. His weary hand reached for his face. His glasses were missing. The end of a cup wedged itself into his agape mouth. Cool water slid down his sandy throat. He drank, helplessly parched. The liquid brought little comfort. A lump was wedged inside of his pipe, and the water didn't force it down. His body felt like mush, his tongue unable to form words.

"Sleep," a voice encouraged him.

He obeyed, allowing himself to drift into darkness. In his dreams, he saw his father's swollen face glaring at him, choking for air he couldn't get. He saw Jax's split skull and the torn skin flashing bits of white bone. He saw the mayor and the way the blood from his neck flowed out like water from a faucet. He saw Zei's predator eyes

feeding on the fears of dying men, her metal arm humming as the two-pronged hook dug at the air. He saw his own arm and the way his flesh bubbled into the roots.

When his nightmares became too much to bear, he jerked awake from the bed. His body was coated in sweat. He opened his eyes, but everything was blurred. His hand rubbed the mattress below him. He was in a large bed with high-rising posts, and elaborate décor furnished the walls. He blinked heavily. His chest tightened. A lone, burning candle rested on top of the table next to the bed, the tiny flame flickering. He assumed he was somewhere inside the mayor's estate. He wiped his face with the white bedsheets and realized he was completely naked. He moved a bit, groping over the table for his eyeglasses. He couldn't find them.

"Can you speak?"

Samuel squinted, trying to make out the figure as it approached his bedside. When the figure leaned over into the light, he was able to recognize the outline of Elizabeth Tulsan. She tucked a loose strand of hair behind her ear before taking up his chin, stiffly turning his head from left to right.

His tongue moved like slosh. "Yes," he groaned.

The doctor pressed a cold hand across his bare chest, feeling for his heart. Samuel eased his muscles at her touch.

"Be still," she commanded. She took his right arm and lifted it to her face. The arm was wrapped in a thick layer of gauze. The doctor unfastened the bindings. Samuel winced.

"The burns are deep, but clean. Your leg is what I was most

worried about. Don't touch either."

Samuel nodded, trying to ignore the pain as the doctor applied a fresh coat of paste over his burns. His eyes watered heavily. He involuntarily kicked his legs, and when he did, he felt the stinging of his left calf.

"It'll hurt," the doctor said. "But this blend promotes tissue growth and prevents infection. You need it. Three coats a day for the next two weeks."

Samuel clenched his fingers into his palms, struggling to ignore the hurt. His neck craned, and he studied the glossy burn marks. He couldn't make out the details of the lines. He brought his arm closer to his nose. The details weren't as flawless as his father's mark. A few of the roots were jagged and uneven.

"The scarring is permanent," the doctor noted dryly as she grabbed a fresh roll of gauze. She took his arm and wrapped it in layers. "Patches and sections may fade over time, but it's unlikely. You're alive. Be grateful for that."

Samuel shook his head. "My father isn't."

The doctor leaned back, rummaging through her medical bag. "I'm sure he prefers it this way. Children are supposed to bury their parents. It's only a tragedy when it's the other way around."

Samuel pulled his left hand up to his face. His skin was clean, void of dirt and blood. Someone must have bathed him. His head throbbed as he reclined deeper into the pillow. Who had found him in the woods? And if someone had found him, they'd also found the mayor. He swallowed, his stomach sinking.

"Does Charles know?"

"Know what?" The doctor took out a green vial, shaking the contents before moving the vial to his lips. "Drink. This next part is going to hurt much worse if you don't take this. With the swelling, I wasn't able to get out the bullet last time I tried. If I don't get it soon, all of this will be for nothing."

Samuel obeyed. The liquid was bitter. He licked his tongue over his teeth, trying to scrape away the taste. The doctor dropped her bag onto the bed and began pulling out her tools. It only took a few minutes for Samuel to start feeling the drug. His body tingled with warmth, and his sight was further hazed. He wanted to see.

"Where are my glasses?"

The doctor pulled back the bedsheets, moving them up past his kneecaps. "The mayor took them this morning. Drove over to Lehles to get them fixed. Should be back by this evening."

Samuel was forced to close his eyes. The spinning room was making him dizzy, and he didn't want to puke. "The mayor's dead too."

The doctor lifted his leg and pulled it into her chest. He could make out the sensation of scraping and cutting, but he didn't feel any pain. Only pressure.

"The new mayor. Why do you think you're here? He's sparing no expense for your treatment and care. You're not a charity case."

Samuel's skin tingled. "Charles doesn't know. He doesn't know I killed him."

"I don't know what you're talking about," the doctor said.

Samuel awoke to the groaning of his stomach. His bandaged arm itched, but he knew better than to touch it. A dull pain throbbed on his calf, no doubt in protest of the doctor's work. He blinked repeatedly, fighting to get the sleep from his eyes. His sight was hazed. An unannounced hand grazed his shoulder. He turned to the side and could make out a female figure standing over him. It was Claudette, her unbound brown hair tumbling onto the bed as she leaned closer.

"Are you okay, Sam?"

Samuel cleared his throat, knowing he had to lie. "Yes."

Claudette skirted a cup toward his mouth. "Are you thirsty?"

He shook his head.

"You need to drink more water," she insisted. "That's what the doctor said." She pressed the glass to his lips. He drank, laboring to force it down. She wiped away the stray drops on his face with the back of her hand. "You must be in a lot of pain. I heard about your father. And your arm. I'm so sorry, Sam."

He bunched his face. "I need more sleep."

"Okay," she said softly. "I'll come back later."

She leaned down and kissed his cheek before stepping out of the room. Samuel forced himself to breathe deep. She deserved someone better than him. He was both a pathetic coward and a murderer, and he wasn't sure how he managed to be both of those things. He grabbed onto the sheets, wanting to cry and sleep and never wake up.

The hinges of the bedroom door creaked, and the sound of new footsteps filled the room. He opened his eyes, tired of pretending to be something he wasn't and lying about everything. He went to push his glasses up, but then realized they weren't there. The blurry figure grunted as it strolled over, sliding up a chair by the side of the bed. Samuel squinted, and he was able to make out the intruder. He felt relief. It was the only person in the world besides Zei he could be completely honest with.

"Wow," the sheriff grumbled as he reclined into the chair, the revolver that was strapped to his side thudding against the chair. "You look like shit."

Samuel smirked a bit, but it faded quickly.

The sheriff cleared his throat as he fumbled inside of his pocket. He pulled out what Samuel assumed was a flask and edged it to his mouth. "Some mess out there. Sixteen people dead. Mostly patrolmen. A few loggers. No women or children. So that's something. Body count doesn't include the redlander. Or the mayor. Two of my men found his body along the edge of the western woods. Throat was slit. Belly stabbed. And that's not all they found there. Some unconscious little fool had gotten himself shot in the leg and had a bloody knife in his jacket."

Samuel's chest burned.

"Who else knows?"

The sheriff wiped his mustache.

"Who knows what?"

"Does Charles know?"

"I told my boys to keep their mouths shut if they didn't want to end up like that fat dead mayor. Not like that's a guarantee. Nobody listens to me." The sheriff took another swig from his flask and smacked his lips. "Honestly? Didn't think you had it in you."

Samuel breathed deep. "I killed him."

"The little mayor isn't crying over his dead daddy," the sheriff said. "If that's what you're thinking. He's the new mayor of Haid. As is his birthright." He tapped his boots onto the floor. "A thank-you would be nice."

"Huh?"

"Me helping you. A thank-you would be nice."

Samuel leaned into the cushions. "My father is dead. You didn't help me."

The sheriff huffed.

"You're here. Alive. Which is a hell of a lot more than you deserve after the shit you pulled. Who do you think let out that monster? Who do you think single-handedly brought this town to its knees by setting that monster loose?"

Samuel tried sitting up, but the pain of his leg stopped him.

"What?"

The sheriff laughed to himself, smacking his thigh.

"Do you know what some of the citizens are saying? That death, the dark servant of Azhuel, came to Haid in the form of a red-haired child to enact vengeance on the citizens, because some of them had broken the law by touching your old man and murdering him in the dead of night. Now that's really funny. Almost as good as that demon theory. But it gets better. The latest rumor is that you're the one that summoned her." He wriggled his fingers over Samuel's face. He laughed again. "Death. Demon. Monster. Little shit. Whatever that thing is, it's good at killing. Really good. Really fucking good."

Samuel arched his spine, the bones popping. "Why did you let her out?"

The sheriff nodded to himself, fiddling with his flask. He offered Samuel a sip, but he refused. "Maybe I just wanted my jailhouse back. Or maybe I'd had enough of our fat mayor. Maybe that little brat came banging on my door in the middle of the night telling me that you'd gotten caught, crying and saying he'd do anything to save you. Saying he needed my help. Saying that we could stage a coup in the process. Saying I could have my wages doubled as well as more control over my patrolmen. Anything I wanted if I saved you."

"Why would Charles do that?"

The sheriff smirked. "You're not that stupid, are you?" He laughed. "Anyway. It was his idea to set the little beast free, because he said she'd rescue you. I told him he was out of his damn mind, but he insisted. Said that monster wouldn't hurt you, and he'd take the blame if it didn't work. I said I'd kill him myself if it didn't."

"You hate her."

"Damn right." The sheriff closed the flask and stashed it in his pocket. "I know what that thing is capable of. Told the men I trusted to sneak through the neighborhoods and spread the word that something bad was coming. Tell the citizens not to leave their houses or open the shops or head to the woods. Most everyone listened. Those that didn't went to the grounds for military training. They would've sold their souls to make a few extra coins."

"People died."

"Coming from you? That's rich. None of this would've happened if it wasn't for you."

Samuel's burned arm twitched, and a wave of pain forced his eyes closed. "I know that."

The sheriff sighed. "I let the monster out myself. Undid the locks and chains. Told her I'd shoot her dead if she so much as made a move at me. Told her where you were and that you needed help. And I let her go."

Samuel remembered how Zei had burst into the blacksmith's shed, the way she'd slain the foreigner and Jax as if it were nothing. He remembered the way she looked at him, her hands stained wet with blood.

"Did she help you?"

"Yes."

The sheriff shook his head, rubbing his hands over his face. "No shit?"

"How long am I stuck here for?"

"Right now, we're keeping you hidden." The sheriff stood, jamming his fingers into his belt. "There's been some grumblings about how you're the one to blame for all the carnage. Simple minds.

Superstitions and all that. The little mayor wants you to stay in Haid, but I think it's a bad idea. My opinion? You need to get out of this town."

"Wait," Samuel called out before the sheriff made his exit. "Mikael. The foreigner. He called Zei ... he called the demon a Halyre. Do you know the word?"

"Are you serious?" The sheriff snorted. "Like I speak redlander."

Samuel fumbled around the room, searching for his clothes. Instead, he found a stash of Charles's clothes stuffed inside the large dresser. He picked a pair of fitted jeans, which he assumed Charles had outgrown several years before. He guided his bandaged leg inside of the pants, doing his best to avoid rubbing the wound.

He shoved his other leg in without as much effort, then wriggled the jeans up to his waist. He rolled up the pants twice, trying to prevent the bottoms from covering his feet. Dressing was an odd sensation. He'd been naked underneath the bedsheets for over a week, leaving them only to relieve himself. He slipped on a thick shirt and an oversized sweater before slowly making his way back to the lounge chair.

Samuel pushed his newly repaired glasses farther up his nose. Charles had paid a craftsman in Lehles not only to repair the damaged frames, but also to slightly increase the prescription strength of the lenses. Because of it, Samuel had never seen things more clearly.

He winced. His arm prickled with irritation, so he carefully patted the burned skin with the back of his palm. Not only did the burns ache, but they itched as well. He braced himself against the wall before snatching his coat up from the floor.

After he'd finished dressing, Samuel took cautious steps back to the bed. He got down on his knees and rummaged underneath the bed until he found his leather boots. He sat on the bed, lethargically slipping the shoes on and lacing up the strings.

Charles burst into the room, Samuel's backpack draped over his shoulder. He smiled. "I bought you fresh clothes, you know. You can totally have those too. It looks good on you."

Samuel smirked. "Thanks. It's better than a uniform. What happened to my old clothes? The ones I was wearing?"

"Oh. Tossed them out. They were filthy." Charles paused. "Covered in blood."

Samuel picked at sweater sleeves. "Thank you, Charles."

Charles blushed. He whipped Samuel's backpack onto the bed. "Your money's all there. Put in a little extra for you. Oh, and the blacksmith gave you some new throwing knives and sharpened your hunting knife. He says he's sorry about what happened."

Samuel nodded. He wasn't angry with the blacksmith anymore. The man responsible was dead.

Charles got closer. He brushed back Samuel's hair, his fingers lingering. "You should fix your hair. It's a mess."

Samuel nodded.

Charles cleared his throat, pulling away. He straightened his suit jacket and popped the stem of his smoking pipe between his teeth. "You ready?"

A soft rapping came from outside the hallway. Samuel turned. Claudette stood by the doorframe, her arms slung around it. Her four-cord braids fell down her shoulders like a still painting. Her brown eyes stayed downcast.

Samuel dug his fingers into his palm. His muscles tightened.

"Can we have a minute?"

Charles glanced at Claudette. He nodded, took his exit, and closed the door behind him.

Soft light peeked through the lace curtains. Samuel shifted his weight, the floor creaking below his feet. He opened his mouth to speak, but nothing came out. She was beautiful. Inside and out. Pure. He never deserved her.

"Where are you going?" she asked with a tinge of sadness.

Samuel rubbed his thumb across his jacket. "I don't know."

Claudette's voice got sharper. She held herself. "What does that even mean? I don't understand. Every time I come to see you … " She paused. "It's not your fault, Samuel. None of this is your fault. You don't have to run away."

"I killed him," Samuel said.

"What?"

"The mayor. I killed him. I did it."

"You killed him?"

Samuel nodded.

Claudette came closer. She took his face into her hands, her touch sending chills. "I don't care," she said evenly. "He was a bad man. He was cruel. What he did to my father? To yours? He deserved to die."

She embraced him.

"I'm glad you did it, Sam. Can't you see? I'm happy. Please. Don't leave me."

Samuel's mouth puckered. He tasted bile, his jaw clenched. He didn't know if he had the strength to do it. He didn't want to leave her. He wanted her to hold him. He wanted a life with her. But none of those things were possible. He couldn't lie to her anymore. She needed to know the truth. To see him for what he really was.

"No," Samuel said firmly. "I have to."

"Don't say that!"

"I lied about your father. I was there. I watched him die."

Claudette released her hold. Samuel stepped back and slouched his shoulders. He couldn't bear to look at her. "That day. The mayor brought him to the jailhouse. I was there." Samuel nibbled on his tongue. "I watched him die."

Claudette put her hands near her stomach. "What?"

"I didn't do anything to stop them. I didn't try."

"You didn't kill him," Claudette said. She shook her head forcefully, tears running down her cheeks. "I know you didn't. That's not who you are. I know it was the mayor. What did he do? Tell me."

Samuel couldn't say anything else. Zei was the one who held the knife, but that blood was on his hands. He owned it.

Claudette's lip trembled. "Tell me. Please. Just tell me."

The room grew silent until Claudette's feet struck the floor. She reached her hand back and slapped it across Samuel's face. Her eyes sweltered with a fresh wave of tears.

"Tell me!"

Samuel's cheek throbbed. He wanted to throw his arms around her waist and beg her forgiveness. He wanted to confess everything. But she deserved better. It didn't matter what he wanted. He knew he couldn't stay with her. He couldn't stay in Haid. It was more than the sheriff's warnings about superstitious citizens. There were too many ghosts. This town had brought out something dark in him. He tried not thinking about it, but his mind always found its way back to death. She couldn't understand that. He hoped she never would have to.

The snow-laden graveyard was littered with rows of erect wooden sticks. Some of the stripped branches had fallen over, while more had been buried underneath the white powder. Samuel followed Charles, his backpack bouncing. His boots stepped on snow and dried wood. His arms dangled by his sides as he tried not to move any of the sticks still mounted in place.

Samuel hadn't said a word since leaving Claudette alone at the estate. Charles allowed him time to sit in silence on the drive to the burial grounds. The 250 acres of reserved land was deep on the north side of Haid. The grounds were far away from the neighborhoods and square and tucked between the eastern and western woods.

"It's a little farther back," Charles said, zigzagging in between the posts.

"How do you know?"

"I oversaw the burial."

Samuel nibbled on his cheek. "You sure you'll remember where it is?"

Charles sighed loudly. "I marked the stick. Trust me."

Samuel wasn't paying attention, and his elbow accidentally struck the tips of several mounted sticks, knocking two of them over. Samuel stopped. He bent down, and his body tingled with pain. He repositioned the sticks, turned around, and continued following Charles. This time, he shoved his hands inside his pockets. The sun's rays managed to seep through his jacket, and his arm throbbed wildly. He tried not to contort his face. It was almost like it was being burned all over again.

No one was supposed to mark grave posts. It was specified in the Laevis Creed. Politicians, citizens, clerics, even foreigners were to be buried with one another in the same communal burial grounds. If Charles had marked his father's stick, then he'd willfully broken the law on Samuel's behalf. He swore to himself he'd never forget that.

Charles stopped by a cluster of sticks. He bent down and nodded. Samuel tried widening his strides, ignoring the pain in his leg. The stick in front of him was stripped of its outer bark. He thought of his father's frozen body underneath the snow and hard dirt. He squatted beside Charles, slid off the backpack, and placed it beside the post. He retrieved the hunting knife.

"Thank you," Samuel said. "For everything."

"It's no trouble when you're the mayor," Charles bragged. He kicked up a bit of snow. "Crazy how things happen. I always hated my dad. But now that he's gone. I don't know. It's weird. I didn't think your pet monster would actually kill him. I mean. I guess it had to happen one way or the other."

Samuel swallowed. "Yeah."

"I know what my dad did to yours. And I'm sorry. I don't want you to hate me. I care a lot about you." Charles looked down. "I love you."

"I know." Samuel forced a grin, putting a hand on his friend's shoulder. He didn't know if the sheriff was rambling nonsense or telling truth. Either way, he loved Charles. He was a better person than his father. And he didn't want to hurt him. "I don't hate you. I swear. I care about you a lot. That's why you need to stay away from me."

Charles tsked. "You're so dramatic."

He lit the tobacco inside of his pipe and sucked. His face seemed somewhat older as he allowed the cloud of smoke to roll out his open mouth. It reminded Samuel of the last mayor, but he pushed the thought aside.

"Guess I'll go ahead. Be waiting for you with the sheriff."

"Okay."

"Take your time. Do what you have to do."

Samuel bowed, and Charles waved as he made his way back to the sheriff's jeep.

For a long while, Samuel stood still, his ungloved hand gripping the knife's handle. The weight felt heavy. The last time he held a knife, he slit a man's throat with it. He curled the blade up and looked at his father's grave.

There was so much he could have said. His cheeks started aching. He blinked heavily, refusing to let out the tears. Words and tears wouldn't bring him back or right all the wrongs. He sniffled as he raised his open palm. "We are but dirt," he mumbled as he slid the blade across his hand. The blood came slowly at first, but then gushed out freely in between the creases of his fingers. He'd made the cut too deep. He should've known better than to slice the skin that way. He didn't care. He deserved to bleed. "To dirt we shall return."

Samuel paused. It was as if he'd forgotten everything. He'd watched his father perform the rites a hundred times over, but this time was different. This time, he was the one holding the knife. He knew he was supposed to read a passage, but he didn't have the scriptures with him. He closed his eyes.

"What am I supposed to do?"

He waited for a voice, or at least some sort of inward reassurance he wasn't speaking to nothing. But nothing came. Samuel opened his eyes.

The old butcher.

The verse came back to him. He dribbled the blood over his father's grave before folding his hands together.

"'For Azhuel will draw out your flesh and pain, and in Him you will grow again, connected to His roots. In Him, there is always life.' Azhuel, lord of all, I ask that your roots would wrap around my father. Draw him back into you. Give him peace. Please. Just give him peace now."

Samuel rested the side of his head on the passenger window. His bandaged hand clutched the strap of his backpack. They made their way past the neighborhoods and over the railroad tracks. The sheriff edged the jeep up to the cabin, parking near the front of the wooden shed. He petted his mustache, and his glazed eyes stared at Samuel through the front mirror.

"Don't do this."

Samuel picked his head up. Charles was leaning over the center console, his slicked-back hair glistening. "I could drive you to another town. Somewhere you'd be safe. I'll even take you to the border if that's what you want. Let me help you."

Samuel looked away, watching through the window. The limbs from the pine trees danced in the breeze, their piney branches swaying. He couldn't hear their rustling over the rumbling engine.

"I have to do this alone."

"No, you don't," Charles said authoritatively. It sounded forced. "You're not some martyr, you know."

Samuel didn't answer.

Charles tapped Samuel's leg. They looked into each other's eyes. Heat rose in Samuel's chest, but he kept a hard face. He couldn't admit it to himself before, but he could now. He loved Charles as much as he loved Claudette and Zei. He loved things he couldn't have.

"Charles."

"I'm the mayor of Haid. I can protect you. You'd be safest with me. Don't you see that? The dumb citizens will get over their stupid ideas about you. Just give it time. I can have a dozen patrolmen guarding you at all times. At least until things calm down."

"No," the sheriff said abruptly. "You're not about to ask that of my men. Or me. Everyone's already spooked after what happened. I'm trying to maintain trust and respect. You know that can't happen with him still around here, mayor."

Charles let out a groan. He pointed to Samuel's leg. "What about that wound? You're still hobbling. We're just supposed to drop you off and let you stagger out of town like that? What about that butcher girl? You going to leave her too?"

Samuel reached for the door's handle. He didn't want to argue.

"Let him be," the sheriff said calmly. He gave a nod in the direction of the mirror. "Don't be soft, Samuel. Stay alive."

"Thank you," Samuel said.

"You're family," the sheriff said with a mumble. "No need to say thanks. Get your ass out of my jeep."

Charles sank into the seat, crossing his arms. "You'll come back," he said stubbornly. "You'll have to come back. When everything settles down. Promise me, Sam. You will come back."

Samuel gave a reluctant nod before hopping out of the jeep. It was best for him to do nothing and not to look back. The groan of the engine faded as Samuel opened the front door to the cabin. He waited for his eyes to adjust to the cabin's darkness. He went to the fireplace and started a fresh fire, the flames illuminating the room. He tossed his backpack to the ground, reacclimating himself with the place that had been his home for so long. He went to the kitchen and grazed the counter with his fingers. The place smelled the same, like burnt wood and herbal spices. He got on his tiptoes and rummaged through the high cabinets, finding the canister of his father's tealeaves. He brewed himself a cup, the smell permeating his nostrils. He sat down by his father's desk, staring at the old photograph of his mother. Her dark eyes radiated through her thick-framed glasses.

Samuel rubbed the photograph with his thumb. If only his father had lived a different life. He could've grown up knowing a mother's touch. He could've experienced a softer side of his father, one that wasn't plagued by guilt and regret.

Samuel winced. His breathing stopped for a moment as he waited for the pain to dull. The burned mark on his arm reminded him he couldn't escape the roots. As hard as he tried to forget, his father's words would always be with him, pushing him, tormenting him, guiding him. He would rather nurse his doubts and curse his father's faith as misguided. But he couldn't. He didn't know if he could ever be sure if there was some benevolent being watching over humanity. He didn't know if there was such a thing as life after death. Even so, Samuel hoped against hope that his father's soul would be forever connected to Azhuel's roots, that he would rest alongside his mother, and that they both could lie together in peace the way they never could in life.

Samuel's breaths were constricted. There was a constant weight pressing on his chest that he couldn't keep ignoring. He hated himself. He was a liar. A coward. And now, a murderer. He was the reason why Claudette's father was dead. He should've stopped Zei, but he didn't. He was the reason why his father was dead, because he sent him off into a trap. He was the one who slit the mayor's throat. The citizens weren't wrong in their resentment of Samuel. He was the reason so many of them had died. He was the reason Claudette would cry herself to sleep for nights on end.

Samuel propped his chin and saw the leather-bound scriptures resting on the opposite end of the desk. He grabbed the book and slid it closer. There was something tucked inside of the scriptures that bulked up the pages. He opened the book and saw the throwing knife he'd given to his father after Wilkens's funeral. The knife was tucked into the spine.

He carefully lifted the knife and began to read.

The wind rapped against the outside walls, and the wooden planks creaked along with every rhythmic gust. Night had come. Samuel jabbed the smoldering embers with the poker. He scooted back and pulled the ends of the woolly blanket over his shoulders. The flames inside the fireplace cackled as they consumed the glowing logs. The heat rose.

Samuel slipped his left hand deeper inside the blanket and touched the layered gauze wrapped around his forearm. The doctor instructed him to leave the bandage on for another day before removing. She told him the wound was nearly ready to heal. He didn't believe her. It hurt too much. His fingers moved down from his arm and onto the bloody bandage covering his palm. It took a long while for the bleeding to stop. It was as if his right arm was cursed.

He stared at the old backpack beside his father's desk. It held so many knives: the hunting knife, seven throwing knives, and the obsidian-colored blade he'd used on the mayor. It also held the scriptures. He would leave the cabin at morning's light. It was too dangerous to travel through the woods in darkness. He had wasted too much time. He didn't care. A part of him wasn't ready to leave the cabin. This was his home. His real home. But he knew he didn't have a home anymore. He couldn't stay in Haid. He didn't know where he would go next. He recalled his father's pleas for him to seek sanctuary with a nearby cleric, but he couldn't recall the name. It didn't matter. He wasn't going to do that. He was no cleric or patrolman. He glared at his arm.

He was nothing.

A burst of wind struck the outside walls with force, causing the wood to squeal. Another storm was coming. Samuel could feel it. He rubbed his eyes and cleaned his new lenses with the tail end of his sweater. Afterward, he curled deeper into the blanket, but a strange rapping on top of the roof caught his attention. He rationalized it to be nothing more than a fallen tree branch, but there were no pines close enough to touch the cabin. It couldn't have been a squirrel, because the rustling sounded louder than any rodent could muster. What if it was someone?

Samuel sat up and let go of the blanket. He scrambled to his feet and ran to the door, flinging it open. The cold wind struck him hard, the gust nearly taking his breath away. He stepped outside. All he could see were the empty pines and the barely visible moon peaking above.

"Zei?"

He waited for what seemed like ages. But no one came.

"I don't know if you're there," Samuel called out. "But I'm sorry. I was a bad friend to you. I should have helped you more. I didn't. And I'm sorry. For those things I said. I didn't mean them. I care about you. I didn't think I could anymore, but I still do. I never stopped. I don't think I can ever stop."

He took a step back.

"I want you to be safe, Zei. Please. Just don't hurt anyone else … unless they really deserve it? Promise?"

The only response Samuel was given was that of the rustling tree branches. When he could wait no longer, he went back inside and curled up by the fireplace. He should've gone up the ladder and slept in his old bed, but being up in the loft would only bring back more memories. He closed his eyes, trying to force himself to sleep.

Minutes or hours passed before the flames inside the fireplace turned to embers, and Samuel awoke to his own shivering. He needed to get closer to the fire, but his muscles felt like mush.

An unexpected gust of cold wind hit the back of Samuel's legs, but after a squeak, the wind was gone. He kept his eyes closed, curling deeper underneath the blanket. He could've sworn he had heard the door open and close. He shoved his hands over his face. His head throbbed, and he couldn't get himself to think clearly.

Someone was inside the cabin. He could feel it.

He closed his lids tighter. He was terrified, but he fought the urge to turn around. What was the point in trying to run away? He wasn't strong enough to make it through the northern woods all by himself, especially not with winter approaching. What did he even hope for? He could never have a normal life. How hard would he have to work to keep his right arm covered, knowing its exposure would only raise questions, fears, and, in all probability, lead to his arrest? Could he seek refuge in some northern town closer to the coast, one with no knowledge of what had happened in Haid? Could he find any sort of freedom in the chaotic greenlands? Could he somehow find a way to get down to the redlands? He knew the answer.

There was nowhere safe for him.

Muffled footsteps rapped behind him, but still, Samuel refused to turn around. A gentle weight pressed against him, and his body felt the warmth of another's body. He cracked his eyelids, his chest rising and falling with every breath. The burn mark on his arm twitched. This wasn't a dream or a nightmare. Someone was lying beside him.

From the smallest crack in his eyelid, he could see red strands of hair falling over his bandaged arm. He couldn't look. He was terrified to look. He remained motionless as he was warmed from the body heat.

Zei wasn't going to kill him. She hadn't before, and she wouldn't now. What was it that she wanted from him? Did she care for him? Did she notice he was cold? Could a demon be capable of love?

Halyre.

He said the word in his mind, remembering the foreigner's rushed words. If Zei was some sort of forbidden creature, then who had made her? On her last visit, the doctor closed the guestroom door and came to Samuel. "I want to tell you something," she said somberly. "Because, I think if anyone needs to know this, it's you. I took a sample of that child's blood and mailed it off to a colleague I know. She owns the only microscope in the state." The doctor paused. "It's a blood substitute, of course. But it's more than that. A symbiotic entity dwells inside the liquid that tries to engage and feed off its host. It's incompatible with human genetics. And yet, it lived inside that child like a thriving virus, only the effects are … different. Strengthening. Regeneration."

Samuel didn't understand what the doctor meant. Was Zei sick? What had latched onto her? No. Zei was not a girl. Samuel understood that more than before. They were Halyre.

Could Zei have something to do with the old wars? Would Zei tell him if he asked? Perhaps he needed to find answers elsewhere. The foreigner seemed to know things. As a former officer, he must have had access to the banned books and technologies. The redlands military was responsible for safeguarding the past. If Samuel headed south, how many days would it take him to reach the redlands? With the chaos ensuing between the whitelands and the greenlands, would he even have a chance of crossing two borders? Would Zei come with him?

Questions and anxieties plagued him until his thoughts bled into one.

Samuel scooted his body back, edging himself closer to Zei. He felt the soft drag of their fingers across his hair and the pressing of their knees onto his calves. After a while, when his mind had exhausted itself beyond its limitations, he began to settle. Despite all the blood and death, he could sleep with Zei beside him. The humming of gears in the prosthetic arm lulled him. After several hours, his muscles relaxed, and he drifted off.

ACKNOWLEDGMENTS

To my partner, Elise. Thank you for choosing to love me unconditionally, for taking care of our daughter while I'm holed up in a coffee shop writing words, being the moody emo trans kid you fell in love with a decade ago, and for letting me cuddle you every night. You are my safe place. I hope I can always make you proud.

To my daughter, Sansa. Thank you for always being a light in dark places. You are the strongest person I know, and I mean that. I am so thankful to be your mom.

To Jane Delury. Thank you for being a phenomenal writer and mentor and for helping me find diamonds in the rough. To Jessica Welch and Tracy Gold. Thank you for supporting my writing and for being beautiful friends. A sincere thank-you to Andrew Sargus Klein, Justin Sanders, Kendrel Dickerson, Mary Adelle, Abby Shaffer, Mandy May, Chris Warman, Ron Kipling Williams, Tyler Mendelson, Mia White, Kendra Kopelke, Steve Matanle, Pantea Tofangchi, Meredith Purvis, Jennifer Jericho, and the rest of the UB Creative Writing family. I have grown so much as a writer because of you all. To my agent, Amy Tipton. Thank you for your hard work and dedication to getting underrepresented writers on the bookshelves! To Georgia McBride and everyone at Month9Books for all of your hard work on this project. Thank you so much for taking a chance on me.

To Bailey Pope and Kelley Anderson and Leah Canner and Max Canner and Bharathi Vallalar and Jamie Doucette and Alex Doucette and Brittany Wight and Ky Tran and Lyle Greco. Thank you for loving me as I am, for showing me that family is a choice, and how to make pretty things out of any mess. I owe you everything. I love you completely.

To God. Despite my neurosis and need to control everything, I will never not need you.

NIKKI Z. RICHARD

Nikki Richard is a sensitive queer writer with moods and coping mechanisms. An MFA graduate from the University of Baltimore, she lives in the city with her hot wife, amazing daughter, and fluffy cat.

CONNECT WITH US

Find more books like this at http://www.Month9Books.com

Facebook: www.Facebook.com/Month9Books
Instagram: https://instagram.com/month9books
Twitter: https://twitter.com/Month9Books
Tumblr: http://month9books.tumblr.com/
YouTube: www.youtube.com/user/Month9Books
Georgia McBride Media Group: www.georgiamcbride.com

OTHER MONTH9BOOKS TITLES YOU MIGHT LIKE

THE MISSING
THE SPONSORED